"You enjoy laughing at me, don't you?"

That wasn't what Audrey had intended to say to Zach at all. But it was too late to retract her words.

"Why would I want to laugh at you?" he asked.

Because he thought he was better than her. Because it was the way of handsome, entitled, arrogant men to be amused by lessor beings.

But she wasn't about to say either of those things out loud. She wouldn't give him the satisfaction. Instead, she braved through with the most obvious—and innocuous—response.

"Because you always smile when you see me."

His eyebrows shot up, as though she'd astonished him. "Did it ever occur to you that maybe—crazy idea—I might actually enjoy your company?"

It was her turn to be astonished. They'd spent so little time together it was impossible for him to enjoy her company. "No. You and I come from very different places in the world."

He stared at her. Up close, his eyes appeared almost gray instead of dark blue. The gunmetal color of the ocean before a storm.

"You know what?" he said slowly. "I'm going to take that as a compliment."

Dear Reader,

In our household, this book will forever be known as The Lost Book. See, just as I hit Save at around the 70,000 word mark, my hard drive died. And I hadn't backed up in quite a while. As you can imagine, there were tears and wailing and banging of heads against hard surfaces. Then I calmed down and found a data recovery company who worked magic and salvaged my book.

It took them three weeks to accomplish the miracle and I lived in hope the entire time. I also thought about Audrey and Zach's story. A lot. By the time I got the manuscript back, I knew I had to sacrifice almost a third of my word count to take the story in a new direction. But I did it, because I was confident I knew Audrey and Zach by then and I knew what their story needed to be.

As you can imagine, writing this one has been a bit of an obstacle course, but I was desperate for these two slightly damaged souls to understand they needed to be together, so I hung in there. I hope the effort was worth it and you enjoy Zach and Audrey's story.

Happy reading,

Sarah Mayberry

PS—I love to hear from readers! Contact me through my website at www.sarahmayberry.com.

Her Favorite Rival

Sarah Mayberry

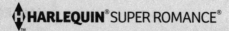

Recycling programs
for this product may
not exist in your area.

ISBN-13: 978-0-373-71872-6

HER FAVORITE RIVAL

Copyright © 2013 by Small Cow Productions Pty Ltd.

Printed in U.S.A.

ABOUT THE AUTHOR

Sarah Mayberry lives by the sea near Melbourne, Australia, with her husband and a small black cavoodle called Max. She is currently enjoying her recently renovated house—complete with gorgeous new kitchen!—and feeling guilty about her overgrown garden. When she's not writing, she can be found reading, cooking, gardening, shoe shopping and enjoying a laugh with friends and family. Oh, and sleeping. She is inordinately fond of a "nana nap."

Books by Sarah Mayberry

HARLEQUIN SUPERROMANCE

HARLEQUIN BLAZE

Other titles by this author available in ebook format.

Where to start with all the thanks?
My brother,
for holding my hand through the initial crisis.
All my fabulous writing friends
who texted or tweeted or emailed to let me know this
had happened to them and to hang in there and hope,
with a particular nod to the fabulous Anna Campbell.
My editor, Wanda,
for being so damn unflappable and positive and
believing, as always, in me.
And Chris,
for your wonderful calm and for making me laugh
when I didn't think I could and for all the ferrying to
and fro of computer bits...
You are, indeed, the shiz, my love.
Last, but not least, to Max,
for all the licks and snuffles and walks and cuddles.
Whatever did we do without you?

CHAPTER ONE

IT WAS STILL dark when Audrey Mathews used her swipe card to enter Makers Hardware Cooperative's headquarters on the southern outskirts of Melbourne. Her new shoes pinched her feet as she made her way to her office, but she figured the pain was worth it. The new CEO, Henry Whitman, started today, and she wanted to look sleek and professional and sharp when she met him. She wanted him to take one look at her and know she was up for anything he might throw at her—including a promotion.

Hence her best suit and new shoes and sleek updo.

Her stomach did a slow roll as she remembered the profile on Whitman she'd read over the weekend. She was a big believer in being prepared, and she'd dug up a bunch of old *Business Review Weekly* articles on her new boss. To an article, they described him as ruthless, hard-nosed and utterly unsentimental; a man who habitually cut companies to the bone to produce results. One article had even reported that his employees referred to him as the Executioner.

Formidable stuff. But she figured if he was so focused on results, he would appreciate someone who was goal-oriented and hardworking and ambitious.

And nervous. Don't forget nervous.

Because even though she was prepared to do her damnedest to prove herself—including waking up at the crack of dawn to make a positive first impression—if Whitman ran true to form, there were going to be a lot of retrenchments in the next weeks and months, and there was a chance she might be one of them. Which was why she'd updated her résumé this weekend, too.

She might be an optimist, but she wasn't stupid.

She checked her watch. One of the articles she'd read claimed Henry Whitman started work at six-thirty every day, without fail. Which meant he should be arriving any second now.

She gathered an armful of papers and strode toward reception. No matter where he entered, Whitman had to pass through the foyer to get to the executive offices, and she planned on being very visible when he did so.

She felt more than a little foolish as she took up a position to the rear of the foyer. For all she knew, Henry Whitman might not even register her when he arrived. Or maybe he'd see right through her ploy and mark her down as a horrible little suck-up.

She glanced over her shoulder, wondering if she should give up on this crazy idea, go back to her desk and use her early start to put a dent in her workload instead of trying to manipulate events.

She wavered for a moment, but something inside wouldn't let her back away from her plan to be noticed. Probably it was the same something that kept her at her desk many nights when most of her colleagues had gone home. If she had to try to distill it down to its component parts, she guessed it would be one part making up for lost time and two parts sheer grit and determination to carve out a useful, productive niche for herself in the world.

She might not be a doctor or a lawyer, but she was damned good at what she did, and that counted for something. Well, it did with her, anyway.

The sound of the door from the underground parking garage opening and closing echoed up the corridor. Lifting her chin, Audrey tightened her grip on her papers and stepped briskly into the foyer, trying to look as though she was on her way somewhere vital and important and urgent.

She pulled up short when she caught sight of the tall, broad-shouldered man striding toward her.

Not Henry Whitman, but Zach Black, fellow buyer and all-around thorn in her side. Why was she not surprised *he* was here ready to grease up to the new head honcho? The man oozed ambition; it was a miracle he hadn't set up camp outside Whitman's office in order to get a jump on everyone else.

She ignored the little voice that pointed out she was here to do exactly the same thing and cocked an eyebrow. There was the smallest of hitches in Zach's stride as he saw her, then his mouth settled into the familiar, amused curve he always wore around her. As usual, he looked ridiculously, almost offensively handsome in a charcoal pinstriped suit, his pink-and-white checked shirt and pale gray tie managing to somehow straddle the fine line between professional and stylish.

"Mathews. You pulling an all-nighter or something?" he asked as he joined her.

Funny. Not.

"You read the *Business Review Weekly* article, didn't you?" she guessed.

"Of course." His dark blue eyes scanned her body. "New shoes. Nice touch."

She fought the urge to squirm. So what if she'd put her best foot forward—literally—today of all days? It wasn't a crime to be keen to impress your new boss.

"You had your hair cut," she pointed out.

"It was due."

She arched an eyebrow again. Who was he kidding? Like

her, he'd clearly come prepared to smooch maximum butt this morning.

"Is he here yet?" he asked, glancing over her shoulder in the direction of the CEO's office.

"Not yet."

"Hmm." He frowned and checked his watch. "Maybe he's taking meetings off-site today."

"Maybe."

"Talking to some of the key suppliers."

"Could be."

A lock of almost-black hair flopped over his forehead, lending his good looks a more approachable, boyish appeal. An illusion, of course. Zach was a shark in a suit. He'd been recruited to Makers six months ago, bringing with him a reputation as a wunderkind who'd gone to the right schools and rocketed his way up the corporate ladder at light speed. She'd recognized him as her only real competition for the next category manager's job that came up the moment she laid eyes on him, and time had done nothing to prove her instincts wrong.

Zach checked his watch again. "Might as well get some work done, I guess."

She watched as he walked away, her gaze gravitating to the firm muscles of his backside. She had a running bet with her friend Megan that he had his suits specially tailored to flatter his rear. That was the only explanation for how good his butt looked and why he was universally known as the Man With the Golden Ass among the women in the building.

Good thing she was more of a leg woman.

She returned to her own office, frustrated that her grand plan had gone astray—and that she wasn't the only one who'd had the genius idea of ambushing the new CEO.

Bloody Zach Black.

It took her a moment to get past the prickliness he always seemed to inspire in her to see the humor in the situation: the two of them getting up before sunrise to race into work to impress each other. If it was anyone else, she'd be laughing with them in the staff room over a cup of terrible instant coffee.

But it wasn't anyone else; it was Zach. It didn't help that he was three years younger than her with many years less experience in the industry, yet thanks to impressive academic qualifications and a short but stellar CV, had walked into a job on the same level and was probably getting paid more than her. She knew that was the way the world worked—that women, on average, earned 78 percent of what their male colleagues did in equivalent roles, and that the business community tended to value academic qualifications over working-your-way-up-the-ladder, hands-on experience—but it didn't make it any easier to swallow.

Nor did his fancy suits and sleek European car and general air of swanky-well-groomed-well-bred-ness. The way he spoke, the way he dressed, even the car he drove seemed designed to let the world know he was that little bit better than everyone else.

Even if it was true, she didn't need her face rubbed in it.

She also didn't need to sit at her desk brooding over him. A few hours from now, the office would be buzzing with people who all wanted a piece of her busy schedule. In the meantime, she had a full in-tray to work her way through. More than enough to keep her mind off her pesky colleague.

ZACH TRIED TO concentrate on the spreadsheet on his computer screen. He was developing a new store-brand power-tool range with one of Makers's big suppliers, and the information in front of him was important. Unfortunately, all he could think about was Audrey Mathews in her navy suit and new shoes.

She'd beaten him in. If he'd taken the time to think about it, he might have guessed she would do her homework on Whitman, that she'd note the man's six-thirty start time, and that she'd be here early to impress the man, the same as him. As a general rule, though, he tried not to think about Audrey too much. Not only because he preferred to run his own race. There was something disturbingly distracting about her shiny brown hair and warm golden-brown eyes. Then there was the way she looked in her neat little suits. He shook his head and refocused on his computer. There were too many offerings in the cordless battery range at the budget end of the market. It was crazy to waste shelf space on what was essentially the same product with some minor tweaks.

Maybe he was being paranoid, but he got the distinct impression that he wasn't Audrey's favorite person. Which was fine. He'd allocated himself two years at Makers to win a promotion to category manager. He didn't have time for distractions.

There were ten buyers in the merchandising department, but he'd worked out early on that Audrey was the only competition he needed to worry about. She was one of a handful of female executives, but she never played the gender card to get what she wanted. She was thorough, smart, calm in a crisis and determined. She also had a long history with the company and was well respected. In short, a serious contender for the next category manager opening.

Pity he was going to be the one who got it.

Registering that he was once again thinking about Audrey, he swung away from his computer. Coffee was clearly needed to jump-start his brain. He'd had to forgo his usual morning run to get in early, so caffeine would have to act as a substitute for fresh air and endorphins.

As luck would have it, he had to pass Audrey's office on the way to the small staff room situated between the marketing and merchandising departments. Her dark head was bent over her desk as she wrote something on a notepad. He wasn't sure he approved of her new hairstyle. It was too severe for her round face. Made her look like a repressed librarian or school principal.

Still, there was something to be said for repressed librarians. All that pent-up passion…

As if she'd sensed his errant thoughts, Audrey glanced up from her work. She was wearing a pair of dark-framed, rectangular reading glasses, and her gaze met his briefly over the top of the frames, accentuating the schoolmarmish vibe.

She wasn't schoolmarmish, though. He'd seen her at the office Christmas party, laughing and dancing and enjoying herself. She was fun, when she let her hair down. Fun and more than a little sexy.

Okay, definitely time for coffee.

He made a point of keeping his gaze dead ahead on the return journey and lost himself in his work once he was at his desk. Over the next two hours, the office slowly came to life as the rest of the staff trickled in. He looked up a couple of times as people called out greetings to him, but otherwise he was undisturbed, and he managed to finalize his notes to the supplier.

As nine drew closer, a familiar tension settled into the back of his neck. He waited until nine-thirty before picking up the phone. It was a Monday, after all, and he always checked in with Vera on Mondays.

"Hi, Zach," she said when she picked up.

"Vera. How are things? Did your daughter have her baby yet?"

"She's due next week. Although from the size of her I'm beginning to think she's having twins." Vera laughed, years of smoking giving the sound a husky roughness.

"This'll be your third grandchild, right?"

"You've got a sharp memory."

He did. For lots of things, good and bad.

"How's Mum doing?" he finally asked.

Might as well cut to the chase, since neither Vera nor he was under the illusion that he was calling to talk about the imminent arrival of her grandchild.

"All quiet on the western front at the moment. There might be a new boyfriend on the scene. It's hard to tell sometimes."

He pinched the bridge of his nose. A new boyfriend. Great. His mother had disastrous taste in men.

"But otherwise everything is good?"

"As far as I can tell."

"Thanks, Vera. I appreciate it." Next time he visited his mother, he'd drop by next door, too, and give Vera a box of the Scottish shortbreads she loved and some passes for the movies. She refused to take anything more from him, even though he'd done his best to convince her otherwise over the years.

"You look after yourself, sweetheart," she said warmly, then he was listening to the dial tone.

He couldn't stop his mind from racing ahead to what the future would almost inevitably hold if what Vera had said was true. None of it was good. If his mother had a new boyfriend and he ran true to type, there would be hospital visits in the near future. Police visits, too. Then the inevitable binge as his mother drowned her sorrows post-breakup.

Acid burned in his belly. He'd been looking out for his mother one way or another for more than twenty years, and the cycle of ups and downs was always the same. Neverending. Relentless. And it was always going to be that way, until the day she died.

Suddenly he felt infinitely weary. As though gravity had doubled, dragging him down. He stared at his desk blotter, lost in a world of worry.

The ping of an email arriving cut through his thoughts. His gaze shifted to the screen.

There was work to do—there was always work to do. Reaching for his keyboard, he pushed his troubles aside and concentrated on the matter at hand.

THE NEW SHOES had been a mistake. By the time midmorning rolled around, Audrey's feet were throbbing so much she wanted to sob with every step she took. Every time she was safely behind her desk she toed them off, which only made squeezing her now-swollen feet back into the shoes every time she needed to leave her office even more painful.

A lesson learned. Next time she bought new shoes, she would run a marathon in them before she so much as considered wearing them to work.

The "best" thing was that Henry Whitman still hadn't set foot in the building. The steam off the office street was that Zach's guess had been right—Henry had taken breakfast meetings with the company's top five suppliers. Which meant her early start and painful shoes had all been for nothing.

Awesome.

She had a slew of phone calls leading up to lunch and was about to rush out to a sandwich shop to grab a bite when she saw her fellow buyer and friend Megan hustling past her office with her head down. Spider senses tingling, Audrey followed her to the ladies' room. She entered in time to see her friend's face crumple with misery. She didn't hesitate, opening her arms and pulling Megan close for a hug.

"Is this what I think it is?" Audrey asked.

"Yes."

"Megsy, it'll happen," she said quietly. "By hook or by crook, it'll happen."

Megan and her husband had been trying to get pregnant

for a while now, having suffered a miscarriage early in their relationship.

"I'm so sick of this. Why won't my body work? What's wrong with me?" Megan's voice was thick with tears, her small-featured face flushed.

Audrey pressed a kiss to her temple and squeezed her a little tighter. Megan was going to make a great mum, and Audrey didn't doubt for a moment that somehow she would get there, whether through the old-fashioned way or IVF or adoption, but it was a long, exhausting row to hoe.

"Hang in there. It'll happen. And if it doesn't, you'll find a way to make it happen."

"I know. It's just…hard." Megan sniffed loudly and Audrey released her, leaning across to pluck a handful of tissues from the box next to the washbasin.

"Thanks." Megan blew her nose, then took a big, shuddery breath. "Do I look like a panda?"

They both turned to consider her reflection in the mirror—smudged eyes, sad mouth, wavy blonde hair down to her shoulders.

"I'm thinking raccoon. Or Lady Gaga the morning after," Audrey said.

Megan gave an almost-smile. "I wish."

"Want me to go get your handbag?"

"Would you?"

Audrey gave her a gentle punch on the arm. "Even though it's a feat on a par with landing a man on the moon, I will. Because it's you, and because I'm that kind of girl."

By the time she'd returned and helped Megan repair her makeup and talked some more about her friend's recalcitrant ovaries and uncooperative uterus, the window for sandwich-grabbing had well and truly closed. Audrey was due in her office for a phone hookup with some interstate colleagues. Not that she minded, at all. Megan had saved her sanity more times than she could count, and Audrey would have been happy to hold her friend's hand all afternoon.

Still, by two-thirty hunger was gnawing a hole in her belly, and she hobbled to the staff room to collect the tub of emergency yogurt she had stashed in the fridge. She did a little air punch when she saw that a generous colleague had left a bunch of bananas on the table with a note taped to them: *Help yourself.* Banana and yogurt—practically a three-course meal.

She took a seat before pulling the largest and ripest fruit from the bunch and peeling the top off her yogurt. She'd just eased her shoes off and taken a big bite of banana when a tall, gray-haired man in his late fifties appeared in the doorway. She recognized him instantly as Henry Whitman and nearly choked.

"Excuse me, can you tell me where Gary O'Connor's office is, please?" The man smiled thinly, his gray eyes flicking over her in efficient assessment before taking a quick inventory of the staff room.

Audrey swallowed a mortified moan. She'd dragged herself out of bed at the horrific hour of four-thirty so she could be in a position to make a good first impression on this man, and instead she got to meet him with bulging cheeks and an enormous half-peeled banana in her hand.

She chewed like crazy and tried to force the lump of banana down her suddenly tight throat. The silence seemed to stretch as he waited for her answer, eyebrows slightly raised. She was on the verge of attempting to mime directions to Gary's office when the banana finally slid down her throat.

Thank. God.

Eyes watering, she summoned what she hoped was a gracious, professional smile. "Sorry about that." Her voice sounded funny. As though she'd choked down a chunk of banana, in fact. "Gary's office is the first on your left around the corner. The one with the Father Christmas suit hanging from the coatrack."

"Father Christmas. Right. Thank you."

She started to introduce herself, but he was already turning away. A heartbeat later, he was gone.

Audrey swore under her breath and groped under the table with her feet, searching for her shoes. Had he noticed that her feet were bare? God, she hoped not. She so did not want her new boss's first impression to be of her barefoot and chipmunk-cheeked, holding the world's most phallic food.

She was sliding her right foot into its shoe when Zach cruised into the room, coffee mug in hand.

"Mathews." He gave her a casual salute.

She stood. She wasn't in the mood for his mocking smiles right now. She'd just crashed and burned, big time. Despite her careful plotting and planning, her scary, intimidating new boss now thought she was about as dynamic as a cud-chewing Jersey cow.

"You know, something's been bugging me, Mathews." Zach leaned against the counter and crossed his arms over his chest, his tone serious but his eyes laughing. "We were the only people here this morning—so where exactly were you headed so urgently with all those important papers?"

"Wouldn't you like to know." Not the world's wittiest comeback, but it was the best she could do at short notice.

"That was the point of me asking, actually."

She wasn't sure what devil prompted her next words. Maybe it was the way Zach was laughing at her, or maybe it was because she was disconcertingly aware of the fact that his crossed-arm posture accentuated the breadth of his shoulders and the muscles in his biceps.

"So, what do you think of Whitman?" she asked.

"I don't know. I haven't met him yet." Zach's eyes narrowed. "Why, have you?"

"We had a little chat."

Very little, but he didn't need to know that.

"Yeah? What about?"

"This and that. Christmas, that kind of thing." She waved a hand to suggest a broader conversation.

"What was your impression?"

She thought to the moment when she'd looked into Whitman's cold, steely eyes.

"Surprisingly approachable, actually."

Zach would find out soon enough that their new CEO was a cyborg, but it wouldn't hurt to keep him off-balance in the short term.

"Good to hear," Zach said. "Makes the range review presentations a little less daunting."

She'd been turning to leave, wanting to exit on a high, but his words brought her up short.

"The range reviews? What's he got to do with the range reviews?"

Regularly reviewing and assessing the performance of the products within the various departments under her purview was an integral part of her—and Zach's—role.

"He's sitting in on them. Didn't you hear?"

She blinked rapidly, trying to get her head around his announcement. The range reviews were tomorrow. She'd assumed she'd be presenting to the merchandising manager, Gary, as usual, as well as the panel of store owners who sat on the catalog committee. Since Makers was a cooperative, its 645 member stores liked to have a say in what was stocked and how it was promoted, and the representative store owners on the committee spoke on their behalf. They could be a force to be reckoned with at times, but she was used to dealing with them.

Henry Whitman was a whole other story, though.

"When did you find this out?" Her voice was high with surprise.

"Last week sometime."

Which meant he'd had days to make his presentation as kick-ass as possible, while she had—she checked her watch—less than twenty-four hours.

Aware of Zach watching her, she forced herself to shrug as if she didn't have a care in the world. "Should make it a bit more interesting than usual."

"Absolutely." He grinned, the epitome of cocky arrogance.

She forced her mouth into what she hoped was an equally confident smile and headed for the door, making an effort not to hobble in her too-tight shoes or show by the flicker of an eyelid that she was battling a panicky wash of adrenaline. Showing any weakness in front of this man was the equivalent of a limping gazelle bathing in gravy and handing out paper plates and serviettes to the waiting lions. She wasn't about to make it easy for him.

In her office, she dialed her boss.

"Gary, what's this I'm hearing about Henry Whitman sitting in on our range reviews tomorrow?"

"Oh, yeah. I meant to let you know. He wants to get a feel for our systems, see people in action."

"Right." She bit the single word out. Gary was a good guy, but sometimes he forgot to pass on things and this was a classic example.

"Relax, Audrey. You'll do fine."

"Sure. Thanks."

She tossed the phone onto her desk and called up the range review file. She'd opted to rationalize the portable heating range and had arranged her points neatly in a slide show presentation, complete with product specifications, images and pricing. It was fine, perfectly adequate, but there were no bells or whistles or extras. She knew without a doubt that Zach's would have all of the above, and more.

"Crap."

You can do this. You've got all night to make this better. Take a deep breath and think.

She stared at her computer screen, but instead of neat bullet points, she saw her bank statement. She'd stretched herself so she could buy the small one-bedroom apartment she called home. She had car payments to meet, too. If she failed to impress tomorrow and the Executioner put her head on the chopping block, it wouldn't take long before her life unraveled at the seams.

She shook her head in instinctive rejection of the scenario. She had all night. It would be enough.

She would make it enough, if it killed her.

CHAPTER TWO

IT WAS NEARLY seven by the time Zach switched off his computer and slid the paperwork he was taking home with him into his briefcase.

A single light shone on the other side of the department. Audrey's office. He hesitated, then changed course. He couldn't help smiling when he stopped in her doorway. The sleek, put-together woman from this morning was long gone. Her hair had been released from the updo and hung to her shoulders in a rumpled mess. Her jacket had been discarded and her sleeves rolled up. Her shoes were abandoned in the corner, lying on their sides. She glanced at him before her gaze returned to the computer.

"If you're looking for the quarterly report, I passed it on to Tom already," she said, referring to a dense, complicated report they circulated among the department to save on paper waste, one of Makers's feeble attempts at being environmentally aware.

He knew without asking that she was working on her range review; it was what he'd be doing, too, if he'd just learned that his new boss was going to be breathing down his neck during the presentation.

"Unclench, Mathews. Your review is probably word perfect, as always. Go home and get some food and sleep."

Her gaze lifted to his again, her expression incredulous. "As. If."

Which was exactly what he'd say, too, if their positions were reversed.

"If you're overtired, you'll make mistakes."

"I'll be fine."

"Humor me and at least stop for dinner, then."

She frowned, as well she might. What did he care if she ate or not? She was his rival, not his friend.

"This may come as a shock to you, but I've been looking after myself for a few years now. I think I have the hang of it," she said.

Fine. He wasn't even sure what impulse had driven him to swing by her office, anyway. Whatever it was, it had been a mistake.

"Suit yourself." He started to turn away, then hesitated. "If you get to the point where you're ready to chew your arm off, there's a stash of protein bars in the bottom left drawer of my desk."

She blinked, clearly surprised by his offer. He lifted a hand in farewell and headed for the exit, unsettled by his own altruistic impulse. For a long time now, his energies had been focused on only two things—protecting his mother from herself and establishing himself in his career. Everything else— women, friendships, outside interests—had taken a backseat. It was the reason his last girlfriend, Tina, had walked. She'd said he didn't care enough, and in the eight months since their breakup he'd come to acknowledge that she'd been right. The bottom line was that there were only so many hours in the day, and he had only so much energy. Which was why he'd been sleeping alone since Tina bailed on him.

So why was he looking out for Audrey, worrying about whether she was skipping dinner, for God's sake?

He threw his briefcase onto the backseat of his Audi sedan and slid behind the wheel, uncomfortably aware that part of his motivation might be that Audrey was about his age, with a damn fine figure and a low, sexy voice that had always intrigued him.

Yeah. Hard as it was to admit, apparently he wasn't immune to the urgings of testosterone.

Well, his gonads were going to have to find someone else to fixate on, because there was no way in hell he was going to so much as look sideways at a work colleague. He'd seen too many people undone by workplace affairs to be stupid enough to go there.

It took him half an hour to drive across town to his place in Surrey Hills. He'd bought his down-at-the-heel three-bedroom Victorian cottage as an investment and was renovating it in slow stages. Once it was finished he planned to sell it and upgrade. All part of his five-year plan.

The air still smelled faintly of paint when he let himself in, despite the fact that he'd redecorated the front part of the house more than four months ago. Maybe if he cooked a little more, there would be competing smells to drown out the paint odor. He wasn't about to start tonight, though.

There was leftover Chinese in the fridge, and he nuked it before sitting at the kitchen counter and going over the papers he'd brought home.

Tomorrow was a big day. He had a friend from university who had worked under Henry Whitman at his previous company, so Zach knew Whitman's reputation for making lightning assessments. If he screwed up his presentation or failed to impress, things were going to get tense.

They might get tense, anyway. It all depended on what Whitman's mandate was from the retailers who'd employed him to lead their company. Build and cultivate, or slash and burn.

He put his paperwork into his briefcase at nine and grabbed his car keys. What he really wanted was a hot shower and an early night, but ever since he'd spoken to

Vera this morning there'd been an alarm sounding in the back of his mind, and he knew he wouldn't be able to sleep until he'd checked on his mother.

He drove west until he was wending through the streets of his childhood in the working-class suburb of Footscray. He stopped in front of his mother's house, but didn't get out of the car. Now that he was here, he couldn't bring himself to face her. In all likelihood she would be high, and he wasn't up to managing her tonight. Familiar guilt tugged at him, but he'd learned long ago that no matter what he did, he would always feel guilty. A tougher lesson had been learning that he was also entitled to a life. Nothing would be gained by his sacrificing everything on the altar of his mother's addiction.

The lights were on in the front room, the flicker of the television visible through the thin net curtains. There was no car in the driveway or any other sign of a boyfriend. He sat staring at the lit window, hoping like hell that Vera had it wrong. After ten minutes he started the car and drove off.

He stripped and stepped beneath a hot shower when he got home. Moments from the day flashed across his mind's eye as he let the water run over his shoulders and back, but the one that stuck was the picture of Audrey striding so purposefully and self-importantly across the foyer at 6:30 a.m., a stack of papers in hand. The look on her face when she'd realized it was him and not Whitman…

He laughed out loud. She'd been so damned annoyed. Mind, so had he. But it hadn't taken her long to find her feet again, calling him on his haircut, just as he'd called her on her new shoes.

It was a pity they worked for the same company, because if he was free to follow his instincts where she was concerned—

What? You'd date her for a while and then screw that up, too?

The smile slipped from his lips.

It was irrelevant. As he'd established more than once today, Audrey wasn't exactly his biggest fan, and he'd never make a move on her, even if she was.

He turned his face into the spray, reminding himself that there were worse things in the world than being lonely and horny.

Just because he couldn't think of them right now didn't mean it wasn't true.

AUDREY RUBBED HER temples, willing her aching eyes to focus on the screen. She was so tired she could barely see straight. She'd tweaked her presentation within an inch of its life, but anxiety kept her at her desk, going over and over each page. She wanted to knock it out of the park tomorrow. She wanted Henry Whitman to remember her as the go-getter with the awesome range review, not the chipmunk-cheeked banana-eater from the staff room.

She wanted—

The low, demanding growl of her stomach echoed. She'd been ignoring her belly for the past two hours, but now she was getting to the sick stage of hunger where she was feeling more than a little shaky.

Ever heard of the law of diminishing returns? Time to go home, princess.

She knew the voice in her head was right. Her brain was mush, her judgment out the window. As much as it killed her to admit it, Zach had been on the money when he'd said that if she was overtired, she'd make mistakes.

She hit Save, then—to be safe—made a backup of her presentation and emailed it to herself. She was shutting down her computer when her phone rang in her handbag.

She grabbed it and recognized the number as her parents'. She hesitated, not sure if she was up to a conversation with her mother right now. Then she straightened her spine and took the call.

"Hi, Mum."

"Audrey. Have I caught you at a bad time?" Her mother's voice was cool and briskly efficient, as though she was working her way down a to-do list and talking to Audrey was the next item to be crossed off. Knowing her mother, it was probably not far from the truth.

"No, no, you're good. How are you? How's Dad?" She could hear the polite stiffness in her own voice but was powerless to stop it. After years of agonizing over their relationship and trying to make up for the mistakes of her past, she had come to accept that this was simply the way things were—not so bad, but not so great, either.

"We're well, thank you. I won't keep you, but I wanted to ask you to save the seventeenth for Leah's birthday. Your father is keen to take her somewhere special for lunch."

"Sure. I'll put it in my calendar now." It was her sister's thirtieth, so it made sense that their father would want to make a splash.

"She's been working so hard lately, she deserves a treat."

Like both their parents, Leah was a doctor, but while Karen and John were both G.P.s, Leah was training to be a cardiothoracic surgeon, something their mother had always wanted for her.

"How many years left now?" Audrey asked.

"Four. Which seems like a long time at the moment but the sky is literally the limit when she's completed her training." There was no missing the pride in her voice.

And why not? Leah had always been the best at everything. High school had been a walk in the park, she'd graduated at top of her class at university and she'd secured a place in the cardiothoracic program without breaking a sweat. It stood to reason that once Leah finished her training she would have a stellar career that would make their mother even prouder.

"Well, she's on the downhill run now," Audrey joked. "She can start taking it easy soon."

"I don't think your sister knows how. We had a spa day together last week and she spent the whole time checking her messages and making phone calls. Typical high achiever." Her mother gave a fond sigh.

Audrey picked up her pen and started drawing circles on the notepad beside her phone.

"How's everything else? Did you sort out the problem with the lawn?"

"What problem with the lawn?" Her mother sounded completely blank.

"The drainage. Last time we spoke you'd had some problems with flooding down the back."

"Oh, that was months ago. Your father had someone come in and dig a ditch or something. Anyway, it's all fine now."

"Good."

They talked about the weather and her parents' garden for a few more minutes, then her mother insisted on "letting her go."

Audrey closed her eyes, aware of the old, old hollow feeling behind her breastbone. Every now and then, her mother or father or sister said something that gave her a glimpse into the world they shared with one another—cozy dinners for three, outings to the theater, European holidays. Last week, a mother-daughter spa day.

And Audrey hadn't spoken to any of them for over a month. Even after so many years, it hurt to know it all went on without her. She'd be lying if she pretended anything else.

"Definitely time to go home."

Before she became completely maudlin and pathetic.

She snagged the strap of her handbag and her briefcase

then stood. The room spun crazily as the blood rushed from her head, and she slapped her hand onto the desk to steady herself.

Whoa. Someone has low blood sugar.

She held out her hand, and sure enough it was shaking. It was nearly ten, and she'd been at her desk since six-thirty in the morning. Lunch had been two bites of banana and a snack-size yogurt—*hours* ago.

So much for knowing how to look after herself. Barefoot, she made her way to the staff room in the hope that there were some bananas left. No such luck. The cookie jar was empty, too, only a few crumbs in the bottom to taunt the truly desperate. She opened the fridge and eyed the detritus left from other people's lunches. Squishy-looking fruit and dry, curled sandwiches. Blurg.

If you get to the point where you're ready to chew your arm off, there's a stash of protein bars in the bottom left drawer of my desk.

She shut the fridge door. There was no way she was raiding Zach's stash. There was something about the idea of accepting a favor from him that made her uncomfortable.

Her stomach growled, an audible counterargument to her thoughts. She looked around the kitchen a little desperately. She'd make herself another cup of coffee with lots of sugar. That should do the trick. She opened the fridge in search of milk, only to find none.

Damn it. She hated black coffee with a passion.

Stop being so bloody precious. Eat his protein bar and go home and get a good night's sleep. Like a grown-up.

Gritting her teeth, she marched out of the staff room before she could think the matter to death. Zach's office was on the opposite side of the department from hers. She paused in the doorway, then committed herself to his domain.

Like her, he had a company-issue desk made from blond

wood veneer. The bookcase and filing cabinet were also standard-issue, but he'd hung a series of black-and-white framed photographs on the walls, arty shots of old buildings and other architectural features, as well as bringing in an old-fashioned wood-and-brass desk lamp. She'd been in his office for only brief moments before, and she paused in front of one the photographs. A moody photograph of a European street, it was stark and simple. She wondered if he'd taken it himself.

She gave herself a shake. She was here for sustenance, not snooping. She couldn't stop herself from noticing his pristine desktop as she pushed his chair back to access the drawers, though. His blotter was unblemished, his in- and out-trays empty. By contrast, her own desk looked like a war zone: piles of papers, catalogs bristling with sticky notes, crumbs in her keyboard, a million reminders to herself scribbled across the blotter. She hadn't sighted her in-tray for over a month, it was buried beneath so much paperwork. She prided herself on the fact that, if pushed, she could lay her hand on anything within thirty seconds, but the fact remained that Zach had her beat, hands down, in the anal tidiness stakes.

She slid the bottom drawer open. Sure enough, a box of protein bars was inside. There were two flavors, Dutch chocolate and French vanilla, and she chose vanilla. She was about to shut the drawer when her gaze fell on a bottle of aftershave. She reached for it and lifted it to her nose, inhaling a light citrus scent with surprising spicy base notes. Mmm. Nice. She sniffed again, closing her eyes as she tried to identify what it reminded her of. The beach in summer? No, it was more intimate than that. Perhaps—

Abruptly she registered what was she was doing—hovering over Zach's desk, sniffing his aftershave. She whipped her hand away from her face so quickly she almost dropped the bottle. She returned it to the drawer, being careful to put it exactly where she had found it, then closed the drawer. There was a memo pad beside Zach's computer and she reached for the nearest pen to write him an IOU. It wasn't until she felt the weight of the thing that she realized she wasn't holding an ordinary plastic ballpoint. Black and shiny with warm golden accents, the pen had real heft to it. When she pressed it against the paper, it rolled effortlessly, silkily across the page. Then she spotted the tiny telltale star logo on the end.

Montblanc.

Wow. No wonder his handwriting was always so crisp and elegantly formed.

Must be nice to be able to drop three figures on a fancy pen. She made a noise, unable to imagine a universe where she would have enough money to spare to allow herself that kind of indulgence.

She returned the pen to the caddy on Zach's desk and escaped his office, taking with her the slightly guilty sense that she'd invaded his privacy. Checking out his photos and sniffing his aftershave and using his fancy-schmancy pen was hardly on a par with riffling through his underwear drawer, but if their positions were reversed, she knew she wouldn't be thrilled to know he'd lingered over her personal effects. In fact, the thought of him examining her space in that way made her toes curl into the carpet.

In her office, she tore the wrapper off the protein bar and ate it with stolid determination, chewing and swallowing until the thing was gone and the edgy, shaky feeling had passed.

She let out a sigh of relief, then grabbed her bag, briefcase and shoes and headed for the garage.

Whether she liked it or not, Zach had saved her bacon tonight. She would make a point of thanking him for his generosity tomorrow—as well as replacing the bar, of course. Under no circumstances would she try to get close enough to find out if he was wearing any of that delicious aftershave, though. And she definitely wouldn't ask him to confirm her guess about the photos on his office wall.

He was still the enemy, after all. Or, at best, her fiercest rival. It would never pay to forget that.

"How did it go?" Megan asked.

Audrey sank onto the bar stool next to her best friend and let her bag slide to the floor. "I'm alive. That's about all I'm willing to commit to right now."

Twenty minutes ago she'd left the conference room after delivering her range review and enduring nearly an hour and a half of brutal, probing questions courtesy of Henry Whitman. He'd asked about her range initiative, grilling her on every possible detail, then branched out into asking about her strategy for the department, her thoughts on the retail hardware sector in Australia, her experience in the industry...

Even though it was only five o'clock when she emerged, she'd been so exhausted and wrung out she hadn't hesitated to bail when she found Megan's note indicating that she'd be waiting at Al's Place. She'd said goodbye to her assistant, Lucy, and made for the exit as though the hounds of hell were on her tail.

Megan slid a glass of red wine along the bar toward her. "Here. You look like you could use this."

"Does it come in IV form?" Audrey slumped forward, propping her elbows on the bar.

Megan pushed her hair over her shoulder. "Wow. He really gave you a going-over, huh? I pretty much said my piece, answered a few questions from the retailers and then buggered off."

Audrey stared at her. "Really? He didn't grill you on everything from your favorite color to whether you believe in the Easter Bunny or not?"

"It was an Easter Bunny–free conversation." Megan's brow puckered. "Do you think that's a good thing or a bad thing?"

"I have no idea."

"I think it's a bad thing. He was obviously interested in you. Me, not so much." Megan shrugged philosophically, her expression clearing. "Oh, well. As soon as I'm knocked up I'm out of here anyway, so it probably doesn't really matter what the Executioner thinks of me."

"I think we need a different nickname. The Interrogator is much more accurate," Audrey said.

"The Interrogator. Nice. Has a good, intimidating ring to it."

Audrey sucked down a mouthful of wine. "We should probably eat something with this."

They both had to get behind the wheel to drive home, after all.

"Already on it. Cameron is bringing curly fries."

"I knew there was a reason we love it here."

They'd discovered Al's Place a couple of years ago. A dark and dingy little bar in the strip of shops across from Makers, the rest of their colleagues gave it a wide berth, making it the perfect place for post-work bitch sessions and two-woman mutual sympathy parties. The floor was sticky and the decor firmly stuck in the eighties, but Cameron always gave them lots of pretzels and was never stingy with his pouring.

"Okay, the big question for you," Megan said, twisting so she faced Audrey more squarely. "If Whitman came over all Robert Redford in *Indecent Proposal* with you, would you or wouldn't you?"

Audrey let out a crack of laughter. Trust Megan to find such a unique, irreverent way to put the afternoon's ordeal into perspective.

"Come on." Megan nudged her. "Would you sleep with him to keep your job or not?"

Audrey considered that. Whitman had to be in his late fifties, maybe early sixties, but he was in good shape, no spare tire or jowly chops. If she squinted and the lighting was right, he might be considered a silver fox. But there was no amount of squinting that could erase those steely, all-seeing eyes.

"Not in a million years," she said.

"What was it that did it for you? The sausage fingers or the seagull eyes?"

"The eyes. I didn't even notice his fingers."

"Oh, you will, trust me. They're hard to miss." Megan shuddered, then took a sip.

Audrey huffed out a laugh. "Have I told you lately that I love you?"

"I'm thinking he's a socks-with-sandals kind of guy, too. I bet he breaks them out at the conference, along with bad floral shirts with short sleeves."

Audrey nearly choked on her wine. "God, I'd forgotten all about the conference."

She'd been so consumed with researching her new boss it had slipped her mind that she and her colleagues would soon be flying to sunny Queensland for three days of intense business powwows with more than six hundred member retailers.

"Only ten days to go." Megan raised her glass in mock toast.

Audrey didn't lift her glass in return. This would be her second conference in the capacity of buyer, and she wasn't looking forward to being cornered by random retailers and taken to task over some imagined slight or oversight or deficiency. Throw Henry Whitman and his X-ray vision and hard questions into the mix, and the conference began to look like an endurance test of epic proportions.

"Look at it this way—it's three days' worth of sucking-up

opportunities. We can all sing for our supper and make the big man feel suitably powerful, then come home again and get back to business as usual," Megan said matter-of-factly.

"You really think it will be business as usual?"

Megan's blue eyes became serious. "No. I think Whitman is going to go through us like a combine harvester. But there's nothing I can do to stop that from happening, so I am going to do my best and live my life and take the worst as it comes, if it comes."

They were both silent as they contemplated the truth of Megan's words. Cameron broke the moment by sliding a bowl of golden fries in front of them.

"Enjoy, ladies."

"Bless you. Animal fats to the rescue," Audrey said.

They both reached for a handful of potato curls.

"Who do you think will go first?" Audrey asked.

Megan sighed. "I don't know. Maybe Barry? And possibly Gordon. In my experience, guys like Whitman always have their own team they want to bring on board."

Since Barry and Gordon both worked in the financial area, Megan's assessment made sense.

"Out of us, I wouldn't want to be Tom." Megan referred to the buyer in charge of building materials.

Audrey nodded in agreement. Tom was a lovely man, but he was close to retirement age and definitely old school in his approach.

"I tell you who won't be going, though—Zach. Fifty bucks he gets a promotion out of all of this."

Audrey reached for the fries. "He's not that good."

"Sorry, sweetie, but he is. He's smart, he's good at what he does and he could charm a snake out of its skin."

Audrey rolled her eyes. "You're only saying that because you have a soft spot for him."

"Yeah, it's called a vagina."

Audrey shook her head at her friend's outrageousness. "You are so lucky no one from work comes here."

Megan stuffed a fry into her mouth before cocking her head. "You honestly don't think he's hot?"

"Who?"

"You know who."

Audrey did know. She shrugged. "He's okay. A bit too perfect, pretty-boy for my taste."

"He's not a pretty boy. He's got that little bump on the bridge of his nose like he's been in a fight. And he's got that cowboy-to-the-rescue walk." Megan mimed Zach's confident swagger from her seated position.

"Does your husband know about your little obsession?" Audrey asked.

"What he doesn't know he can't use in the divorce proceedings. You know, if you were a true friend, you'd go there for me and give me a full report."

"You're a pervert, you know that?"

"Okay, don't give me a full report. But for God's sake don't let an opportunity like Zach Black pass you by."

"He's just a man, Megsy. He takes his pants off one leg at a time. He probably has trouble finding the clitoris like every other male on the planet."

"Honey, Zach knows *exactly* where the clitoris is. All you have to do is look into his eyes to know that."

An odd little shiver ran down Audrey's spine. She knew what Megan was talking about—the knowing, dirty glint in Zach's eyes that spoke of tangled sheets and roaming hands and healthy, earthy curiosity.

"Stop it. I don't want to think about Zach in relation to my clitoris or any other body part."

"Ahem."

The sound came from behind her, and had a distinctly masculine tone. Belatedly she noticed the cool brush of air on the nape of her neck—as though someone had recently entered—and the tide of color rising up Megan's chest and into her face.

Everything in her went very still. She closed her eyes. "Please tell me Zach isn't standing behind me."

"I *could* tell you that, but it wouldn't be true," her friend replied.

Audrey mouthed a four-letter word as embarrassed heat flooded her face. She told herself to turn around and face the music, but her body was rigid with mortification.

"It's not going to get any easier, Mathews," Zach said. "Might as well get it over and done with."

She knew exactly what expression he'd be wearing—smug, slightly self-satisfied. How…appalling.

Slowly she turned. Contrary to her expectation, his expression was carefully neutral. For the life of her she couldn't tell if he was pissed or amused or something else entirely.

"I tried your phone, but it went straight to voice mail, and Lucy said to try over here. A courier dropped off a delivery in the parking garage and backed into your car."

"What?" Audrey slid off the stool and onto her feet, concern for her car momentarily trumping her humiliation.

"It's not major, but I figured you'd want to know about it. Lucy's got the guy's insurance details."

Her thoughts rushing ahead to insurance claims and the inconvenience of repairs, Audrey collected her bag and turned to go. At the last minute she remembered the bar tab and turned back.

"Don't worry about it. Your treat next time," Megan said, waving her off.

It wasn't until she was exiting Al's Place and blinking in the bright late-afternoon sunlight that Audrey realized she'd have to make the walk back to the office with Zach at her side.

If she'd stopped to think for even a second, she would have made some excuse to send him ahead of her—anything to avoid the awkward, loaded silence that descended as they made their way to the traffic lights. She pressed the button and stared across the four lanes of road separating her from her place of work. Never had a few meters of asphalt seemed to stretch so far.

She sneaked a look at Zach out of the corner of her eye. He was staring straight ahead, his expression still unreadable. She wondered how much of the conversation he'd heard. Obviously, the bit where she'd referenced her very private body parts and his name in the same sentence. But had he heard the bit where Megan had admired his prowess? Or the bit where Audrey had dismissed him as a pretty boy?

She was still hot from the first wave of embarrassment, but she could feel a second, deeper heat stealing into her cheeks. So much for Al's being a safe place of refuge. She would never sit with her back to the door again for the rest of her life.

The light changed and they strode onto the road. Audrey kept sneaking glances at Zach, but he had the best poker face she'd ever come across.

Finally she broke. "Look, I know it must have sounded pretty bad, but what you heard was totally out of context."

They'd reached the center island and Zach stopped, forcing her to stop, too.

"Maybe I'm a bit thick, but I can't come up with too many contexts that feature your clitoris and me in the same conversation that aren't *exactly* what I'm thinking."

Dear God. She couldn't believe she was standing in the middle of a freeway listening to Zach refer to her lady parts as casually as if he was discussing the weather.

"We were actually discussing the likelihood of you being promoted," she said a little desperately.

He slipped his hands into his trouser pockets and considered her for a moment. "Okay, I'll bite. What on earth has that got to do with your clitoris?"

She gritted her teeth. "Could you stop saying that, please?"

"What? Clitoris?"

"Yes."

A truck blew past, making his jacket flap.

"Would you prefer me to call it something else? Little man in the boat? Love button?"

He was enjoying himself, she could tell by the creases around his eyes. And maybe she deserved to suffer a little. If she'd caught him having the same conversation about her with one of their male colleagues, she would be justifiably outraged.

"I would really, really like you to erase the last five minutes from your memory."

He turned and hit the button to trigger the pedestrian lights. When he faced her he shrugged.

"Okay."

She stared at him, but there wasn't much else she could do or say. He'd caught her having an inappropriate conversation with a friend, and she was going to have to live with the knowledge that Zach now believed she and Megan habitually talked about him in intimate terms in their spare time.

The light changed and they walked in silence the rest of the way. Zach led the way to the garage before standing back while she inspected the large dent in the side of her little hatchback. She was very aware of him as she ran her hand over the damage.

"Ugly but drivable," she said.

"Yeah. His insurance should cover the repair."

She looked at him. Humiliation aside, he'd gone out of his way to find her so she wouldn't return and find her car all banged up. A pretty nice thing to do.

And he'd fed her last night.

"Thanks for coming to get me. I appreciate it."

"It was no big deal." He buttoned his suit jacket. "See you tomorrow."

He headed for the stairs, no doubt going back up to his office to put in more overtime. She watched him walk away, begrudgingly agreeing with Megan—he was too manly and masculine to be a true pretty boy, even if his face *was* very pretty.

But it seemed he wasn't just an attractive face. He could be nice, too, as well as considerate.

She frowned. She didn't want to start seeing the human side of Zach. He got under her skin enough already. If they were in a meeting together, it was always his comments she remembered the most clearly afterward. At large work functions, she always knew where he was and who he was talking to. And when he took leave or traveled interstate, the office felt too quiet and slow in his absence, as though some vital element was missing.

She didn't want to be so aware of him. In fact, it was the very last thing she wanted. Half the women in the building had a crush on him, and she steadfastly refused to join their ranks.

Besides, even if he was a nice person under his well-cut suits and perfect hair, it didn't change the fact that he would throw her under a bus if he thought it would further his career.

Admit it, you'd give him a shove, too.

Maybe. Part of her liked to think she would. She worked in a male-dominated industry, and it was important to be as tough, as emotionless as many of the men she had around her. The other part of her questioned if any role or pay raise was worth all the stress and exhaustion and worry.

She squared her shoulders. It was worth it. The alternatives—sitting in the corner waiting to be rewarded for being a good little girl, or giving up entirely and finding something less demanding—were not really alternatives. She could no more walk away from this job and her ambition than she could change the color of her eyes or her skin. She needed to prove herself. She needed it like she needed oxygen.

Turning her back on her scratched and dented car, she headed back to her office. If Zach was putting in the long hours tonight, she needed to be, too.

That was just the way it was.

CHAPTER THREE

ZACH WASN'T ABOUT to kid himself—there was no way he would get any work done with Audrey's words bouncing around inside his head.

I don't want to think about Zach in relation to my clitoris or any other body part.

He'd entered the bar just in time to catch Audrey's words, and he was burning to know what she and Megan had been talking about before he arrived.

Him—obviously—but had the conversation been led by Megan or Audrey? And had it been the kind of conversation a guy liked to think women might have about him when he wasn't around, or the kind that could leave a man scarred for life?

He made a frustrated noise as it hit him that he would never know. The odds of Audrey ever willingly broaching the topic again were slim to none, and he certainly wasn't going to harangue her into confessing. That would give her too much power.

He would simply have to learn to live with the mystery. Yet another unanswered question where she was concerned, to be added to the host of other things he wanted to know about her.

Like what she did when she wasn't working, and why he found her so compelling, and if the pale, downy skin at the nape of her neck was as soft and fragrant as he imagined....

He loosened his tie and gave himself a mental slap, pushing thoughts of Audrey into a dark, deep corner. Where they were going to stay, for the sake of his peace of mind and his career.

He made a point of not noticing if Audrey's office was still lit as he made his way to his car an hour later. He drove home via the supermarket and walked in the door just after eight o'clock. He kicked off his shoes, made himself a chicken sandwich and ate in front of the TV. Even though he was tired, he felt wired, his brain unable to focus on the screen.

Maybe he should go out, catch a movie or something. Or maybe read a book. He walked to the bookcase in his study and checked out the shelf he'd reserved for fiction. Two lonely, dusty spy thrillers sat there, and he'd read both of them. Still, it had been a while. The odds were good he'd forgotten enough of the plot to still go along for the ride.

He returned to the couch, one of the books in hand, and muted the TV. He settled down with his legs outstretched, a cushion behind his head. He opened the first page and started reading.

He was intensely aware of the silence in the house, so much so that his own breathing sounded loud in his head. It hit him that this was the first time in months that he'd taken some time for himself, and even though he was ostensibly chilling out, there was still a voice in the back of his mind telling him he should check his email and go over another report.

He set the book down on his belly and let his head drop back. Was it possible to lose the ability to relax? Because if so, he was there.

He stared at the stain on the ceiling from where the roof had leaked and wondered what Audrey was doing tonight.

"Idiot."

He stood abruptly, the book sliding to the floor.

This little crush he was developing stopped *now*. No more self-indulgence. No more flirting with the possibilities.

Even though it was dark outside, he changed into his running gear and hit the street. An hour later, he was drenched in sweat, his thigh muscles burning. Most importantly, his mind was blessedly clear.

It would stay that way, too. He had the conference coming up, then a series of catalogs to plan for. Plus whatever drama Whitman would no doubt stir up.

Then there was his mother.

More than enough for one man to handle.

AUDREY ARRIVED AT work the next morning with a plan: to acknowledge Zach's generosity in helping her with her car while simultaneously avoiding him as much as possible in the hope that they could both forget the clitoris thing. On the surface they were two agendas at odds with each other, but she was hoping she could swing it. She started her campaign by leaving a box of protein bars on his desk, complete with a breezy note. *Thanks for your help yesterday and for the much-needed snack the other night. Both much appreciated. A.*

It had taken her a whole hour last night to compose those two sentences, and while she wasn't entirely happy with them, she figured her note covered the first part of her plan. The second part—the avoidance part—would require more effort and vigilance. The merchandising department might employ in excess of thirty people, but it was essentially a fishbowl and they all swam around one another all day. There were multiple opportunities to run into Zach in the hall, in the staff room, at the printer, near the photocopier, so she needed to stay sharp and be quick on her feet.

And spend a lot of time hiding in her office.

A couple of days should do it, she figured. Long enough

for her to stop blushing every time she remembered that moment in the bar, and hopefully long enough for him to forget what he'd overheard.

All went well, avoidance-wise, until midafternoon when she arrived three minutes late for the weekly departmental meeting to find only one seat left. Right next to Zach, naturally.

Well, shit.

Shaking a mental fist at fate, she slid into the empty seat. Zach glanced at her briefly before focusing on Gary, who had the floor. Audrey flipped to a new page in her notebook, determined to get past this silly self-consciousness where he was concerned.

So, she'd said something stupid and potentially revealing in front of the one colleague whom she really didn't want to do any of the above with. It wasn't the end of the world. Right?

Right?

Megan sat diagonally opposite, her eyes dancing with suppressed laughter. Audrey pressed her lips together, sure her friend was remembering last night.

At least someone was getting something positive out of the situation. That was nice.

Gary talked about the sales results for the first week of the current catalog, and she made notes to compare some of the figures with her own data. She steadfastly refused to glance sideways at Zach, but she could feel heat stealing into her face anyway, a slow, steadily growing burn.

She concentrated fiercely on her notes, taking down almost every word Gary said, and slowly her embarrassment subsided—that is, until Zach shifted beside her, bumping her shoulder, and the whole rising-tide-of-heat thing started all over again.

By the time the meeting ended she had damp armpits and

was desperate for five minutes alone to regain her equilibrium. The moment Gary signaled they could go she was on her feet, gathering her things as though school had been let out for summer.

"Audrey, could I have a word?" Gary called as she all but sprinted for the door.

She pulled up short. "Sure. Of course."

She joined him at the head of the table, mentally reviewing her to-do list. Maybe he wanted to talk about the new proposal they'd had from one of their lighting suppliers. Or the additions she wanted to make to the rechargeable battery range.

But Gary's gaze was focused over her shoulder. "You, too, Zach."

Of course he wanted to talk to Zach at the same time. Today was clearly her day. Not. She hugged her papers to her chest as Zach joined them.

"I've got a meeting in ten so I'll cut to the chase," Gary said. "Whitman has asked us to put together a competitor analysis. Strengths, weaknesses, growth areas. You know the drill. I thought maybe you two would like to handle it."

Okay, now she knew fate really was dicking with her. The last-remaining-seat situation was one thing, but offering her a chance to score some major corporate brownie points while linking that same opportunity to her having to work hand-in-glove with Zach? That was simply cruel.

"Sounds good," Zach said easily. "But I'm happy to handle it on my own if Audrey's snowed."

She blinked, drawn out of her own thoughts by his casually worded attempted coup. She *bet* he'd be happy to handle the analysis on his own. He'd probably love to give Whitman a little shoulder rub and polish his car, too.

"Oh no, I'm up for it," she said brightly.

Only belatedly did she consider how her words might be

construed, given what Zach had overheard her say last night. "I mean, I'm not snowed." That didn't sound good, either. Not when she was talking to her immediate boss. "Don't get me wrong, I'm busy, but I'd like the opportunity."

"Good. You've got two weeks. Whitman wants a presentation after the conference." Gary gave her a curious look before heading for the door.

She cleared her throat and faced her temporary partner in crime. Determined to be professional about this, no matter what.

"So…how do you want to do this?"

"I guess we should divide up the workload. Write our sections separately, then pool data and conclusions," Zach said.

She forced herself to look at him directly for the first time all day. He was wearing a dark blue shirt, the color lending extra depth to his eyes. For once he wasn't laughing at her. A small win.

"Sounds good. Do you want to reconvene after five, draw up a schedule…?"

"Can we make it six? I've got a conference call with some of the guys from Perth."

"Sure, suits me."

He gestured for her to precede him from the room and they parted in the hallway.

In her office, she gave herself a little pep talk. This report was an opportunity, and she was going to hit it out of the park. End of story.

She applied herself to her task list with a Terminator-like zeal, aware that she would have to carve out the time to research and write her share of the analysis over the coming week. Since no one had miraculously added a couple of extra hours to every day, she was going to have to work harder and smarter to fit everything in.

Accordingly, she was armed with some initial thoughts

when she made her way to the meeting room at six. Zach hadn't arrived yet, so she set herself up at one end of the long table, spreading printouts and past reports in front of her.

Makers had three major rivals—two corporate "big box" type retailers and a group of smaller independents that had banded together. While Makers kept a keen eye on all players, the company hadn't commissioned a comprehensive competitor analysis for more than four years. A major oversight, in Audrey's opinion, and she wasn't surprised Whitman had made it one of his first priorities.

She worked her way through the last report, highlighting figures that would need updating in fluorescent pink.

"Sorry. We had a bad connection and the call went over." Zach dropped into the chair next to her, sighing heavily. He considered all the printouts she'd laid out. "You've been busy."

"I pulled some old reports. Most of them are irrelevant now, the market has moved on so much. But there's good background information in some of them we might be able to use."

"Good plan."

He leaned across to grab one of the reports and a spicy, mellow scent drifted her way. She recognized it as the aftershave he had stashed in his desk and shifted uncomfortably in her seat. She didn't want to notice his aftershave. Even if it was really delicious.

"We need to pull in a lot of data," she said. "I'll put out a shout to the state marketing coordinators tomorrow to get them started on some figures."

She was aware of Zach looking at her, but rather than make eye contact she turned another page and lifted her hand to tuck her hair behind her ear.

"If we're going to divide this up, how do you want to do it?" she asked.

When he didn't answer immediately, she lifted her gaze. He was watching her, his eyes crinkled at the corners. Clearly amused by something. As always.

"I could take on Mathesons, and you could do Handy Hardware. Which leaves us with Home Savings—we can split that last one," she suggested.

"Sounds good. Gary mentioned a consulting firm we can call on for industry data?"

They talked over the details of the project for half an hour, making notes and plans. Every now and then she glanced up and caught him smiling that small, amused smile, but he didn't offer to share the joke and she wasn't about to ask. The cup of tea she'd had before joining him was starting to make its presence felt.

"Won't be a moment," she said as she stood.

He was busy making a notation in the margin of one of the older reports as she left the room. She rolled her shoulders as she made her way to the ladies'. She really needed to learn to loosen up around him; her shoulders felt like they were set in concrete.

She saw the mark on her face the moment she entered the bathroom—a big fluorescent pink streak from the middle of her cheek up into her hairline.

"What the—?"

Then she remembered pushing back her hair with the highlighter in her hand. D'oh.

No wonder he'd been smirking at her.

"Thanks for the heads-up, buddy," she muttered to herself as she scrubbed her face clean. She took care of business, then returned to the meeting room, aware that she was, yet again, at a disadvantage where he was concerned. Just once it would be nice if he was the one who looked like a dick.

She waited for him to say something about her face—finally—when she entered the room, but he simply gave another one of those small almost-smiles and pushed a print-out her way.

"There's some good stuff in here about projected revenues. We can springboard off historical predictions and talk about how the entry of the second big-box retailer into the market has changed the environment."

"I'll make a note of it."

She tried to concentrate on what she was doing, but she couldn't let go of the fact that he'd sat next to her for more than half an hour, laughing privately at her striped face, amusing himself at her expense.

The more she thought about it, the more steamed she got, and finally she couldn't hold it in any longer.

"You could have said something."

"Sorry?" He looked up from the page he was reading, his expression distracted.

"The highlighter on my face. You could have said something."

His gaze went to her cheek. "Could I?"

"Yes, you could have."

"But then we would have gotten into the whole 'where is it?' and 'have I got it all?' thing. Next thing you know, I'd be spitting on my hanky and wiping your face." He smiled, inviting her to share the joke.

At last.

"You enjoy laughing at me, don't you?" The words popped out of their own accord.

He frowned. "Do I?"

"You know you do."

"Actually, I don't. Why would I want to laugh at you?"

Because he thought he was better than her. Because it was the way of handsome, entitled, arrogant men to be amused by lesser beings.

But she wasn't about to say either of those things out loud. She wouldn't give him the satisfaction.

"We don't have time for this." She made a big deal out of sorting through the papers in front of her.

"You brought it up, not me."

"Forget I said anything."

"You can't throw an accusation like that out there and then shut down the conversation. Why on earth would you think I was laughing at you?" He looked and sounded genuinely perplexed.

"Because you always smile when you see me, for starters."

His eyebrows shot up, as though she'd astonished him. "Did it ever occur to you that maybe—crazy idea—I might actually enjoy your company?"

It was her turn to be astonished. "No."

"Wow. Okay." He shook his head as though she'd confused the hell out of him.

"You want the next category manager's role. Don't pretend you don't. And you know I'm your toughest competition."

"So, what, we can't be friends?"

She didn't even need to think about it. "No. My career is too important for me to screw it up by allowing other considerations to enter into the equation."

"That's uncanny. You sounded exactly like Gordon Gekko in *Wall Street* when you said that."

"I'm not ashamed of being ambitious. I'm the only person in the world I can rely on, and if I don't make things happen, they don't happen. I'm not going to apologize for that."

Suddenly he looked very serious. "You think I don't understand that?"

She caught herself before she scoffed out loud. He had to be kidding. He was a walking advertisement for indulgence, from the luxury watch to his silk-and-wool suit to his Italian leather shoes. His pen alone represented a mortgage payment on her tiny place. As the daughter of two hardworking GPs, she'd grown up in a house where money had never really been an issue, but Zach reeked of a whole different level of privilege. The kind where houses were "estates" and children had numerals after their names to differentiate them from their noble forebears.

"There's a difference between wanting something and needing it. For example, I'm sure you *want* your polo pony, but I *need* to pay my electricity bill."

He blinked. Then he sat back in his chair. He looked... *stunned* was the only word she could come up with. As though she'd sneaked up and goosed him.

"You think I have a polo pony?"

She had no idea how the other half lived—or, more accurately, the one percent—but her point still stood. No way would he ever be as hungry as she was.

"If you've got it, flaunt it, right?" she said.

When he continued to look baffled, she pointed to his shoes. "Hugo Boss." She glanced at his wrist, where the gleam of his slim, elegant rose-gold watch peeked out beneath the cuff of his jacket. "Patek Philippe." She indicated his suit. "Armani."

"Okay. I like nice things. Your point is?"

"That you and I come from very different places in the world."

He stared at her. Up close, his eyes appeared almost gray instead of dark blue. The gunmetal color of the ocean before a storm.

"Look. Maybe we should just concentrate on getting this project sorted and we can both get on with our lives," she said.

He still didn't say anything and she shook her head slightly. She didn't get why he was looking so gobsmacked. Did he really think people hadn't noticed he was different?

"I'll take this stuff home and draw up an outline for my sections. If you do the same, we can meet again tomorrow after work and finalize our brief before diving in. How does that sound?"

His frown was gone now, his expression impenetrable. "Whatever suits."

"Good. Same time tomorrow?"

"That works for me."

He stood and scooped up his things.

"Hang on, I think you've got my phone…" she said, frowning.

He flipped up the protective cover and checked. "You're right, sorry," he said, his tone clipped as they swapped handsets.

She was about to tell him that it was an easy enough mistake since they all had the same company-issued handsets and covers, but before she could say another word he was gone. She stared at the empty doorway. She felt uncomfortable about what had just happened. She should have bitten her tongue and swallowed her impulsive words, for the sake of the project if nothing else. If she hadn't been feeling so dumb after the highlighter incident, maybe she would have, but she'd hated the thought of him being amused at her expense. Sitting there laughing at her up his sleeve while she'd been doing her best to make this project fly.

She made a growling noise in her throat.

Why did she always wind up second-guessing herself where Zach was concerned? No one else in her world made her feel so self-conscious and uneasy.

She didn't know what it was, but she didn't like it. The sooner this project was over, the better.

CHAPTER FOUR

APPARENTLY, HE WAS an elitist snob, born with a silver spoon in his mouth.

How 'bout that.

Zach threw another folder into his briefcase, trying to work out if he was flattered by Audrey's insanely inaccurate take on who he was or if he was, in fact, supremely pissed at being dismissed as a trust-fund playboy dabbling in a career for fun.

He'd grown up with nothing, in both material and spiritual senses. Any money that came into the household had gone straight up his mother's arm, and the only reason he was still alive today was because of the people in his mother's life—various hangers-on and fellow addicts and the few persistent, stubborn family members who had persevered in maintaining contact with his mother over the years, despite her many, many abuses of their trust.

His school uniforms had been secondhand; his textbooks, too. He worked after school and earned himself scholarships and held down two part-time jobs to support himself while at university. No one had handed him anything, ever.

Yet, according to Audrey, he came across as a snotty-nosed rich kid. Someone who'd had every good thing in life gifted to him on a silver platter.

How…bizarre.

It had never occurred to him that anyone might take him for anything other than what he was—a poor kid who'd made good. He liked nice things, but he hadn't bought his car or his watch or his suit because he wanted other people to look at him and think he was something he wasn't. He'd bought them because he could. Because he'd admired and wanted them, and he'd had more than enough of missing out in his life. Seeing something beautiful and fine and knowing he could make it his own was a power he would never, ever take for granted and never, ever tire of exercising.

Screw it. Who cares what she thinks? Let her believe what she wants to believe.

An excellent notion, except for one small problem: he did care what Audrey thought of him. And not only because he wanted to get her naked.

She was smart. She was determined. She was funny. There was something about her, a tilt to her chin or a light in her eye or…*something* that spoke to him. He wanted to know more about her. Where she came from, who her parents were, what her school years had been like, if she was all about chocolate or if vanilla was her poison of choice. He wanted more of her.

I'm the only person in the world I can rely on, and if I don't make things happen, they don't happen. I'm not going to apologize for that.

They were her words, but the huge irony was that he could just as well have spoken them himself. Certainly they reflected his philosophy in life.

Audrey might not recognize it, but they had a lot in common.

He mulled over the other things she'd said as he drove home, especially the stuff about him laughing at her. Did he really always smile when he saw her? He thought back over their recent interactions, but couldn't remember what he'd been doing with his face when he'd been talking to her. Certainly, he always relished the opportunity to be in the same room as her. Was it possible his enjoyment manifested itself in the form of a gormless grin?

He shook his head in self-disgust. He really, truly needed to get a grip on himself if that was the case, for his own personal dignity if not for sound business reasons. The last thing he wanted was to be cast as the unrequited desperado in their little office drama.

Not a look he'd ever been keen to cultivate.

By the time he got home he'd decided the best thing he could do—the smartest thing—was to get through this project as quickly and painlessly as possible. Do his bit, keep to himself, keep things purely professional. And make sure he was aware of what his mouth was doing when he was around her.

Simple.

Which didn't explain why he woke at two in the morning and spent twenty minutes rummaging through dusty old boxes in the back of his closet until he'd found what he was looking for: the official grade two school photograph from Footscray Primary, circa 1989. The corners were curled, but there was no missing his scrawny, scrape-kneed seven-year-old self in the front row. He stared at the image for a long moment. The thin, unsmiling kid in the photo had been grappling with both his mother's and his father's destructive lifestyles at the time the picture was taken, learning that the things other kids in his class took for granted—meals, loving supervision, care—were only ever going to be sporadic features in his own life.

Happy times. Thank God he'd survived them.

Pushing the carton back into the depths of the closet, he crossed to his briefcase and slipped the photograph into a pocket.

The thought of it burned in the back of his mind the whole of the next day as he debated the wisdom behind the urge that had driven him out of bed in the early hours.

He didn't want Audrey to mistake who he was. He didn't want her to misunderstand him. Probably a futile, dangerous wish, given their work situation and the pressures they were both currently facing, but her misconception of him was eating away at his gut and he was almost certain he couldn't simply suck it up and move on.

Probably that made him an idiot, but so be it. He'd been called worse things in his time.

Still, he was undecided about what he was going to do with the photograph right up until the moment he joined Audrey in the meeting room. She'd beaten him to the punch—again—and was writing something in her notebook when he entered, a small frown wrinkling her brow, her glasses balanced on the end of her nose. Her head was propped on one hand, the chestnut silk of her hair spilling over her shoulder. She looked studious and serious and shiny and good, and something tightened in his chest as he looked at her.

Then she registered his presence and her expression became wary and stiff. She slid off her glasses. "Oh, hi. I was about to grab a coffee. Do you want one?"

In that second he made his decision, for good or for ill. Placing his briefcase on the table, he flicked it open and pulled the photograph from the inside pocket.

"Thanks. But there's something I want to show you first."

Then, even though he knew it was dumb and that it would serve no purpose whatsoever, he slid the photograph across the table toward her.

AUDREY STARED AT the photograph Zach had pushed in front of her. Why on earth was he giving her a tatty old class photo?

"Is this something to do with the analysis?" she asked stupidly.

Then her gaze fell on the small, dark-haired boy in the front row and she understood what this was and who she was looking at. Zach was smaller than the other children. He was also the only one who wasn't smiling. Both his knees were dark with gravel rash, and his hair very badly needed a cut. Her gaze shifted to the plaque one of the children was holding: Footscray Primary School, Grade Two, 1989.

Slowly she lifted her gaze to his.

"You went to Footscray Primary?" She could hear the incredulity in her own voice. She *felt* incredulous—there was no way that this polished, perfect man could have emerged from one of Melbourne's most problematic inner-city suburbs. It didn't seem possible to her. Although Footscray had enjoyed a renaissance in recent years thanks to the real estate boom and its proximity to the city, for many, many years the inner western suburb had been about stolen cars and drug deals and people doing it tough.

"Footscray Secondary College, too," Zach confirmed.

She blinked as the full import of what he was saying hit home. All the assumptions she'd made about him and all of the niggling little resentments and moments of self-conscious inadequacy that had sprung from those assumptions... All wrong.

All of it.

Oh, boy.

She'd judged him from day one, slotting him neatly into a tidy little box that accorded with her view of the world. All because she'd looked at his expensive suits and smooth good looks and fancy car and decided he was one of God's gifted people. But it hadn't only been about him—about her perception of him, anyway. It had also been about her, about the chip she carried on her shoulder because no matter how hard she worked and how far up the food chain she climbed and how carefully she colored in between the lines, there was a part of her that would always feel like an impostor thanks to the lessons of her childhood and the mistakes of her teenage years.

"You know, I think that's the first time I've seen you truly stumped for a response," Zach said.

"Hardly." It seemed to her that she was all too often speechless and incoherent when he was around. "I've made a lot of assumptions about you, haven't I? I'm sorry. That was…really dumb and rude of me."

"I didn't set the record straight because I wanted an apology. I figured if we were working together it would be good if we were on the same page."

Very decent of him. Not that she deserved it. When she thought of all the different ways she'd misjudged him… It literally made her toes curl inside her shoes. When had she become such a horrible, narrow-minded, threatened person?

"I feel like an enormous idiot, if it's any consolation to you." Along with a lot of other things—petty, smug, stupid, to name a few.

"To be fair, I do own a Patek Philippe watch."

She realized a little dazedly that he was smiling, and she understood that he was very generously letting her off the hook.

"Don't forget your Hugo Boss shoes," she said after a short pause.

"And my Armani suit. Although today it's Ermenegildo Zegna."

"Pretty impressive." She meant it, too. Not because she was impressed by luxury brands, but because he'd clearly shaken off a behind-the-eight-ball start in life to get to a point where he could buy himself such beautiful things. That kind of commitment and hard work and determination took gumption and smarts and whole host of other damned fine characteristics.

"The point has never been to impress anyone."

She believed him. He'd never been ostentatious about his belongings. If anything, he'd been understated—to the point where she'd assumed his nonchalance stemmed from contempt bred from familiarity.

She picked up the photograph, studying seven-year-old

Zach again. How she could have gotten it so wrong for so long was a question that was going to keep her awake into the small hours, squirming with discomfort. Which was as it should be.

"It's not a big deal, Audrey. I just wanted to clear the air."

She looked at him, studying him through the prism of her new understanding. The bump in his nose took on new significance, as did the breadth of his shoulders and the bright directness of his gaze. It struck her that she'd been right when she'd judged Zach as being different—she'd simply misunderstood the why of it.

The beep of her phone registering an email broke the silence. She blinked and looked away from him, suddenly aware that ninety-five percent of the reasons she'd used to keep him at arm's length had just dissolved in a puff of smoke.

Instead of being an arrogant, overprivileged pretty boy with cockiness to spare, Zach was suddenly an approachable, high-achieving man with a very hot body and the world's most delicious aftershave.

And she was stuck in a meeting room with him for the foreseeable future.

"Well. We should probably get stuck into this, or we'll be here all night," she said.

They launched into work, reading over each other's proposals and suggesting areas where more research might be required. Zach was sharp and focused, and her pride demanded that she bring her A-game, too, no matter how off-balance she felt. By seven-thirty they'd agreed to the parameters of the report and identified the data they would require to complete it.

"Right. I guess we need to write up our separate parts and then meet again sometime next week to go over everything," Zach said, leaning back in his chair and stretching his arms over his head.

She did her damnedest not to notice the way his shirt pulled across his belly and chest, but wasn't sure she succeeded.

"What day suits you? I've got late meetings Monday and Tuesday."

"We leave for conference Friday. Will Wednesday be cutting it too fine?" he asked.

She called up the calendar on her phone and checked her schedule. If they had a first draft written by Wednesday night, they'd have Thursday night to finesse things into some kind of coherent presentation. A close call, but not impossible, and maybe they could find some time during the conference itself to do a dry run so they were prepared to present to Whitman when they returned.

"I think it's doable," she said.

"Okay. I'll block out Wednesday and Thursday nights."

She sighed. Sleep and downtime were obviously going to be scarce commodities in the next week or so.

"It could be worse. Gary could have asked someone else to do it," Zach said.

She couldn't help grinning. He was totally on the money—she would be so ticked off if someone else had won this opportunity instead of her.

"True."

They packed up their things in comfortable silence, the first Audrey could ever remember them sharing. Together they walked back to the merchandising department, both of them loaded down with files and laptops.

"To infinity and beyond," Zach said when it was time for them to part ways.

It wasn't until she was back in her office that Audrey recognized his words as a quote from Buzz Lightyear. It made her think of the photograph he'd shown her, of that skinny, raw-kneed boy with the too-long hair and too-serious expression.

It was strange, knowing so much about him. What he looked like as a child. Where he grew up. The fact that he'd earned everything he had with his own efforts.

And yet they weren't friends. Not by a long shot. She wasn't sure what they were.

Not enemies anymore. Rivals? Colleagues? Both words didn't feel quite right.

Audrey gave herself a mental shake. It was late; she was tired and hungry. It was time to go home and pretend she had a life.

ZACH SPENT THE bulk of his spare time for the rest of the week working on the competitor analysis. He pulled company reports from Mathesons off the internet, paid for a media search, and spoke to various suppliers and industry bodies. He spent Saturday pulling all the information he'd gathered into some kind of shape, staring at his laptop until he was bleary-eyed. The only upside of any of it—apart from the potential payoff at the end when Whitman was blown away by the report—was knowing that Audrey was in the trench with him.

Three o'clock. Sunday morning found him tapping away on his laptop, driven from his bed by restless thoughts. He swore out loud when the email notification pinged loudly in the quiet of the living room, startling him, then shook his head when he saw it was from Audrey. Nice to know he wasn't the only one having trouble sleeping.

What's wrong, Mathews? Did you wet the bed?

He was tired enough that he'd hit Send before it occurred to him that even though their working relationship had improved since their little cards-on-the-table chat the other night, it might not be up to incontinence jokes just yet.

"Good one, smart-ass," he told his computer screen, scrubbing his face with his hands.

A second later, another ping.

Had to get up to see Sven and Lars out. Crazy night. Think we might have broken the bed.

He barked out a laugh at her bold response.

That's the problem with the Swedes: too enthusiastic, he typed back.

He stared at the screen, waiting for her response.

Is there such a thing as being too enthusiastic? I'm not sure. Speaking of...I've finished my first draft. Want to correct my grammar?

Thought you'd never ask. Here's mine, just so you don't feel left out. In an attempt to preempt any ridicule, I freely admit that spelling is not my forte. Have at it.

Thanks for taking all the fun out of it. I was going to print off your worst offenses and show them to Megan on Monday.

Feel free. I've already posted your comments about Whitman's sausage fingers on Facebook.

I don't believe I've ever mentioned Whitman's freakishly overinflated digits to you before, so I'm not sure what you'll be posting...oh, wait...

He laughed out loud again and pulled the laptop a little closer to the edge of the coffee table.

Your secrets are safe with me, he typed.

Seriously, though...Those sausage fingers. Megan and I thought we were the only ones who'd noticed.

Dude, you'd have to be hard of seeing not to notice those puppies.

I haven't been called "dude" since the Teenage Mutant Ninja Turtles were big in primary school.

My pleasure.

There was a short pause before the next message appeared.

Hey. I just realized Can't Stop the Music is on. And they say insomnia is bad.

????

You haven't seen it? Dude, you are missing out. Let me sketch a few details for you: Steve Guttenberg, roller skates, New York City. And if that doesn't clinch the deal for you, it was a movie vehicle for the Village People.

Sold.

He grabbed the remote, flicked the TV on and changed the channel. Cheesy music blasted into the room, while the screen filled with a cityscape, complete with a man in white jeans roller-skating down the street, Walkman clutched in one hand.

Wow, he typed.

I know. I'll leave you to enjoy in peace. My gift to you, fellow workaholic.

He stared at the computer screen, only now registering how much he'd been enjoying their exchange. How engaged he'd been, imagining Audrey sitting up in bed tapping away at her laptop, wearing nothing but one of those tight little tank tops and a pair of lacy panties....

Yeah.

Maybe it was just as well she'd signed off, before he let lack of sleep and the intimacy of the early hour lead him into dangerous territory.

Audrey might be sexy and funny and smart, but she was still his coworker. He had no business thinking about her panties. Especially while he and Audrey were coauthoring the competitor analysis together.

He shut his laptop, in case he was tempted to renew contact, and settled back on the couch to watch what promised to be a spectacularly bad movie.

He liked the idea that somewhere in Melbourne, Audrey was doing the same thing.

In a tight little tank top.

And black—no, red—panties.

He was only human, after all.

"So. How's it going?" Megan took a slurp from her milkshake and wiggled her eyebrows suggestively.

"I'm going to go out on a limb and guess that when you say 'it' you're referring to my working relationship with Zach," Audrey said drily.

It was Thursday, one day before they flew out to Queensland for the conference, and her last day of working hand-in-glove with Zach.

"Quit stalling. Have you had wild monkey sex yet? Have you seen him without his shirt?"

Audrey rolled her eyes. "You're obsessed with sex, you know that?"

Although it was very telling that the thought of Zach sans shirt made her heart rate go a little crazy.

"Hello? Trying to get pregnant over here. Sex *is* my life. Not wild monkey sex, though, sadly. We have slightly dutiful procreational sex. Still fun, but not very spontaneous. I think it's all the mucous checking."

"What on earth—" Audrey caught herself and held up a hand. "Actually, you know what? I don't want to know."

"I'll spare you. I'd hate for there to be no surprises for you if you ever decide to have children."

"Thank you. You're very generous."

"So, I'm thinking eight inches, solid girth…?"

"Jesus, Megan." This time Audrey glanced over her shoulder, even though she was pretty sure no one else from work was currently patronizing the food court at the local shopping mall.

"What?" Megan asked, a devilish glint in her eye.

"I don't want to think about Zach's…girth, okay? We're working together."

Not that she hadn't given some consideration to the more intimate aspects of his body over the past week, most notably when she'd been drifting back to sleep at four o'clock Sunday morning, picturing Zach doing the same thing on the other side of town. She was only human, and he was the sexiest man she'd ever spent so much time with.

Hands down.

All he had to do was walk into the room these days and she could feel her body warming. She didn't even want to imagine what he could do if he put his mind to it.

Okay, she did. But she wasn't going to, because she loved her job, and she wanted to get ahead, and sleeping with Zach was the best way she could think of to destroy both those things.

She would dearly love to discuss all of the above with Megan, however, because that was what they did best. It would be so good to get her friend's perspective. But Megan would make a big deal out it, along with encouraging all sorts of reckless fantasies and behavior, and Audrey so did not need that kind of encouragement right now.

It was bad enough dealing with her own inappropriate thoughts and feelings.

Megan sighed heavily. "I knew it. You're wasting this golden opportunity by squabbling with him, aren't you?"

"No."

Not since the night he'd forced her to see him as he really was. Nope, since then they'd been getting on just fine. Chatting in the staff room. Popping into each other's offices to pass on new pieces of information they'd dug up. Emailing each other in the dead of night and having inappropriate, unprofessional conversations.

"Why are you smiling like that?"

Audrey adopted a more serious expression. "Is that better?"

"You'd tell me, wouldn't you, if you and Zach were doing the dirty?" Megan asked beseechingly.

Audrey suspected her friend was only half kidding.

"You'll be the first to know. Outside of Zach, of course."

"Cross your heart and hope to die?"

"Stick a needle in my eye," Audrey promised.

It wasn't as though it was ever going to be an issue, after all. She might be sexually frustrated, but she wasn't an idiot.

"Okay, fine." Megan pointed to the half a sandwich still left on Audrey's plate. "Are you going to eat that?"

"It's all yours."

"Thank you. That sub barely touched the sides. I think I'm having a growth spurt."

Audrey managed to change the subject then, but Megan's words popped into her mind as she hit the mall afterward to shop for a present for her sister.

The truth was, she was finding it incredibly difficult to believe that she had ever not liked Zach. He was funny. He was cheeky. He said amazingly clever things that made her brain hurt trying to keep up. And he was also one hundred percent male.

Hot, firm, hard male.

Yesterday, they'd shared a pizza and worked into the night

as they pasted their separate sections of the analysis into one coherent report and massaged it into shape. At some point he'd loosened his tie and she'd kicked off her shoes. She'd been tired after days of doing her normal job as well as working every spare minute on the project, but Zach had made it fun.

Be honest. He made it more than fun.

Okay, he'd made it exciting. Sitting in the same room with him when the rest of the building was dark and silent had created a special sort of intimacy. They'd laughed and told jokes in between bouts of intense productivity. And they were doing it all over again tonight.

There was no denying the frisson of excitement that fizzed through her belly at the thought. There was also no denying that she'd dressed with particular care this morning, choosing a black pencil skirt and fitted latte-colored silk blouse that made her feel like a heroine in a forties movie. And yes, she'd even spritzed on perfume, something she didn't usually bother with for the office.

"He's your coworker," she murmured to herself, in case that rather important fact had slipped her mind.

"Excuse me, ma'am? Can I help you?"

Audrey lifted her gaze from the scarf display she'd been eyeing and realized that the sales assistant had overheard her talking to herself. Such a good look.

"I'm just browsing, thanks," she said with a sheepish smile.

"For yourself or are you looking for a gift?" the young woman asked.

"It's a gift, for my sister. Her thirtieth, actually."

"Something special, then? Were you thinking a scarf? We have some lovely French silk scarves …."

Audrey blinked at the display. She had no idea, really, why she'd stopped in front of it.

"I was thinking maybe a watch, actually. Or a piece of jewelry."

"Lovely. Jeannie is over in the watch department. She'll be sure to help you out," the saleswoman said, already drifting away to serve another customer.

Audrey made her way to the shiny glass display cabinets in the jewelry department, finally locating the watches. She did a slow circuit of the cabinets, running her eye over the range, hoping something would jump out at her as being perfect for Leah.

Her gaze moved from watch to watch, doubt and indecision gnawing at her. Despite the fact that there were only four years separating them, she and Leah had never really been close. She had no idea whether her sister would be all over a watch loaded with shiny bling, or if she would prefer a more conservative, traditional model.

Funny, because she could still remember how excited she'd been when she'd learned her parents would be bringing home a little sister for her from the hospital. She'd mistakenly believed that it would be her and Leah against the world.

She did a slower circuit, this time stopping when she saw a small-faced gold watch with a leather band and distinctive art deco styling. She thought it was beautiful, but there was no telling whether Leah would. For a moment Audrey was filled with a piercing, ineffable sadness that she knew so little about her own sister's likes and dislikes.

"Excuse me. Could I take a closer look at this one, please?" Audrey called out to the saleswoman.

"Of course, let me grab my key."

Half a minute later, Audrey was wrapping the thin leather band around her wrist. It really was gorgeous. Maybe she should take a punt on it, go with her gut and hope for the best. She flipped the dangling price tag over and blinked in shock when she saw the price.

Twelve hundred dollars.

Whoa.

She did a mental check of her savings account, but she already knew the watch was beyond her budget.

"So, what do you think?" the saleswoman asked.

"It's lovely, but I might look around a little more before I make my final decision," Audrey said.

She smiled politely and handed the watch back before resuming her slow cruise of the display. Nothing else caught her eye, and after five minutes she left the store and headed for her car. Her thoughts kept returning to the watch as she drove back to Makers, however. If she extended the limit on her credit card, she could swing it, barely. It would take a bite out of her savings and make life a little less fun for a few months, but she could do it.

It was her little sister's thirtieth, after all. She wanted to mark the occasion.

What you really mean is that you want to try to buy your way into her favor.

It was a sobering realization, so profound that she didn't notice the traffic light change and had to be honked to awareness by the driver behind her.

Amazing, the way the past could keep coming back to bite her on the ass, even when she was sure that she'd dealt with it and reconciled herself and gotten on with things. Because she'd thought she was done with trying to make amends, in the same way that she'd thought she was beyond feeling hurt by her outsider status in her own family.

She drove into the garage and parked in her allocated spot. She didn't immediately get out of her car. She needed a moment to get herself together.

If she could go back in time, if she could change one decision, undo one choice, she would return to the moment when her angry, resentful, achingly lonely sixteen-year-old self had stuffed a handful of clothes into a duffel bag and climbed out the window and into the waiting car of her boyfriend.

But she couldn't, just as she couldn't undo any of the foolish, dangerous things she'd done in the eighteen months following that night. Stealing from her parents and her sister. Endless rounds of binge drinking. The way she'd allowed herself to be treated by Johnny and his friends for fear that she'd lose the one person who had ever really seen her and believed in her and loved her. Or so she'd thought at the time.

She closed her eyes and leaned her head against the headrest. God, she'd been so young and so hungry for approval and attention. The great irony was that the two people she'd most wanted to sit up and take notice—her parents—were the two people who had never quite forgiven her for the months of worry and heartache and shame she'd inflicted on them as they searched and fretted over their runaway daughter.

They pretended they had. Everyone was perfectly civil and polite to one another once she'd moved home and embarked on the never-ending mission of redeeming herself. But the truth was that that rash, reckless dash into the night when she was sixteen had permanently cemented her black sheep status, and she'd never been able to claw her way back.

Not with good behavior. Not with heartfelt words. And not with gifts.

And certainly not by buying her sister a very expensive watch for her birthday.

She breathed in through her nose, held her breath for a handful of heartbeats, then released it fully. Then she opened the door and climbed out.

How did that L.P. Hartley quote go? "The past is a foreign country." And she didn't have the time or the energy to go there.

Not today, anyway.

CHAPTER FIVE

SHE WAS WEARING perfume. Something light, with sweet vanilla undertones.

Zach looked up from the page he was proofreading and glanced at Audrey's profile, trying to gauge her mindset. They'd been going over the finished analysis for the past hour, correcting typos, adding information, finessing the layout. Not by the flicker of an eyelid had she indicated that tonight was any different from last night or any of the other times they'd met to work on the report—except she didn't usually wear perfume.

Maybe he was a deluded optimist, but he couldn't help hoping she'd worn it for him.

She typed something into her laptop. "Typo, page twenty," she said without looking up.

"Mine or yours?" he asked.

"Mine."

"So that makes us even at four all, right?"

"You still trying to count that outdated pie chart as one mistake?" she said, shooting him a dry look. "I don't think so."

"Technically, it *was* only one mistake."

"Sure, in the same way that the guy steering the Titanic only made one mistake."

He propped his elbow on the table, work forgotten for the moment. More than anything, he liked matching wits with her.

"So you're suggesting a slightly inaccurate pie chart is on a par with the one of the greatest maritime disasters of all time?"

"Yes. Yes, I am." She tried to keep a poker face but her mouth kept curling up at the corners.

"You're full of it, Mathews," he said, returning to the page he was proofing.

What he really wanted to do was ask if she'd like to grab a drink together after they'd finished tonight. He wasn't going to do that, though. The whole point of this analysis was to impress Whitman and get on the man's radar—in a good way. Given Zach's track record with women, using the fact that he and Audrey were working together as a springboard into starting something else would be a very bad idea.

Tina, for example, had not walked away a happy woman. She'd been angry and hurt that he'd repeatedly put his work ahead of her. She hadn't understood about his mother, or how important it was for him to put as much distance, time and money between himself and the past as he possibly could. Probably because he'd never told her, but that was a whole other ball of wax.

The point was, he couldn't afford to indulge himself where Audrey was concerned and then risk having a pissed-off woman glaring at him across the meeting room table every week. Only an idiot would open himself up to that kind of potential disaster, and he'd like to think he wasn't an idiot.

"Do we need pizza yet?" Audrey asked.

She was toeing off her shoes again, wiggling her stockinged feet into the carpet. He watched avidly, like a teenage boy getting a glimpse through the bathroom window.

She had great feet. He'd never really noticed a woman's feet before, but hers were delicately arched, the toes straight and neat. He had the sudden, incredibly inappropriate urge to offer her a foot rub, so he had an excuse to get his hands on them.

You sick, horny, pathetic bastard.

"I don't know if I can face pizza again. Isn't there a Malaysian place up the road?" he asked.

"Let me see." She stretched and flexed her fingers like a virtuoso pianist preparing to play a complicated concerto, then started typing. "Okay, yes, there is. And I have a take-away menu."

"Oh, you're good."

"Thank you. Come take a look so we can order."

He moved to stand behind her chair. She shifted the laptop so he could see the screen. He rested a hand on the back of her chair and leaned forward over her shoulder so he could read the small text.

Big mistake. He could smell her perfume and what he suspected was her shampoo, and he could see down her top enough to know she was wearing a lacy chocolate-colored bra beneath her shirt.

He straightened. "I'll have Singapore noodles."

"That makes it easy, because that's what I'm having, too."

He moved back to his seat as she grabbed her phone and placed an order for two servings of Singapore noodles.

"Ten minutes," she said when she ended the call.

"Cool."

He told himself not to even think of taking his eyes off the page, but it didn't stop him from glancing across at her breasts to confirm that, yes, he could see the faint outline of lace beneath the silky fabric of her shirt. He wondered what the rest of her bra looked like, and if she was wearing matching underwear. He had a real thing about French knickers. Maybe she was wearing a pair, all chocolate satin and lace.

He could feel himself growing hard, desire starting up a drumbeat of demand in his groin.

Good one, doofus.

Exactly what he needed, an inappropriate hard-on. What was he, fifteen?

Very deliberately, he thought back to the brief encounter he'd had with Henry Whitman earlier in the week. They'd crossed paths in the corridor and the other man had pulled Zach up and fired a series of questions at him about his product selection for the upcoming summer catalog. He'd questioned Zach's favoring of one brand over another, suggesting strongly that he reconsider his decision, his manner brusque and steely. Zach had been left feeling like a naughty kid, not something he particularly relished at the ripe old age of thirty. Worse, he'd been left with the impression that Whitman wasn't exactly overwhelmed by his performance to date.

He glanced down at his crotch. Yep, that seemed to have done the trick. Erection well and truly gone. Nothing like imminent castration via job loss to take the heat out of a man's libido.

"I'll be back in ten. You want anything to drink?" Audrey said, pushing back her chair and standing.

"I'll go," he said, reaching for his jacket.

"You went last night."

"What can I say? I'm a homemaker. I love to feed people."

She smiled. "Funny. But it's my turn."

"Why don't we both go? Then we can argue about who's paying all the way there and back."

Her eyes widened with outrage. "I'm paying. You paid for the pizza. That is absolutely nonnegotiable."

"We'll see," he said.

True to his prediction, she argued her side every step of the way to the garage, only shutting up when he beeped open his car and held the door for her.

"Wow. This is like the first-class section on the plane.

Not that I've ever sat in first class, mind you. But I've taken a peek through the curtain."

She slid into the seat, one hand stroking the leather arm-rest reverently. Never in his entire life had he been so jealous of an inanimate object.

"I guess this makes the commute a whole lot more fun, huh?" she asked as he slid into the driver's seat.

"It takes some of the pain out, yeah."

He started the car and drove out of the garage, very aware of her watching him work the clutch and change gears. He reminded himself that now would not be a good time to stall.

"Why do men always buy manual cars?"

"Because we like to be in control. Why do women always buy automatics?"

"Because we like to conserve our energy for more important things."

"I have plenty of energy left to spare, don't worry."

The moment he said it he regretted it. So far, they'd kept their banter strictly PG, but he knew she hadn't missed the innuendo in his tone.

So much for keeping his eye on the ball.

"I think the Malaysian place is up here in that group of shops," she said after a small pause.

"Got it."

He stayed in the car while she went inside to collect their meal, punishing himself for his slipup by only allowing himself a one-second glance at her ass as she disappeared through the door. Whoever invented those figure-hugging skirts knew what she was doing, that was for sure.

He gave himself another lecture while he waited, reminding himself of everything they had at stake. The report. Their jobs. Their future career prospects.

There had been rumblings around the office lately, rumors that Whitman had been meeting with outside personnel consultants. That could only mean one thing—layoffs. Only an absolute idiot would put his head in the noose by having a hot and heavy affair with a colleague.

Still, what a way to go…

He started as the passenger door opened and Audrey slid into the seat.

"They gave us a free serve of roti bread."

She was clearly delighted by the gesture.

"Someone's won a customer."

"Yep. I freely admit that I am a sucker for the unsolicited extra portion."

The conversation remained light as they returned to Makers and grabbed cutlery from the staff room, although he was aware that they were both working at it, thanks to his stupid energy-to-spare line. Back in the meeting room, Audrey passed him a napkin and slid his noodles toward him.

"May the best man win," she said.

Even though he was starving, he didn't immediately start eating. Instead, he watched as she peeled her lid off and wound her first mouthful around her fork. Even though the extra workload had been the exact opposite of fun, he was suddenly fiercely glad Gary had chosen her to be his coauthor on the report. And not only because it gave him a chance to strut his stuff for Whitman. For months he'd watched Audrey laugh with everyone else instead of him. It was good to be on the receiving end of one of her smiles. Good to know that he could make her laugh. Good to get to know some of what went on behind her golden-brown eyes.

She glanced up and caught him staring. "What?"

"Just waiting for you to be the first one to spill something down your shirt. Lets me off the hook," he said easily.

She tilted her head ever so slightly to one side and he knew she didn't believe him. Not entirely. But she wasn't about to call him on it, for the same reason he wasn't about to be honest.

They both had too much to lose.

AUDREY WORKED FROM home the following morning, answering emails and taking calls in between packing for the conference. She also managed to put on a load of washing—a miracle—and empty the decomposing matter from the bottom of her crisper. It was hard to tell for certain, but she thought it might have once been a packet of carrots and a bunch of celery. Martha Stewart she was not.

She was more than happy to be busy, because it stopped her from dwelling too much on what had happened with Zach last night: the moment in his car when he'd made that sexy little comment about energy not being a problem, then that moment later when she'd caught him watching her so closely.

There had definitely been a vibe there. An intense, very adult vibe that had robbed her of several hours' sleep last night as she tossed and turned and tried not to think about what she was thinking about.

Zach's body.

Zach's mouth.

Zach's hands.

At twelve she shut down her laptop, tucked it into its travel bag and called a cab. She was at the airport by one-thirty, perfect timing for her two-thirty flight, since she wasn't one of those travelers who got a buzz out of running down the concourse screaming for the attendants to hold the gate.

She off-loaded her luggage, bought herself a giant latte and went in search of her departure gate. She caught sight of Megan when she arrived, and waved before making her way to her side.

"Bring on the pain," Megan said drily as Audrey dropped into the seat her friend had been saving.

"Three days of sucking-up opportunities, remember?"

Megan pulled a face before delving into her handbag and producing a muesli bar. "You want one? I came prepared for bad airline food."

"I just ate lunch, thanks."

"Me, too. But I could eat my own head I'm so hungry. I don't know what's wrong with me at the moment—I can't stop eating."

Audrey narrowed her eyes. "You said that the other day. Are you sure you're not…?"

"Since I had my period last week, I'm thinking no," Megan said.

"Don't some women still get their periods even though they're pregnant?" Audrey asked.

"I don't feel pregnant. I feel hungry." Megan took a big bite from the muesli bar.

The boarding call came over the speaker and they both stood, pulling their passes from their handbags.

"If we'd been smarter, we would have coordinated our check-in so we'd be sitting together," Megan said.

"That would have been smart. Want to bet we're on opposite ends of the plane?"

They compared cards and discovered they were several rows apart.

"Figures," Audrey said.

"Exactly. If we hated each other, they'd sit me in your lap."

They gathered their bags and walked the small distance to the gate. Audrey was seated closer to the rear of the plane than Megan, and she bid her friend farewell as she continued up the aisle.

She spotted Zach as she drew closer and closer to her row. He had the window seat, but the seat beside him was empty. The aisle seats both before and after his row were empty, too. She glanced down at her boarding pass. She had an aisle seat.

She held her breath as she drew closer, counting down the rows. Huh. She was seated in the row behind Zach. Bummer.

He glanced up from whatever he was reading and made eye contact with her.

"Afternoon. Braced for paradise?" he asked as she shuffled past his row.

"Ready as I'll ever be."

She was very aware of him watching her as she opened the overhead locker and attempted to stow her bag. It was already very full, however, and the only way to get her bag in place was to slip it in behind someone else's. She was straining on tiptoe, conscious of her shirt pulling free from the waistband of her trousers, when Zach slid out of his seat.

"Here, let me."

Before she could object, he was behind her, reaching for her luggage.

"Up the back, yeah?" he said.

They were standing so close—her back to his chest, her backside brushing his hips—she felt his words ruffle the hair near her ear. If she turned around, her breasts would be pressed against his chest. She'd only have to lean forward an inch, maybe two, to kiss him.

His body moved against hers as he pushed her bag into place. Desire washed over her like warm, sticky toffee. She closed her eyes, trying to quell the longing rising inside her.

How long had it been since she'd had sex? Really good, earth-shaking sex, the kind that made a woman forget her own name?

Too long. Way too long.

"There we go. Sorted."

One minute Zach was behind her, the next he was gone, sliding back into his seat. She blinked, feeling distinctly robbed. Having him rammed up behind her had been the most fulfilling sensual encounter she'd had all year.

Then she remembered where they were, and exactly how many of their colleagues were seated around them right at this minute.

Dear God, and she was standing in the aisle, gasping like a landed fish, her face warm, her blouse untucked.

She shut her mouth and hastily retucked her blouse before dropping into her seat.

"Thanks for that," she said belatedly.

"Not a problem," Zach said casually.

She stared at what she could see of his profile through the gap in the headrests. He sounded very calm, while she felt as though she'd just stepped out of a Turkish sauna. Was it possible he could have this effect on her yet be immune to her himself?

A middle-aged woman stopped beside Audrey and gave an apologetic smile. "That's me," she said, pointing to the window seat. "Sorry to be a pain."

"All good," Audrey said, unclipping her belt and standing to let the woman take her seat.

She couldn't stop herself from glancing at Zach before she sat back down and saw that he was reading his way through a very familiar-looking document.

"Is that ours?" she asked, leaning forward to get a better look, even though she knew the smartest thing for her to do right now was to go stick her head under the tap in the tiny bathroom until her unruly hormones calmed the freak down.

He glanced up at her. "Giving it one last go-over. Just in case."

"You nerdy nerd."

"Bet you've got a copy in your bag."

She smiled her best mysterious, Mona Lisa smile. "Maybe I do, maybe I don't."

"Good try, Mathews, but you're as much of a nerdy nerd as I am," he said, laughing at her.

It was a little scary how much she liked making him laugh. And how much she wanted to do it again. Anything to prolong their conversation. She was about to send a suitable insult his way when the flight attendant cruised past and asked her to fasten her seat belt, effectively saving her from herself.

It was a two-hour flight to the Gold Coast, and she spent most of it chastising herself for her heated response to Zach's proximity. She really needed to be more careful around him if a little bit of close-talking and the most innocuous of body contact could get her so turned on. It was just as well that the report was all but finished. Once they'd presented it to Whitman, there would be no reason for them to spend so much time together.

She caught a cab to the hotel with Megan, and after they'd checked in they made their way to the lifts. Zach was waiting there, and the three of them entered the one elevator car. It was odd taking the lift up to their rooms and discovering that he was only one floor below where she would be sleeping for the next three nights. Megan gave her a look as the elevator doors closed behind him.

"Needle in your eye, remember? More binding than a pinky promise," she said.

"Relax. Nothing is going to happen," Audrey replied, distinctly worried by the lack of conviction in her own voice.

THE CONFERENCE KICKED off with a cocktail party that evening, an event she'd been dreading. She hated small talk, but as this was the only occasion when she had access to so many of the cooperative's influential retailers and suppliers under one roof, she knew she had to make hay while the sun shone. So, she went to battle dressed in her best little black dress, friendly smile at the ready.

She spotted Zach the moment she entered the ballroom, even though he had his back to the door. He was wearing a gunmetal gray suit, and she knew before he turned around that the color would do amazing things for his eyes. Then he turned and she forgot to breathe for a moment as his stormy gaze met hers.

Wow. How was it possible for one man to contain so much hotness in one body? One very muscular, very hard, very toned body? And how was it possible that he kept getting better-looking? Because he definitely was. It wasn't simply her imagination.

"Here."

Megan slid an icy champagne flute into her hand.

"Bless you." Audrey tore her eyes from Zach before her friend could notice and start campaigning again.

"How long does this thing go for again?" Megan asked out of the side of her mouth.

"Two hours."

"Meet you in the bar afterward?"

"Deal."

They clinked glasses and parted ways. Audrey threw Zach one last glance before diving into the fray. He was talking to one of the retailer's wives, and the woman was gazing up at him with a small smile on her face. As if she couldn't believe he was real, and that she was talking to him.

Audrey hoped she didn't look like that when she was talking to Zach. It would be too humiliating and far too revealing.

She spent the next two hours schmoozing, cajoling, defending various decisions the merchandise department had made and laughing at bad jokes. It was nearly 10:30 by the time she could legitimately slink off, and she made her way to the bar and found a booth in its darkest, most hidden corner. She closed her eyes for a precious minute. Her feet ached and she was absolutely starving, the catering having been on the stingy side. Her throat was sore from speaking up to be heard over the crowd, and it would only get worse as the conference progressed.

"Oh, I thought that would never end," Megan said as she slid into the seat opposite her.

Audrey pushed the drinks menu across the table. "Choose your poison, my dear."

Megan gave her a grateful smile. "Have I ever told you what an awesome friend you are? Do you have any idea how many times my head would have exploded over the past five years if I didn't have you keeping me sane?"

"Ditto, babe. The feeling is entirely mutual."

They ordered nachos for two and a bottle of wine and bitched and moaned and strategized until they were both yawning and possibly a little tipsy.

"Bed for me," Megan said.

"God, yes."

They made their way to their floor and parted company in the corridor.

"Don't do anything I wouldn't do," Megan said as she teetered up the hallway.

Audrey kicked her shoes off the moment she was inside her room, shimmying out of her dress before pulling on a tank top and pajama pants. She slept in the buff at home, but there were far too many unexpected intrusions in hotels for her to feel comfortable doing so tonight.

Megan's words echoed in her head as she brushed her teeth. *Don't do anything I wouldn't do.* She entertained herself by wondering where, exactly, her friend would draw the line.

Eating every chocolate bar in the minifridge?

Making prank phone calls to their fellow conference attendees?

Knocking on Zach's door and making him an offer he couldn't refuse?

Okay. Where had *that* thought come from?

As if you don't know.

Audrey spat out toothpaste and rinsed her mouth, then met her own gaze in the mirror. If they didn't work together, she would be seriously tempted to follow through on the idea.

But they did.

She made a frustrated noise before walking to the bedroom. She flicked off the lights, then lay stiff as a board between the cool, starchy hotel sheets and tried to clear her mind.

But she couldn't. All she could think about was Zach, and the crazy, reckless urge to find out if the way she felt when she was around him translated into the kind of mind-blowing sex she suspected it might.

After a few minutes of battling her own hormones, she gave in and let herself imagine what might happen if she really did go knocking on Zach's door.

There was no harm in imagining, right?

She'd have a shower first, of course, and dig out the matching black bra and underwear she'd brought to wear beneath her dress for the gala dinner. She'd spray on perfume and do her best femme fatale makeup, then she'd slip into something that would be easy to take off again—no point pretending she was there to do anything but get naked with him.

She imagined herself striding up the corridor and stopping outside Zach's door. Her stomach gave an odd little hop-skip, even though this wasn't real.

She'd never propositioned a man in her life. But this was pure fiction, so she might as well go for broke. It wasn't as though she would ever have the real thing, after all.

She'd knock, and Zach would open the door, and she'd look him in the eye and say something confident and sassy like "What happens at conference stays at conference. Get your clothes off."

She smiled in the darkness, loving her fantasy-self's brashness.

She'd push Zach backward, then she'd kiss him and press her body against his. He'd be hard already and she'd tilt her hips into his, teasing them both.

She shifted restlessly, aware of the growing ache of desire between her thighs. That was the thing with fantasy—it made for great foreplay, but when there was no payoff in sight it became a special form of torture. Her fingers curved to the soft roundness of her mound and she pressed ever so lightly.

She imagined Zach touching her, and her touching him. She imagined pulling her dress over her head and him pushing her onto the bed and peeling off her underwear and sliding his fingers inside her. He'd find her hot and wet and ready for him.

So ready for him.

She slipped her hand beneath the waistband of her pajama pants, but something stopped her from breaching the final barrier of her panties.

If she did this, she would be crossing a line, even if only in her head. It was one thing to admit she was attracted to Zach, another thing entirely to fantasize herself to a climax using him as her inspiration.

She had to work with him. She had to see him every day in the staff room. She had to present their joint analysis to their scary new CEO with him when they returned from conference.

She slid her hand from her pajamas. Her body sent up a silent wail of protest as she rolled onto her belly and very deliberately thought about the repairs she still hadn't booked for her car.

Slowly her body cooled and the ache between her thighs dissipated. A good thing. She'd made the right decision. The smart decision. That was who she was now, since she'd used up her quota of bad decisions when she was sixteen.

One day, maybe, she could let up on herself. But not today. Definitely not today.

CHAPTER SIX

SHE ROSE EARLY the next morning and went for a walk along the beach, figuring she should take advantage of the fact that they were on the sunny Gold Coast. A small and completely harmless pleasure.

When she returned, she met Megan in the hotel restaurant and watched her friend all but backstroke through the offerings in the buffet.

"Feeling a little peckish, huh?" she asked as Megan slid her piled-high plate onto the table.

"I told you, I'm going through a growth spurt. Or I'm sublimating my disappointment at not being able to fall pregnant into growing a food-baby." She patted her stomach. "Either way, this buffet works for me."

Audrey ate her virtuous fruit and granola and watched her friend inhale her meal.

"Better?"

"I feel a little sick. But kind of proud of myself. Is that wrong?"

Audrey passed her a napkin and indicated that she had food on her chin. "We'd better motor, the first sessions start soon."

She stood and turned from the table—and stopped dead in her tracks because Zach was there, standing mere meters away in front of the bread selection, trying to decide between a croissant and a Danish. Images of last night assailed her—

Zach kissing her, Zach pushing her down onto his bed, her slipping her hand beneath her pajama pants…

Even though some of those things had only happened in the privacy of her mind, she could feel guilty, revealing heat stealing into her face.

Ducking her head, she hustled past Zach before he could spot her, stopping only when she was standing in front of the elevator bank.

"Wow, you are really worried about not missing the first session, aren't you?" Megan said.

"I just remembered I need to make some calls," Audrey fibbed.

She still felt warm, and even though she couldn't see her face she suspected it must still be pink. Thank God she hadn't actually gone all the way with fantasy Zach last night. She would have been at real risk of actually self-combusting back there.

The chime sounded, signaling the arrival of the elevator, and she and Megan stepped inside. The doors were about to close when someone called out for them to hold the lift.

Megan hit the open button and they both stood a little straighter as Henry Whitman stepped in. He wore running gear and had obviously been tearing up the streets. Audrey offered him a smile and a bright good-morning before averting her eyes from his bare shoulders, only to find herself looking at his bare legs instead. Really, there was no good place to look when your boss was in workout gear.

She could only be thankful he wasn't an avid cyclist and she and Megan didn't have to contend with a padded Lycra butt, painfully outlined man bits and silly shoes.

"Great day out there," Megan said, super perky. "Sunshine, nice clear skies."

"Yes," Whitman said.

Audrey racked her brain for something to say. She'd had

precious few face-to-face encounters with him to date—the
banana incident, obviously, and the range-review inquisition,
along with a handful of smile-and-nod pass-bys in the cor-
ridors at work. She'd noticed he wasn't exactly the master
of small talk. Or perhaps he simply preferred not to get too
close to the people he would soon squash like bugs.

Either way, it was clearly going to be up to her to initi-
ate conversation.

"Have you had a chance to—"

The lift pinged to a halt, the doors gliding open. Whitman exited after offering them a terse nod.

She and Megan remained silent until the doors closed
again.

"That went well," Audrey said.

"Yes, I thought so. I particularly liked your haiku."

"Thank you. Have you ever considered TV weather girl
as an alternate career?"

They both cracked up laughing.

"Is it just me, or is he super-scary?" Megan asked.

"He's scary. I think he likes it, too."

They parted ways at Audrey's door and Audrey went inside to brush her teeth and make some final preparations for
the day ahead. Her gaze fell on the bright Makers-blue of
the cover of the analysis as she prepared to leave the room
again. Zach would get a kick out of her encounter with the
Great Man. She could almost see his mouth curling up into
an appreciative smile, his eyes crinkling at the corners. He'd
probably tell her—

*So we're both on the same page here, you know what
you're doing, right? Standing in your hotel room, grinning
like a doltish loon over an imaginary conversation with a
man who is never going to be more than a friend?*

She pressed her lips together and left the room. She was

here to work. It would be a good idea if she focused on that fact. Instead of…other things.

SHE DID HER best to avoid Zach for the rest of the day and night, but as fate would have it, he was the first person she saw the next morning when she arrived in the foyer. Hard not to notice him when he was standing in the middle of the lobby, talking to Henry Whitman. Shaking his hand and handing over a thick, spiral-bound document with a bright blue cover.

Time literally stuttered to a halt as neurons fired and connected in her brain. The smile on Zach's face. The manly handshake. The fact that Whitman was walking away with *her freaking analysis in his hand.*

No. No, Zach wouldn't do that to me. He wouldn't. Not after all the hard work we put into that thing.

They'd written it together. They'd rehearsed their presentation together. She couldn't believe that Zach would shaft her so spectacularly by robbing her of her share of the kudos. Not now that they knew each other. Not now that they were friends.

Zach turned away, heading across the foyer toward the restaurant, clearly unaware that she'd witnessed his little confab with Whitman. She scuttled after him, her heels clicking and skidding on the tiled floor.

"Zach. *Zach.*"

He paused, glancing over his shoulder. "Audrey. Hey." He smiled the kind of smile that would normally make her lose her train of thought.

Not today.

"Was that our analysis I just saw you hand to Whitman?" She tried to keep her voice calm.

Because she needed to confirm his perfidy before she gouged his eyes out. Maybe he'd given Whitman a different report and the blue cover was a coincidence. Maybe she was on the verge of lunging for his jugular for no reason at all.

Please let that be the case. Please, please let him not have betrayed me like this.

"Yeah. I bumped into him when I was running this morning and mentioned I had it with me and he asked for it." He shrugged as though it wasn't a big deal.

"So you gave it to him. Even though we're scheduled to present it *together* in a couple of days?"

He frowned, clearly picking up on her tone. "I'm getting the feeling that if I say yes you're going to have a problem with that."

"Oddly, Zach, yes, I will." Her voice rose to a sharp peak and a group of Japanese tourists at the reception desk turned to look at them. "We wrote that report *together*. Equally. Which means we should both get credit for the bloody thing."

"We will. Your name is on the cover, Audrey."

"Oh, thanks. That's going to make all the difference when Whitman reads it, after chatting to you man-to-man while you were out running and having you hand it over to him personally. He's totally going to ignore both those things and read my name on the cover and realize that I wrote half that freaking report, too."

Zach was starting to look pissy. "What was I supposed to do? Tell him to wait for the report he'd commissioned because I wasn't sure if my coauthor would approve of him reading it without her being around? That was never going to happen."

He made it sound so natural that he'd shafted her. As though anyone else would have done the same.

"I'm not an idiot, Zach. Don't pretend you weren't using that report to gain leverage with Whitman."

"Are you telling me you wouldn't have done the same?"

She took a step back, genuinely astounded. "So you're

admitting that you shamelessly used *our* report to adhere *your* lips to Whitman's backside?"

"That's not what I said. Look me in the eye and tell me if you discovered you'd inadvertently scored five minutes alone with Whitman and he'd asked to see the report you wouldn't have handed it over."

"I have no idea, since I didn't go out hunting for him this morning at the crack of dawn. Actually, I *do* have an idea. I was in the lift with him yesterday, just him and me and Megan, and somehow I managed to not even mention let alone *hand over* the report."

"I run every morning. Rain or shine."

"How convenient for you."

"You're overreacting, Audrey. Go get some fresh air and calm down and we can talk about this more rationally."

She blinked at him, momentarily lost for words. Wow. Just…wow. First he did her over, then he tried to minimize his betrayal by making *her* look like a drama queen.

"I haven't had a good night's sleep for nearly two weeks because of that report. And you just climbed over my body to get what you wanted. So don't you dare try to tell me I'm overreacting or dramatizing anything. You patronizing asshat." Her voice was quivering with emotion and she could feel angry tears burning at the back of her eyes.

No way was she going to let them fall, though. No way would she give him that satisfaction.

"I know how hard you worked on the analysis. We both did. And Whitman will know that when we present it to him formally. You'll say your piece, he'll realize you know your stuff, he'll be impressed. You're freaking out over nothing here."

He was so sincere. So convincing.

"I can't work out if you really believe that or if you think I'm a gigantic moron. He's not going to bother sitting through our presentation now that he's got the report, Zach. Why would he waste precious time going over something he's already read? No, you just hit a home run for yourself with *my* work. Congratulations, champ. You'll go far."

She turned on her heel and headed for the lifts.

"Audrey."

She ignored him, stepping into the waiting elevator. The last thing she saw as the doors closed was Zach watching her with a frown on his face. As though he was sincerely baffled by what had happened.

The jerk.

She held on to her tears until she was in the safety of her hotel room. Then she paced, her heels biting into the carpet, fingers wiping away the tears as they plopped hotly onto her cheeks.

She'd worked so hard on that report. She'd brought her A-game, and she'd done good work. And now Zach was going to get the credit. There wasn't a doubt in her mind that that would be the case. She knew the way the world worked, the way people worked. Whitman might see her name on the cover of the report—maybe—but he'd remember talking to Zach about it. And she didn't doubt for a second that Zach had been articulate and smart and sharp as he discussed their findings.

That was what Whitman was going to take away from two weeks of her life—that Zach Black was an intelligent, hard-working young executive with energy and zeal to spare. The kind of guy a CEO should probably promote, if such things were on his mind. Definitely the kind of guy he couldn't afford to lose.

"You sneaky, underhanded, self-serving asshole."

Saying the words out loud helped, but they didn't change how profoundly stupid she felt. These past two weeks she'd done a complete one-eighty where Zach was concerned.

She'd gone from seeing him as a well-fed fat cat, a son of wealth and privilege, to seeing the real him—a driven, highly ambitious guy who had worked damned hard to be able to afford the nice things in life. She'd been impressed. Worse, she'd been lulled and charmed by his undeniable charisma and physical good looks into overlooking his razor-sharp ambition. She'd taken her eye off the ball and focused instead on his legs and ass and shoulders. God, she'd been so far gone that she'd almost cast him as the star of her personal fantasy.

And he hadn't hesitated to sacrifice her for his own means. In fact, she was willing to bet he hadn't even considered how his actions would affect her. Why would he? He wasn't stupid.

Like her.

He hadn't been toying with breaking the cardinal rule of corporate life: don't dip your pen in the office ink. Nope. He'd been busy keeping his eye on the end game. Looking out for himself and his future.

She paced until the first flush of fury had passed, then spent five minutes repairing her makeup. All the while, she picked away at the problem, trying to find some way to recover at least some of the ground she'd lost. The best option she could come up with was to look for an opportunity for a private word with Whitman. She'd mention the report, let him know she was aware Zach had handed it over, then refer to some facts and figures to let him know she was totally familiar with the content. Force him to put a face to the other name on the front cover.

It didn't even come close to the hour she and Zach had had scheduled with him on Tuesday morning, but it would have to do, since she was as sure as she could be that the meeting would be canceled. In fact, she'd stake her career on it.

Still steaming, she left her room. There was no time for her to eat before the first session, but that was okay, since her belly was a boiling cauldron of acid and anger and self-recrimination. Food would not be a great addition to that mix.

One thing was for sure: she would not be letting Zach under her guard again. Not in a million years.

ZACH STARED AT the lift door long after Audrey had disappeared behind it. A part of him was tempted to go after her, but then he remembered the cold fury in her eyes and decided to give her time to calm down before he attempted to fix things between them.

Because the last thing he'd intended to do was disadvantage her. The very last. Contrary to her belief, he had not gone out running in the hope of "accidentally" meeting Whitman. He'd been blowing off two day's worth of rich food, reveling in the clean offshore breeze as he ran along the hard-packed sand at the waterline. He hadn't given a second thought to the lean, gray-haired figure running toward him until they were only a few meters away from crossing paths. Then he'd recognized Whitman and barely had time to raise a hand in acknowledgment before the other man had swept past.

It was only later, when Zach was on his return journey, that he'd spotted Whitman stretching on the dry sand near the stairs to the street. He'd debated going over to strike up conversation, not wanting to intrude on Whitman's down time. Then Whitman had called out to him by name, asking him how he was finding his first Makers conference. Zach said all the right things before Whitman raised the competitor analysis. Zach had been surprised the man even knew who'd been assigned to the task. He'd answered Whitman's questions, made a few observations, and pretty much figured that was that. Then Whitman had asked him to hand the report over at breakfast.

Zach had hesitated. Of course he'd hesitated. He had only

a draft copy, one that he'd discovered a handful of typos in. There was an outside chance he could make the corrections and get a clean copy printed and bound, but not by breakfast. He explained that to Whitman, feeling like an apologist beneath the man's unforgiving, steely gaze. But Whitman had been all easy affability as he waved off a few typos. He could read around spelling mistakes. He'd catch up with Zach at eight in the foyer.

As Zach had told Audrey, he hadn't been in a position to say no to the man. It had been a direct request, almost an order, and Zach was smart and experienced enough to know that you didn't second-guess or disappoint a guy like Whitman.

Had he considered Audrey in any of the above? The honest answer was "not really." The conversation on the beach had happened so quickly, it had been over before he knew it. When he'd gone back to his room to shower and collect the report, he'd definitely thought about her reaction to him handing over a flawed version of their work. She was a stickler for details. But he'd figured she would understand that he hadn't had much choice.

More fool him. She'd been white-hot furious, determined to see the situation as a landgrab from him. Which said a lot about the way she viewed him.

He'd thought they'd become friends over the past few days. He'd thought they liked each other.

Again, more fool him.

Shaking his head, he went to grab breakfast. Despite piling his plate high, though, he found he'd lost his appetite. Having Audrey's words echoing in his head didn't help.

You just hit a home run for yourself with my *work. Congratulations, champ. You'll go far.*

He pushed his plate away. He considered himself a pretty honest guy. Reasonably self-aware. If he'd set out to accost

Whitman and deliberately dangled the report in front of the man, he wouldn't shy away from the fact. He was ambitious. He'd always been ambitious, and he wasn't about to apologize for that. But he hadn't engineered today's meeting on the beach, and he hadn't been the one to bring up the report. He'd been stuck between a rock and a hard place, and he'd done the smart thing. The same thing Audrey would have done, incidentally, had their positions been reversed, because at this stage in their careers, being ambitious meant they had to tug their forelocks on occasion and jump through whatever flaming hoop was on offer. He didn't enjoy doing it, but he endured it because one day he knew he would be in control of his own destiny, in every possible way. It was a promise he'd made himself years ago, and he planned on honoring it.

Audrey had judged him and found him guilty without entering into a discussion. She'd jumped to the most obvious conclusion, and wasted no time condemning him. Frankly, it pissed him off. He didn't like being painted as a ruthless butt kisser who was prepared to do anything to curry favor with the higher-ups—including sacrificing a colleague on the altar of his ambition.

She was out of line. Way out of line.

His self-righteous indignation lasted until lunchtime, when he was standing in the buffet line. He was reaching for a miniature chicken-and-brie baguette when a heavy hand landed on his shoulder.

"Here he is. Zach, I was just discussing your report with Rob. You've given us a great starting place."

It was Whitman, with the chairman in tow.

"I particularly like the sound of this SWOT section you've put together," Rob Atkinson said, his craggy face serious. "We're going to need every advantage we can lay our hands on to hold our own against those big corporates over the next few years."

For some reason he couldn't explain, he glanced to his left. There, on the other side of the buffet, was Audrey. Her face was set into a politely neutral expression, but her eyes were hot with accusation.

This is what I knew would happen, her gaze said. *Thanks for selling me up the river, jerkwad.*

He had to admit, from where she stood, it looked pretty bad. As though her contribution to the report really had been overlooked, despite the fact that her name was right alongside his on the front cover.

Zach returned his focus to the two men in front of him, determined to fix this here and now.

"I can't take all of the credit. Audrey Mathews and I—"

Whitman's hand landed on his shoulder a second time in an unmistakable gesture of farewell. "We can talk about this more another time, Zach. Rob, I wanted to have a word with you and the team from Dulux before you head off on the store tour this afternoon…"

"Mr. Whitman," Zach said, but the two men were already walking away.

He turned to face Audrey, hoping she'd at least witnessed his attempt to ensure that she enjoyed the credit she was due. She wasn't there, though. He stepped away from the buffet and scanned the crowd. He couldn't leave the situation like this. Not now that he knew that her prediction of events was closer to reality than his own.

He spotted her sitting outside at one of the tables in the courtyard. For the moment she was alone, even though seating was at a premium, and he made a beeline for her.

"Audrey," he said when he arrived at her table.

She kept her attention on her plate. For all the world as though he wasn't there.

"Let's talk about this." He reached for the empty chair beside her, only to discover it wouldn't budge beneath his hand. It took him a moment to understand why. Glancing beneath the table, he saw that she'd hooked her foot behind the chair rung and was holding it in place.

"Seriously?" he asked.

She didn't lift her gaze. "Go away."

She sliced off a portion of frittata with her knife, the sound making a very distinct clink as metal hit china. He stared down at her shiny brown hair, trying to find the words to cut through her anger. It had been a long time since he'd cared so much about having someone's good opinion.

"Audrey—"

"If you don't go, I will hurt you with this fork."

"We can fix this—"

She stood so quickly her chair almost toppled over. Still not glancing at him, she walked away.

He was considering his next move when Gary stopped beside him.

"Slick move getting the report to Whitman early. He's happy as a clam." He gave Zach an approving wink before moving off.

Zach gritted his teeth. Even though he knew he wasn't the asshole in this situation, he was getting a pretty clear picture of how things must look from Audrey's perspective. And it wasn't pretty.

He owed her an apology. Not because he'd set out to do her wrong, but because circumstances had left her holding the shitty end of the stick. He might not have intended it to be that way, but it was what had happened, and it wasn't fair.

This time he didn't even consider going after her. She needed space. He'd give her some time, then try when they were in Melbourne. Perhaps he'd even wait until after they'd delivered their joint presentation. Having her moment in the sun with Whitman would surely go a long way toward assuaging her anger.

In accordance with his strategy, he kept his distance for the remaining day and night of the conference. He was thankfully seated at the far end of the plane for the flight home, and he grabbed a cab from the airport rather than pool with his colleagues.

He logged on to the internet the moment he got home, even though it was nearly midnight. It took him ten minutes to find a locally based online florist. He ordered the brightest, biggest bunch of flowers he could find and arranged for them to be delivered the following day. He kept the card simple—*I'm sorry. Can we please talk? I'll even buy the pizza*—and sat back feeling marginally better.

Actions spoke louder than words, after all. Audrey might not want to listen to him, but she couldn't ignore a big bunch of flowers.

At least, he hoped she couldn't. Hopefully they would soften her resolve, and after their presentation Tuesday morning they could talk and put this misunderstanding behind them.

He stared at the order confirmation on his computer, remembering the laughter they'd shared while they worked on the report. He'd always felt as though he was on the outside looking in when it came to Audrey, but she'd let him in during those late nights and early mornings. He didn't want to be on the outside again.

He wanted in. Not sexually, because that would never happen, but he wanted to be on the receiving end of her smiles again. He wanted to have the right to stop by her office and talk for five minutes, or to send her an email, simply because he thought it would amuse her.

Weary, he knuckled his eyes. Flowers. He had to trust in the flowers.

CHAPTER SEVEN

AUDREY HAD A morning meeting with a supplier the following day and didn't arrive at work until midday. Her step was brisk as she made her way to the merchandising area. The first week after conference was always busy, and she'd come armed with a stash of muesli bars, having already resigned herself to no lunch and a late night at her desk in order to catch up.

It wasn't until she was in the middle of the open-plan section of the department that she noticed the heads turning as she passed by. A few people waved; others smiled as though they were in on some secret she'd yet to hear. She smiled and waved and checked surreptitiously that her buttons were all buttoned and her fly zipped.

Yes and yes. Maybe her sparkling presence had simply been missed while she was away. A little bemused, she paused by her assistant's cubicle.

"Hey, Lucy. How was your weekend?"

Lucy was in her early twenties and very pretty and smart. Audrey shared her with two other buyers, but Lucy made no secret of the fact that Audrey was her favorite.

The younger woman's head came up when she heard Audrey's voice.

"Oh, my God, I have been dying for you to get in. I wanted to call you so badly but I knew you were in that meeting. Plus I didn't want to ruin your surprise." Lucy flicked her auburn ponytail over her shoulder, her eyes bright with excitement.

Audrey lifted an eyebrow. "What surprise?"

"You'll see," Lucy said, standing and ushering Audrey toward her office.

Audrey stopped on the threshold, stunned by the towering floral display dwarfing her desk. Orchids and lilies and gerberas and roses and three different types of greenery, all arranged in a glossy black box.

"Get the truck out of here," she said, momentarily awed by the sheer size of the thing.

"I know. It's probably got its own gravitational field. Some of us were worried your desk might collapse beneath it."

"Who are they from?" Audrey asked. Then her brain kicked in—because there was only one person in her life who would think that a floral tribute like this might be the answer to his prayers.

"You don't know?" Lucy asked, frowning.

Audrey bent her mouth into a smile. "They're probably from my parents."

"Is it your birthday or something? I thought it wasn't until March?"

Damn Lucy's amazing memory.

"It is. But sometimes they do random things like this," Audrey fibbed.

A small white envelope was taped to the box. Lucy plucked it off and passed it to Audrey.

"Only one way to find out for sure." She was so tickled by the whole thing. Clearly she thought Audrey had embarked on a new romance or something equally flower-worthy.

Audrey made the mistake of glancing out into the office as she took the envelope. Two of Lucy's fellow assistants had spun in their chairs and were watching unashamedly, indulgent smiles on their faces.

Zach was the biggest idiot under the sun for making such an obvious gesture so publicly. Where on earth was his brain at? If anyone found out he'd sent these flowers, the whole building would be gossiping about them. The office grapevine would have them doing it, engaged and married with a baby on the way by the end of the day.

Her cheeks were starting to ache from smiling as she pulled the card free from the envelope.

I'm sorry. Can we please talk? I'll even buy the pizza—

Pizza. As if.

Audrey quickly slipped the card into the envelope, well aware that Lucy had a preternatural ability to read upside down as well as sideways.

"Yep, from my folks." Audrey gave a small shrug.

"Really?" Lucy sagged with disappointment. "I thought maybe you'd been holding out on me."

"No such luck." Audrey tucked the card safely into her purse. The first chance she got she would burn it.

"Huh. Well, that's a bit of an anticlimax, I have to say," Lucy said.

"Sorry 'bout that."

"Still, nice of your parents to think of you. Really sweet, actually."

"Yeah."

Audrey made a big deal out of dumping her bag and shedding her suit jacket, uncomfortable with telling so many white lies. Thankfully, Lucy took the hint and switched to business mode.

"Two messages while you were out, and I've proofed our page for the summer catalog and flagged a few things for you."

"Great. Thanks. And before I forget…" Audrey pulled out the snow dome she'd bought. Lucy collected them, so Audrey made a point of picking her up a cheesy souvenir from every place she visited.

"Oh, thank you. It's awesome." Lucy shook the dome and

watched flakes of snow settle around a giant pineapple wearing sunglasses. "Do you think it ever occurred to whoever designed this that snow and pineapples don't go together?"

"Somehow I don't think those considerations are top priority at the snow dome factory."

They discussed a couple of other work matters before Lucy headed back to her desk. Audrey sat behind hers, grateful for the wall of flowers that hid her from view from the rest of the office.

Zach was demented—and damned lucky that she knew how to be discreet, even if he didn't. As for his apology... He could stick it where the sun didn't shine as far as she was concerned. She wasn't interested in his mealymouthed excuses or explanations—especially after witnessing him bathing in the kudos from their joint effort firsthand at the conference. She'd almost ground her molars to dust as she stood there listening to Whitman and the chairman pat Zach on the back for all his hard work.

Be fair, he did try to fan a little credit your way. It's not his fault they didn't listen.

Admittedly, she'd been surprised to hear him mention her name when she'd expected him to be basking in his moment of glory. It hadn't changed anything, but he'd made the effort.

Only because he saw me standing right there.

Maybe. But she couldn't help remembering what he'd said that morning.

What was I supposed to do, Audrey? Tell him to wait for the report he'd commissioned because I wasn't sure if my coauthor would approve of him reading it without her being around?

He'd suggested she'd have done the same thing if she was in his shoes, and she'd denied the charge at the time. Now, she forced herself to consider the situation from his perspective. If she'd run into Whitman by chance and they'd talked about the report and he'd asked for a copy, what would she have done?

Saying no would have been out of the question, but she'd like to think that she would have found a way to track Zach down and ensure that the two of them delivered the report together. That would have been the fair, reasonable thing to do. But there was no guarantee she would have been able to pull that off.

She slipped the card from the side pocket of her purse and reread Zach's words. Maybe she should let him buy her pizza and hear him out.

Her email chimed and she reached for her mouse like a laboratory rat at the feeder bar, unable to ignore the electronic cue.

It was from Whitman's assistant, the subject titled "Competitor Analysis Presentation." Narrowing her eyes, Audrey clicked to bring up the email.

Whitman had canceled their presentation. As she'd predicted he would.

She stared at the single line of black type, thinking about all the hours she'd put into that report.

For nothing.

She stood and got a good grip on the box at the base of the arrangement. A spike of greenery tried to take out her eye, but she successfully navigated her way past her interested workmates and into the bowels of the building without suffering bodily harm. Carpet gave way to scarred linoleum as she approached the warehouse offices. Two middle-aged women looked up from their paperwork when she paused in the doorway of the dispatch department.

Jan and Jean had worked for Makers for years. Both were leathery from too much sun and too many cigarettes, with chests like prows of ships. Between them they'd saved Audrey's backside more than once and she figured that if anyone should benefit from Zach's guilty conscience, it should be them.

"Good golly Miss Molly. Where did you get those from?" Jan asked.

"More importantly, what did you have to do to get them?" Jean added.

"They're a gift, but they're way too big for my office. I thought you two might get a kick out of them," Audrey said.

Jean and Jan were only too happy to be recipients of her beneficence, and Audrey left them arguing over where best to position the flowers.

It might not be entirely Zach's fault that she'd been screwed over, but she couldn't stomach having his makeup gesture in her face every time she turned around. She needed to be angry with him right now, and she didn't particularly care if that was fair or not.

Maybe that would change with time, but right now she felt too raw and stupid—and, yes, sulky—to be mature about it.

Zach would have to suck it up, in the same way that she was having to suck it up.

ZACH CHECKED HIS watch as he left his twelve o'clock meeting. A quick chat with Audrey's assistant this morning had elicited the information that Audrey wasn't due in till midday. It was nearly one now. Time to do a cruise past her office to see if his floral sacrifice had made a dent in her righteous anger.

"Zach, good timing. I was about to bring this to you," Lucy said as he stopped at Audrey's office.

He could see Audrey at her desk out of the corner of his eye, but he kept his focus on her assistant, who was offering him a folder thick with press clippings.

"Is this the latest media monitoring?"

"Yep. Your stuff is toward the back."

"Thanks, Luce."

Only when the folder had changed hands did he allow himself to glance into Audrey's office. She was talking on the phone, but her cool, impersonal gaze flicked to him briefly before returning to the notes in front of her. Not a sign of a thaw in sight—and no sign of the mother of all bouquets, either.

Where the hell had it gone?

He turned to Lucy, about to ask, then shut his jaw. The only thing dumber than asking Audrey where the flowers were was asking her assistant. Media monitoring firmly in hand, he flashed Lucy his best friendly smile and retreated to his office.

Where could Audrey have stashed the flowers? Surely she wouldn't have thrown them away? There wasn't a bin in the building big enough to accommodate them.

Unless he counted the huge Dumpsters sitting outside the warehouse.

He shook his head after a second's contemplation. No way would she march all the way through the building to dispose of his offering. She was far too aware of appearances, and people would be bound to talk. No, it was far more likely that she'd put them in her car so she could dispose of them after hours.

Whatever Audrey had done with his flowers, it was clear he was still a long way from being forgiven. This was obviously going to be an endurance test—Audrey's outrage pitted against his determination to make things right.

He was contemplating his next move when he saw the email from Whitman's assistant. He closed his eyes for a brief, regretful moment after he'd read it.

Damn.

Audrey was really going to hate his guts now that Whitman had canceled their presentation. As she'd predicted he would.

He tapped his pen against his desk half a dozen times, considering and rejecting a handful of scenarios before alighting on the only one that seemed remotely viable. He searched until he found the biggest, most decadent chocolate-themed gift basket on the internet. He paused for a moment when he came to the section where he could type in the message for the card.

You were right. I'm sorry things turned out this way. I'm guessing pizza is out of the question now?

He sat back in his chair, considering the few lines of text. Inadequate, but it would have to do.

He hit Send.

AUDREY WAS ABOUT to make her tenth phone call the following morning when Lucy appeared in her doorway, a peculiar expression on her face.

"They want to see you at reception," she said.

Audrey frowned. "What for?"

"There's a delivery for you."

"If it's samples, sign for it and take them to the warehouse," Audrey said, her attention already returning to her work.

"It's not that kind of delivery. And you have to sign for it personally."

Audrey glanced up, confused. Then she saw the glint in her assistant's eye.

No way.

Zach had done it again.

She stood so fast her chair shot backward and banged against the wall. "I'll be back in a minute."

Spine straight, she marched to reception. Sure enough, a delivery man was waiting with a vast cellophane-wrapped wicker basket that appeared to be brimming with goodies.

"You Audrey Mathews?" he asked, offering her an electronic slate to sign.

Audrey smiled tightly. "That's me."

She signed, aware of the two receptionists' interest. Gift hampers and baskets were common enough at Christmas as suppliers tried to curry favor, but the holiday season was still months away.

Bloody Zach.

The delivery man headed for the exit, leaving Audrey with the mammoth basket. She'd barely managed to get her arms around the damned thing and lift it when Henry Whitman stepped out of his office. He zeroed in on her immediately, one eyebrow quirking upward in silent question.

Audrey laughed, the sound sharp and uncomfortable even to her own ears. "I know. Enough to feed a small army, right?"

"Indeed." Whitman scanned the basket. "I take it you have a sweet tooth, Ms. Mathews?"

"Well, chocolate *is* one of the five major food groups."

He surprised her by smiling, his arctic eyes warming. "You sound like my wife. She swears that chocolate is a vegetable, since it's made from cocoa beans."

"I definitely think she's onto something there."

He nodded, still smiling, then walked past the reception desk and around the corner.

He knew her name. How about that. He'd been so distant and cold every time they'd interacted she was convinced he'd barely registered her. But he knew her name. Hopefully that was a good thing.

She was still trying to decide if it was or not when she entered her office.

Lucy bounced out of her seat, following her inside. "Let me guess—another gift from your 'parents'?" Lucy used her fingers to make air quotes.

So much for her buying Audrey's story yesterday.

"I have no idea who these are from."

Lucy's gaze slid to the envelope taped to the basket, but Audrey deliberately didn't take the hint, instead sat at her desk and did her best to look as though she was diving into work. Even though she was aware that the natural, expected reaction to receiving such a luxurious gift would be to tear open the envelope before exploring the bounties given.

After what felt like a long time, Lucy made a small dissatisfied sound and left. Only when her assistant was safely ensconced at her work station did Audrey reach for the envelope. She read Zach's message before hiding it inside her handbag.

He was trying hard, she had to give him that. Although, it was pretty easy to dial up some flowers and some chocolates, wasn't it? Meanwhile, he was the department's golden boy, able to do no wrong in the eyes of the people who counted.

She ground her teeth together.

Yeah. She wasn't quite at the forgiveness stage yet.

She reached for the scissors in her desk drawer and started cutting through the cellophane.

She was about to become the most popular woman in the office.

EVERYONE WAS EATING chocolate, from the two women behind the reception desk to the assistants in their cubicles to his fellow buyers and category managers in their offices. The rustle of bonbons being unwrapped followed Zach like a whisper as he made his way through the building.

He didn't need to ask where all the chocolate had come from. He didn't even need to shark past Audrey's office to confirm his guess.

She'd given his gift away.

He tossed his briefcase into the corner of his office with

a little too much force. This was getting old, fast. He didn't enjoy being the whipping boy for a situation that had been beyond his control. He'd never been a grudge-keeper himself, and he didn't admire people who were.

There was a point where stubbornness became pigheadedness, after all. Where determination became bloody-mindedness and justifiable outrage morphed into holier-than-thou self-congratulation.

What did Audrey want from him? An apology on bended knee? A full-fledged, belly-to-the-ground grovel? Perhaps she'd like him to parade through the department in a hair shirt before prostrating himself in front of her office on a bed of nails?

He pushed his hair back from his forehead, aware that he was getting worked up over what was becoming a farcical battle of wills. If Audrey truly didn't want to accept his apology, there was precious little he could do about it.

Maybe it was time to let it go. To accept that she was going to hang on to her hurt and anger, and he was going to remain in the wrong in her eyes, no matter how unfair he considered that judgment to be. It stuck in his craw, especially when he'd done his level best to apologize and rectify the situation, but he'd swallowed worse compromises in his lifetime.

He was aware of a sense of disappointment as he checked his voice mail. Even though he'd been almost certain he was never going to act on the attraction he felt for Audrey, there was something profoundly depressing about letting go of the possibility of something happening between them. Because that was what his concession meant, essentially—that he and Audrey would never be more than distantly polite work colleagues from now on. The buzz of excitement he experienced when he was around her, the awareness of her scent, the sound of her voice…

None of that would ever amount to anything.

He would never find out if she was as sensual and wild as he imagined she was. He would never trace the curves of her body or get to taste her lips. He would never learn her secrets and unlock her true self.

All things he should never have wanted from her in the first place, given their circumstances. So maybe he should thank his lucky stars that he'd taken that ill-fated run along the beach. Maybe that run had actually helped save Zach from himself by creating this rift between him and Audrey.

"Heads up," a voice called.

He glanced up in time to catch sight of something small and shiny whizzing his way. It hit his chest before ricocheting onto his blotter.

"Don't say I never give you anything," Gary said before continuing on his way past Zach's office.

Zach stared at the shiny bonbon. Even though it was barely ten and the last thing he wanted was chocolate, he peeled the wrapper off. He put the chocolate in his mouth and forced himself to note the smooth, velvety texture as it melted on his tongue. Then he swallowed and was left with nothing but a bittersweet aftertaste.

How appropriate.

Despite his best attempts to put the situation out of his mind, he kept circling back to it all day—until Gary entered his office midafternoon and immediately turned to close the door. Everything in Zach went on the alert. Gary was not a closed-door-meeting kind of guy. Which meant this had to be extraordinarily bad news.

"Hey. What's up?" Zach asked.

Gary stood behind the visitor's chair and gripped the backrest with both hands. "This is about to become common knowledge, but I wanted to forewarn you. Word is we're going to lose some people today."

Zach tensed. Was he about to lose his job? He was the last

hire in the department, after all. "Last on, first off" was an axiom in business for a good reason.

"Okay. Should I be worried?" He hoped he didn't sound as shaken as he felt.

From the moment Whitman had been appointed to the role of CEO, Zach had known this was coming.

Gary looked uncomfortable. "I'd love to be able to reassure you, mate, but the truth is I have no idea. All I've heard from people in the know is that merchandising is the first department he's reshuffling."

"Right. Well, thanks for the warning. Gives me a chance to clear out my desk." Zach managed a smile.

"Hang in there. And know that if I have any say in the matter, you'll be part of my team." Gary grimaced, and it hit Zach for the first time that his boss, too, might be in the firing line.

A restructure was a restructure, after all. In theory, no one was safe.

"Thanks. I appreciate it."

Gary left and Zach slumped in his chair, his mind racing as he processed the implications.

He'd been careful with money from a very young age. When he was fifteen, he'd started a catalog distribution business using the kids at school as labor. He had banked everything he earned, being careful to keep it away from his mother. It had been his get-the-hell-out-of-Dodge money, and by the time he was ready to leave home and go to university, it had become a serious nest egg. He'd used it to make a down payment on a small studio apartment, practically picketing the bank until they gave him a loan, and after four years the apartment had doubled in value and he'd been sitting pretty. Prettily enough to indulge his taste for nice things, anyway, while making sure his bank account remained healthy.

He'd maintained that balance in his life, ensuring that he

always had some money in reserve for the lean times, and he was more than confident there was enough there to survive being out of work for a few months without having to compromise on supporting his mother or be at risk of losing his house or car. He didn't want to be hocking his wares out in the job market, though. He'd researched Makers Hardware extensively before jumping ship with his previous employer and coming on board. Being ousted by a new, carnivorous CEO was not part of his plans.

Damn it.

He took a deep breath. There was no point in freaking out. Nothing he did or thought or said in the next few hours was going to have any effect on decisions that Whitman had already made. All he could do was wait and see.

He did his best to focus on getting through his in-tray, but every time his phone rang or someone stopped in his doorway, adrenaline shot through his belly. By the time four-thirty rolled around, he'd given up the pretense that he could concentrate. Collecting his coffee mug, he walked slowly to the staff kitchen, noting the subdued atmosphere in the department as he went.

Everyone knew that the ax was about to fall, obviously. A few people made eye contact and he nodded acknowledgment. Audrey was standing inside Lucy's cubicle as he passed, her dark head bent over Lucy's auburn one. When Audrey straightened, he saw that Lucy's nose was red and she was clutching a wad of scrunched-up tissues.

For a moment he was tempted to stop and reassure her, too—she was smart and able and a real asset to the team, and if Whitman was culling assistants, Lucy would be one of the last to go. But Audrey clearly had things covered, her hand coming to rest comfortably on the younger woman's shoulder.

As if she sensed his regard, Audrey glanced up. Their

gazes locked and he knew she was every bit as worried for her future as he was for his. He had no idea what her situation was, but he hoped like hell she'd put something aside for a rainy day.

She broke the contact, refocusing on Lucy. He continued to the staff room, filling his mug by rote, even though the last thing he needed was caffeine.

He was walking out of the staff room when he saw Charlie shrugging into his suit jacket and leaving his office. One look at the man's pale face and Zach knew where he was going.

Charlie was one of the most experienced category managers, an old-school guy who still talked about the days when Makers had been a regional rather than national chain. If he was slated for retrenchment, no one was safe.

The next half hour dragged by. Zach shuffled papers around on his desk and tried to pretend there weren't half moons of sweat beneath his armpits. He went over and over every interaction he'd had with Whitman. Preconference, Zach would have said he was screwed. But he'd definitely kicked a goal with the competitor analysis. Whitman had been openly pleased with his work there.

You mean you and Audrey kicked a goal, and that he'd been pleased with both your work. Right?

He swore under his breath as it hit him that the misunderstanding with the report could have very real repercussions today. If Audrey lost her job…

He shook his head. It wasn't going to happen. Whitman might be a brutal, ruthless predator, but he was a smart one, and Audrey was great at her job.

Still, he knew the fact that her work on the report had been overlooked must be burning in her gut right now.

It was five before Gary appeared in his office doorway again.

"Charlie, Ned and Rick," he said solemnly, naming two

category managers and one of Zach's fellow buyers. "And we've lost Annie, Sam and Dan."

Three assistants, for a total head count of six from the merchandising department.

"Is that it?" Zach refused to let himself be relieved until he knew the danger had passed.

"As far as I know. For now, anyway. Marketing's next."

"When?"

"Tomorrow, I think. We're not exactly being kept in the loop." Gary sounded pissed.

Zach reached out and hit the button to turn off his monitor. "In that case, can I buy you a beer?"

Gary let out a short, sharp crack of laughter. "Mate, nothing I'd like better, but I've got a wife to get home to and reassure."

"Sure. I'll see you tomorrow, then."

Gary lifted his hand in farewell. Zach allowed himself a small moment of relief once he was alone.

He was safe. For now.

He wouldn't have to dust off his CV and find some way of finessing the fact that he'd been with Makers for only six months. He wouldn't have to schmooze and network until he'd found himself the next promising thing.

He was safe. And so was Audrey.

It was a little worrying how relieved he was by that last fact.

He grabbed his briefcase. He was wrung out, and he figured he deserved an early night after the rigors of the last few hours. He deliberately left all the paperwork he should be taking home on his desk and grabbed his jacket. His briefcase felt light as a feather as he made his way to the stairs to the garage. He started plotting his evening as he descended. He'd grab some takeaway and a good bottle of wine, find something decent to watch on TV…

He frowned as a picture of himself sitting at home on his own like a sad sack formed in his head. Maybe he'd call one of his friends instead. It was short notice, but with a bit of luck Mark or Finn might be available for dinner and a few drinks.

He sat in his car to make the calls and five minutes later was two for two on the rejection front. Apparently he was all out of luck tonight. He shrugged. Dinner for one it was, then.

He started the Audi and drove out of the garage. It wasn't until he was about to turn onto the freeway that he looked across the intersection and saw the faded neon sign for Al's Place.

What were the odds that there were Makers staffers over there, drowning their anxieties in a few glasses of beer? The light turned green and he drove across the intersection and into the parking lot at Al's.

It took his eyes a moment to adjust to the gloom inside the building. There were three people at the bar, none of whom he recognized as fellow employees. Otherwise, the place was empty.

So much for enjoying a little postcrisis bonding with his colleagues. He'd assumed because he'd found Megan and Audrey over here that it must be a Makers haunt. Apparently, he'd assumed wrongly.

He hovered for a beat, tempted to revert to his earlier plan for the evening. Then he shrugged. Screw it. He was here, and the guy behind the bar undoubtedly had copious quantities of beer to offer up. Being a sad sack in a skeevy bar in the middle of industrial Melbourne was marginally better than being a sad sack at home on his own.

Loosening his tie and unbuttoning the top button of his shirt, he made his way to one of the booths lining the far wall and slid onto sticky, patched vinyl. He'd stay for a couple of beers, maybe treat himself to a greasy burger.

Pretty tragic as celebrations—or wakes—went, but beggars couldn't be choosers.

CHAPTER EIGHT

AUDREY COULDN'T WAIT to leave the building. The whole afternoon had been an unrelenting exercise in corporate torture, and even though it wasn't close to her usual quitting time, she needed to go. If she stayed behind her desk a second longer there was the very real risk she was going to give in to the urge to wreck some furniture like a temperamental rock star.

High heels tapping out an urgent rhythm, she made her way to her car. When she was behind the wheel and sealed in her own personal privacy chamber, she let her head fall against the headrest.

She couldn't believe Whitman had given Charlie his marching orders. Audrey had been Charlie's assistant for two years while she worked her way up the food chain, and she had enormous respect for his patience, wisdom and knowledge. Whitman was an idiot of the highest order for culling one of the company's most valuable walking, talking knowledge bases. As for the way he'd gutted their support staff...

All so the retailers could squeeze a fraction more profit from the business at the expense of any loyalty they'd received from staff.

It made her sick to think about it. Sick and angry and impotent and ashamed—because, of course, mixed in with her outrage on Charlie's behalf was a kernel of relief that she wasn't the one who'd been called to the big man's office.

She sighed heavily. Then she started her car and drove the short distance to Al's. Megan had sent her a text midafternoon suggesting they'd both need a debriefing by the time the day was over, and Audrey had been only too happy to agree. Now, she shed her suit jacket and loosened her hair from its too-tight chignon before getting out of her car and heading for the bar entrance. She needed a cold glass of white wine, deep-fried food and her best friend's shoulder to bitch on. Not necessarily in that order, but she'd take whatever she could get, however it came.

She grabbed an empty stool at the far end of the counter and reserved the one next to her with her handbag in case any of the handful of sodden Lotharios propping up the bar got the mistaken idea she might welcome their advances.

Megan had been on the phone when Audrey left the building, but she'd signaled she wouldn't be long. Audrey checked her watch before giving the room an idle once-over, more to kill time than anything else. Her gaze got stuck on the dark-headed figure occupying a booth in the far corner.

Surely that wasn't…?

She leaned forward in her seat, craning her neck. It was hard to see from this angle, but it looked as though it was Zach.

What on earth was he doing here, of all places? This was her and Megan's secret bolt-hole, as insalubrious as bars came. No one from Makers came here. Ever. So why was he here, of all people?

It's a free world, remember? And his day has been every bit as foul as yours.

Suddenly she remembered the moment when she'd been comforting Lucy. Her assistant had practically been hyperventilating over the prospect of losing her job. Lucy and her fiancé had recently bought a house and land package and she'd been sick that she'd soon be unemployed and unable to meet her share of the mortgage payments. Audrey had been talking her down from the cliff edge when Zach had walked past. His concern for Lucy had been there for any-one to see. There'd even been a small hitch in his step, as though he was contemplating stopping to reassure her, too. Then their gazes had met and she'd felt a current of...*con-nection* was too strong a word. Maybe fellow feeling was a better characterization. As though he knew *exactly* what she was thinking and feeling, because he was thinking and feeling the same things. For those few split seconds, she'd forgotten everything that had gone wrong between them. He was simply her colleague, and they were both secretly terri-fied of losing their jobs, and it sucked, hard.

Now, she stared at his profile. Spurred by the memory of that earlier moment, she stood and walked to his booth. He looked up from the menu, clearly surprised to see her.

"I wanted to say thank you for the chocolates." Because somehow, after today, it felt stupid and petty to be angry with him.

His eyebrows shot up and she knew she'd caught him off guard. After all, she'd been a hard nut to crack, holding on to her outrage like a security blanket.

After a second he nodded. "My pleasure. I hope you en-joyed them."

"I did. Thank you," she lied. She hadn't eaten a single bonbon, no matter how tempting they'd been. Her pride had demanded it.

Stupid pride.

A knowing light came into Zach's eyes and she knew that he knew she'd given his fancy chocolates away to anyone who'd take one.

"What can I get you?" Cameron asked.

"I'll have a Stella Artois." Zach looked at her. "What would you like?"

"Oh." Audrey glanced over her shoulder. Megan still hadn't arrived. "Um. A glass of white wine would be nice, thanks. Maybe that semillon sauvignon we had last week, Cam."

"Done."

She hovered for a moment, then slid into the booth opposite Zach. She could hardly stand while drinking the wine he'd bought her.

"I thought this place would be stuffed to the rafters after the day we've all had," Zach said.

"Most people go to the big pub farther up the road. It's a little less sticky."

"Right." Zach inspected the bar for a few seconds before focusing on her. "But you don't have a problem with sticky?"

"It's not great, but Al's is the bar equivalent of the Cone of Silence. Megan and I know we can bitch and whine to our hearts' content here and we don't have to worry we'll be overheard."

Cameron appeared with a drink in each hand, sliding the beer to Zach and the wine to her. They both nodded their thanks before he headed to the bar.

"So. We survived," Zach said after a short silence.

"We did. For now."

"You think he'll come back for a second pass at the department?"

"I have no idea."

They both drank. She could feel how wary Zach was, could feel her own awkwardness.

She took a deep breath. "Maybe we should get this out of the way—I don't think you were trying to screw me over."

"Good."

"I'm still a little pissed that I put in all that work for no reward, but I acknowledge that what happened was not your fault."

"Good. Because I enjoyed working with you. And I never

intended for any of that to happen. It was just really crappy timing."

"I believe you." She did. She'd been blinded by anger and frustration initially, but the events of the afternoon had been like a bucket of cold water in the face. A wake-up call to quit with the bullshit and let go of anything that wasn't helping her get where she needed to be.

Bottom line: she trusted the impression she'd formed of Zach during those late nights together. She believed he was a decent man. And she believed he'd made the best decision he could in a difficult situation.

She also believed that he genuinely regretted it.

"So if I send you flowers tomorrow, you won't give them to Jan and Jean in the warehouse?"

So he'd discovered what she'd done with his floral offering.

"You don't need to send me flowers."

He pointed the neck of his beer bottle at her. "You're a stubborn woman."

"Wouldn't be here if I wasn't. Neither would you."

He smiled a little, which she chose to take as agreement.

She settled into the booth. "I think this day has to go down as one of my top five, all-time bad days. Just above the time I broke my leg in third grade, in fact."

"What sort of break are we talking? Compound?"

"You know, I'm not sure. But don't tell my parents that—they're both doctors and they'd die of shame."

"Really? How come you didn't go into the family business?"

It wasn't an uncommon response when she happened to mention that both of her parents were doctors. She took a sip of her wine before shrugging casually. "Not smart enough. But my sister is doing them proud, so they've got someone to pass their charts and anatomical models on to. What about you? What do your parents do?"

There was the smallest of pauses as Zach took a pull from his beer. "My parents are dead."

"Oh, God. I'm sorry." Way to put her foot in it.

"Don't be. It was a long time ago."

His voice was utterly uninflected, but she had the sense that there was a lot going on beneath his easygoing demeanor. She wasn't sure how she knew, she just did.

"Hey. Started without me, I see." Megan slid in beside Audrey and lifted a hand to get Cameron's attention. "I'll have what she's having," she called.

Megan and Zach exchanged small talk while they waited for her drink to come.

"Listen, I don't want to cramp your style," Zach said. "Just let me know if three's a crowd."

"Hey, the more the merrier after the godawful day we've all had," Megan said.

Zach was watching Audrey. Waiting.

"Stay," she said.

His shoulders dropped a fraction of an inch, as though he was letting go of a heavy burden. Had he been that worried about her forgiving him?

All evidence pointed in that direction. For some reason, her stomach gave a little nervous twist.

"Can you believe Charlie's gone? And Ned?" Megan asked.

"There'll be more, too, if Whitman's running true to form," Zach said, looking away from Audrey.

Megan swore pithily.

"You said it," Zach said.

Audrey drank her wine and listened as Megan and Zach discussed the severance packages that appeared to be on offer. Then Zach said something about his previous company, and before she knew it an hour had passed and they were ordering burgers with the works and curly fries.

The conversation ranged all over, from the politics at play within the cooperative to their opinions of their competitors' marketing and pricing strategies to Zach's renovation plans and Megan's pregnancy hopes. Audrey found herself talking about her own ham-fisted renovation attempts—the new timber venetian blinds she'd attempted to install the previous summer—and by the time it was pushing eight o'clock she was mellow from wine and animal fats and good conversation with people she enjoyed.

That one of those people was Zach wasn't really too great a surprise. She'd already been well on the way toward liking him before the brown smelly stuff hit the fan at conference. Now they'd come out the other side of their disagreement and bonded over shared peril.

Powerful stuff, at the best of times.

"You want another drink?" he asked as Cameron cleared their sauce-and-grease-smeared plates.

Megan shook her head. "Gotta drive. In fact…" She checked her phone a split second before it began to ring. "There he is, like clockwork." Sliding from the booth, she moved to take the call.

"Her husband," Audrey explained for Zach's benefit.

"I guessed." At some point in the past few hours he'd shifted so his back was against the side wall of the booth, his elbow braced on the table. He'd undone a couple of buttons, too, and a triangle of golden tanned skin showed at his neck. He looked tired and relaxed and more than a little rumpled.

"Thanks for this," Zach said suddenly.

She raised her eyebrows, not sure what he was referring to.

"I was going home to have Chinese on the couch."

She understood then that he was thanking her for the company, for the chance to decompress.

"No problem. It was a horrible day. A bit of fellow feeling goes a long way."

Megan returned to the table and leaned across to grab her handbag from where she'd stashed it alongside Audrey's.

"That's it for me, I'm afraid. I've been lured home with the offer of a foot massage."

Audrey groaned with envy. "You seriously need to talk to Tim about hiring his services out by the hour."

"You need to seek medical help for that foot fetish of yours." Megan slid a sly look toward Zach. "Over to you, Dr. Black." With that, she gave them both a cheeky wink before heading for the exit.

Audrey made a rude noise before calling after her. "I don't have a foot fetish. I like a good foot rub. Perfectly innocent."

"No crime against that. Not that I'm aware of, anyway," Zach said.

She tore her gaze from her departing friend's back.

"It's mostly because I'm crap at wearing high heels," she explained. In case he was inclined to believe she really did have a foot fetish. "If I could get away with wearing sturdy orthopedic shoes to work I'd wear them every day."

"No, you wouldn't." He said it very confidently. As though he knew her inside out.

"What makes you say that?"

Zach shrugged as though it was self-explanatory. "You like to look good. There's no way you're going to ruin all that hard work with lace-ups."

"Are you suggesting I'm vain?"

He laughed. "No. No more than the next person."

"What if the next person is you?"

"Oh, I'm definitely vain. If I wasn't I'd wear a hundred-dollar suit and buy wash-and-wear shirts and rubber-soled shoes."

None of those things would dim his appeal one iota, but she wasn't about to tell him that.

"So. I guess we should go, too," she said.

Because it had hit her that it was just the two of them now. Alone in a dark, slightly seedy bar.

Probably not the best venue for one-on-one interaction with Zach, given the little fantasy she'd indulged in while they were away.

"Where is home for you?" he asked.

He was watching her with a warm intensity that was both unnerving and very flattering. She couldn't maintain the contact, dropping her gaze to his mouth. It was decidedly sultry for a man, the bottom lip a little fuller than the top. She bet he could work magic with that mouth. Bring a woman to her knees.

Okay, not a helpful thought.

"I've got a little place in Ringwood. You?"

"Surrey Hills."

"Right."

She glanced toward the door, aware that she should leave but not quite able to commit to doing so.

"Sure you don't want another drink?" he asked.

She did. Very badly. And not because she craved alcohol—although she was aware that it would make a great excuse afterward if anything were to happen. She wanted another drink because it meant she'd get to spend more time with Zach.

"It's probably a bad idea," she said.

He was silent for a moment. "You're right."

Neither of them moved.

"What would you have done if you hadn't come here tonight?" Zach asked.

"Honestly? I probably would have defrosted a meal and gotten stuck in the work in my briefcase."

He tilted his head slightly. "Do you ever give yourself a break?"

"No. Do you?"

He shook his head. "Can't afford to."

"Ditto."

"I guess you must have a very understanding boyfriend."

It was such a blatant fishing expedition that she couldn't stop herself from smiling.

"That's an interesting concept, but no."

"No boyfriend?" He was smiling a little, too. The faintest curving of his lips.

"No." She hesitated, aware that a smart woman wouldn't ask the question on her lips. "What about you? Are you seeing anyone?"

"Nope. Apparently I'm a bad bet. A workaholic."

"Right."

"Always on the phone or bringing work home with me. Too serious."

"You're not too serious. You're funny." The words were out before she could stop them.

"Next time I need a character witness, I know who to call."

"I'm pretty sure you can handle yourself without my help."

She suddenly registered that she was leaning forward, instinctively trying to close the distance between them.

Bad move. Really bad move.

"I should go," she said for the second time.

"Yeah. I need to get home, too." He slid to the end of the booth and stood.

He pulled his wallet out and she opened her mouth to let him know that she wanted to pay her own way. He nailed her with a single, sharp look. She swallowed her words, knowing without him saying a thing that it would be pointless to protest.

"Okay. But it's my turn next time," she said.

Something flared in his eyes at the mention of a next time. She gave herself a mental kick. There would be no next time. Not if she was as savvy as she prided herself on being.

She gathered her handbag and hovered uncertainly while he settled their tab at the bar. Her heart threw out an extra beat as he turned and started toward her.

He had a really lovely body, and he looked incredibly sexy, all rumpled and disheveled and tired.

Her palms were suddenly damp. She eased them subtly down the sides of her skirt.

Dumb to be nervous because they were walking out the door together. This wasn't a date, after all, this was an accidental meeting between work colleagues. In sixty seconds' time they would both be in their cars, heading to their respective homes, and this evening would be history, important only because it marked the day they'd both survived the first descent of the ax at Makers.

"Ready to go?" Zach said.

"Yep."

They stepped into the dim fuzziness of twilight. She knew without asking that Zach intended to escort her to her car. They walked silently across the gravel lot. The nervous sensation intensified with every step, to the point where she could feel her pulse thumping away in her neck and wrists and between her thighs. Her breathing was shallow, almost choppy, and she had trouble swallowing past the tightness in her throat. She was hyperaware of Zach at her side—the height of him, the breadth, the scent of his aftershave, the rhythm of his walk. It was almost as though he generated his own gravitational field, his presence was so compelling.

"This is me," she said as she stopped by her car. A pointless comment, since he knew her car.

Her hands were shaking as she searched through her keys

for the right one. Dear God, what was wrong with her? Anyone would think she'd never been walked to her car before.

"I'm really glad—" She lost whatever she'd been about to say when Zach took a step closer. Her gaze found his and a voice in her head told her to take a step back, or push him away or cut him down in some way. Whatever it took to prevent what was about to happen. What his eyes told her he was going to do.

She didn't move. Couldn't.

He took another step. She could feel the heat of his body, could see the individual whiskers of his five o'clock shadow. Her heart thrashed in her chest. Without consciously willing it, she tilted her head.

He brushed her temple with his thumb, his touch whisper-soft, before sliding his fingers into her hair. For a moment he simply held her in the palm of his hand, his gaze locked with hers. Then he lowered his head and pressed his mouth to hers.

In that split second she understood that it hadn't been nervousness that had made her jumpy and edgy during the short walk to her car. It had been anticipation. Excitement.

Because she'd been hoping he'd do this.

He tasted of beer and desire. His tongue stroked along the seam of her lips and she gave way easily, eagerly, stroking his tongue with hers before allowing him into her mouth. The feel of him inside her even in such a minimal way sent a shudder of pure need through her. He responded by curling his hand around the nape of her neck and closing the remaining distance between them. The press of his body against hers was an electric, visceral thing, as revealing as the first touch of his mouth had been.

She'd been waiting for this—wanting it—for a long time. Even though she'd known it was stupid and wrong and inadvisable for so many reasons.

He was already hard, his arousal a hot pressure against

her belly. The ache between her thighs demanded that she rub against him, that she slide a hand around his waist and grip his backside and haul him closer still.

He muttered something urgent against her mouth, then his hands were on her breasts, cupping and squeezing them through the thin cotton of her shirt. She gave a small, inarticulate moan when his thumb grazed her nipple, and when he caught it between thumb and forefinger and squeezed she almost dissolved on the spot.

A tidal wave of need threatened to swamp her. She wanted him inside her, slamming into her. She wanted heat and a hard male body bearing down on her. She wanted sweat and sex smells and mouths and tongues and fingers and hands.

She felt dizzy with it, intoxicated. Overwhelmed.

Panicking, she broke their kiss, her hands flat on his chest as she pushed him away.

She needed space. She needed air. She needed to *think*.

He took a step backward and the world snapped into sharp, harsh focus.

She was pressed against the side of her car in the parking lot of a seedy bar situated mere meters from her place of employment.

And she was with *Zach*.

For a long moment they stared at each other, breathing heavily. Despite the power of her wake-up call, a treacherous, reckless part of her still urged her to fist her hands in his shirt and jerk him against her so he could finish what he'd started.

He was that good. *They* were that good together.

She clenched her hands, clinging to self control.

"Well. I guess that answers a few questions."

It was so not what she was expecting that a gust of laughter escaped her. He smiled, and she didn't feel quite so appalled by what had almost happened.

"That was really dumb," she said.

"Yes."

"We work together. There's too much at stake. Especially at the moment."

"I know."

Neither of them moved. Her knuckles ached.

"I'm going to go now," she said.

"Okay."

He still didn't move, which meant it was up to her. She slid along her car until there was space between them, scared of what might happen if she walked too close to him. Zach was still standing where she'd left him, watching her, and she had to concentrate on the simple act of sitting behind the wheel and guiding the key into the ignition. Finally the engine fired and she wound down the passenger window and tried to think of something to say that didn't include the words *Come home with me*. She couldn't, so she offered him a wave before taking off.

The fog of lust began to clear as she hit the freeway. What had seemed highly desirable a bare handful of minutes ago suddenly looked exactly like what it was—the sort of rash, ill-considered misstep that could seriously damage her career.

Thank God common sense had made a belated appearance. Thank. God. Otherwise she had no doubt she'd have her knees around her ears right now as Zach took what she'd so eagerly, willingly offered.

Cold relief washed over her as she turned onto her street. She could all too readily imagine the horror of having to look Zach in the eye tomorrow morning after doing him in the backseat of her Honda.

She'd rather chew glass. As for sitting through hours-long meetings with him on the other side of the table… No. It was too awful to even contemplate.

They'd dodged a bullet tonight. They'd taken the step toward safety and sanity in the nick of time.

It had been close, though. Too close. The taste of him… The strength of his beautiful body… The urgent caress of his hands on her breasts…

Yeah.

It had been pretty damned amazing, and it had taken serious willpower to push him away. Even now she felt thwarted, but that wasn't an insurmountable problem. After all, she was a resourceful, imaginative, dexterous single woman, and there were other ways to scratch the itch Zach had created. Safe, private, non-career-threatening ways that wouldn't require her doing the Walk of Shame the next morning.

Of course, there was always ice cream. Fortunately she had a tub of honey macadamia in the freezer.

Smiling grimly, she took the elevator upstairs and served herself a big bowl of frozen consolation.

CHAPTER NINE

AUDREY HAD BEEN right—kissing her had been a mistake. Not for the reasons she'd stated, though. Kissing her had been a mistake because he couldn't stop thinking about it. About her. About the needy, wordless sounds she'd made when he'd stroked her tongue with his. About the way she'd rubbed herself against him. About how good she smelled. About...

Swearing, Zach rolled onto his back and folded his arms behind his head, the better to stare at the ceiling in his bedroom. He resolutely ignored the hard-on tenting the sheet. He was not going to lie here in the dark and fantasize about Audrey while he took care of business like a sweaty teenager. Not tonight, anyway. It smacked way too much of defeat and desperation—and he wasn't sure he was ready to admit defeat where she was concerned.

A dangerous admission, given their mutual circumstance. Mere hours ago, six of their colleagues had been shown the door. There would be more sackings, too, as sure as night followed day. Having an affair with a coworker was a sure-fire way to garner exactly the wrong sort of attention from the executive team. Especially if that affair turned sour—and what were the odds of that happening?

He mentally reviewed the three office romances he'd witnessed firsthand. None of them had ended well—one in divorce, one in a sexual-harassment charge, the third with tears and public humiliation and rejection. People did weird stuff when their hormones and emotions were involved. Was it any wonder that things went pear-shaped when all of that high drama was wedded to the can't-get-away-from-each-other pressure-cooker of an office environment?

So it would be self-destructive in the extreme to pursue this…*heat* between him and Audrey. An act of gross folly. He should stop thinking about her, stop dwelling on those few minutes when she'd been his. He should definitely quit staring at the ceiling and thinking about the warm, welcome weight of her breast in his hand and think about work instead.

No sooner had he started reviewing tomorrow's schedule than a sense memory hijacked his brain: the small hitch in Audrey's breathing when he'd closed the distance between them.

She'd felt so damned good. Too good.

That was the problem. He'd been thinking about her for so long, a few minutes with her in his arms was never going to be enough. It might be stupid, but he wanted more.

His hard-on throbbed in agreement.

"Bloody hell." He rolled out of bed and walked to the bathroom.

One flick and the cold water was running in the shower. He stared at the flowing water for a long beat, knowing it would be a painful solution to his problem. Then he stepped beneath the icy stream.

Sixty seconds later, he flicked the water off and toweled himself dry, his "issue" momentarily resolved.

Long-term, though…

He needed to get over her. That was the only sensible, smart solution. He needed to exorcise her from his fantasies and move on.

He returned to bed and closed his eyes resolutely.

THE FOLLOWING MORNING, he dragged himself out of bed after a restless night and was at his desk by seven. Audrey, however, was not.

Unusual for her. But maybe she had a meeting first thing.

Fifteen minutes later, a light flicked on on the other side of the office.

Audrey.

His heart rate kicked up as he contemplated going to speak to her.

Probably a bad idea, given that her mere presence in the building was enough to make him hard. He gave his crotch a rueful glance.

Thanks for helping me out, buddy.

It was a grim day, the empty desks in the department serving as a powerful reminder of yesterday's carnage. At midday the rumor went around that the first of the marketing department staff had been let go. By the end of the day, there were eight empty desks there, too. It certainly helped put unrequited lust into perspective.

He left work with a heavy briefcase, but instead of heading straight home he traveled through the city and into Footscray. He had a standing arrangement to catch up with his mother once a month, and tonight was the night. She probably wouldn't register the loss if he failed to turn up, but something in him insisted that he keep the date. Duty, perhaps, or love. Or maybe it was simply guilt.

He stopped at the local shopping center for takeaway Indian, ordering enough for two even though his mother wouldn't touch food if she was high. She was invariably skin and bones, her addiction ensuring that eating food for sustenance ran a poor second to her body's demand for drugs. If he could get some food into her, he'd count the evening a success.

A familiar heavy sensation settled over him as he parked his car in the driveway and walked to the front door. Unlike several of the other houses in the street, the lawns were neatly mown, the rudimentary garden trim and neat. He paid a garden maintenance company to take care of the yard, as well as covering the rent and utilities and ensuring that a regular delivery of groceries appeared on his mother's doorstep once a week.

He knew that some people would consider him an enabler, since anything he did to support his mother invariably meant he supported her addiction, but he'd made an uneasy peace with the arrangement. He'd tried cutting her out of his life, turning his back on her for several years when he was studying. He'd told himself he was free of her, and that she was free of him, too. No more guilt and broken promises and disappointment for either of them.

Great in theory. In practice, it had meant he was called to the E.R. at various Melbourne hospitals two, three, four times a year, late night calls that dragged him out of sleep with his heart thumping, sure that this time would be the last, that his mother's wasted body had been fished out of a slum or a river or a gutter. At some point he had acknowledged to himself that he couldn't live with the uncertainty and had set her up in the house next to Vera, an old family friend, and done what he could to keep his mother alive without giving her ready cash to feed her habit.

Not an ideal solution, but life was full of compromises.

He had a key, but he knocked, anyway. This was his mother's house, her private space, and it had never been his home. After a short silence he heard the sound of someone moving inside the house, then the door opened.

"Zach." His mother blinked sleepily, a beatific smile curving her mouth as she registered his presence. "Hey, baby. I forgot you were coming."

Her face was flushed, her pupils shrunken to pinpricks, her words verging on slurred. Her clothes hung on her frame, her thin arms carefully covered with long sleeves to hide the bruises and track marks.

Same old, same old.

"Hey, Mum. I brought you dinner."

She felt impossibly frail when he embraced her. She'd lost more weight since last month, a worrying sign because it usually meant she was using more.

"Thought I could smell something good." She smiled and pushed her gray-streaked dark hair behind her ear. "You always bring me good things."

She blinked a few times before performing a labored about-face and making her way slowly down the hallway, one hand on the wall for balance. For a heartbeat he remained on the doorstep watching her painful progress, fighting the urge to drop the bag of food and turn tail and run.

There was nothing but despair for him in this house, and he'd had enough to last a lifetime.

He stepped inside and shut the door behind him before following his mother to the living room at the rear of the house. He caught her as she tidied the paraphernalia strewn across the coffee table—the length of stocking she was using as a tourniquet, the spoon she used for cooking her gear, the sterile swabs she used as filters, a box of sterile syringes.

"It's okay, Mum."

"I know you don't like it." Even though her high had left her far from coordinated, she worked doggedly until she'd transferred everything into a wicker basket, which she then took from the room.

He collected a couple of plates from the kitchen and was serving up the food when she returned.

"Butter chicken. My favorite," she said as she sank onto the couch.

She talked a good talk, but he had no illusions that she'd eat anything while she was high. Before he left he'd cover her untouched meal and leave it in the fridge for her to find later.

"So, what's been happening?" he asked as he picked up his own plate.

"Oh, not much. Some new people have moved in up the street. Single mum with a couple of kids. She's been pretty friendly so far, but that will change." His mum pulled a face.

"You don't know that."

"Zach, come on. The moment she finds out there's a junkie on the street, the kids will be warned off and I'll get the silent treatment. And someone will tell her, don't you worry about that." Her words came slowly and it was obvious she was struggling to stay focused. Any second now she'd fade out altogether—"nodding out," in street speak. If her high ran to form, she'd fade in and out for the next hour or so.

Could be worse. She could be strung out.

Last time he'd visited she'd been suffering withdrawal symptoms, pacing agitatedly as she fretted over when her dealer would return her call. His two-hour-long visit had felt like a week.

"You're not a monster, Mum."

"I know that. You know that. But most of the world thinks I'm a waste of space. They might be right, too." She huffed out a laugh before her eyes drifted shut.

Right.

Even though his appetite had completely deserted him, Zach ate his meal. He had a lot of work to get through once he got home, and he needed the energy.

After a minute or two his mother stirred, her chin lifting from her chest, eyes blinking. He kept eating. There wasn't much point restarting their conversation, since she'd only lose track of it in a few minutes when she nodded out again.

"Sorry."

"It's okay, Mum."

It wasn't, but he was past the point of being angry or hurt by his mother's addiction. Judy had been a heroin user on and off for nearly twenty-five years now. Together they'd seen it all: three overdoses, various infections, his mother's hepatitis C diagnosis, brushes with the law, more hospitalizations than Zach could count on the fingers of both hands. His mother had kicked it—gone cold turkey—many times, but the longest she'd stayed straight was a year, and she always found her way back to the life. It had taken him years of pointless railing and fruitless hope, but he had finally understood that something was broken inside her. Whatever it was that she'd been running from or seeking comfort from when she first started using casually had long since been eclipsed by the multiple traumas her addiction had visited upon her. Upon both of them. She was a living, breathing vicious cycle— she took drugs to comfort the pain of living, and the drug-taking made her life disastrous, so she took drugs to escape reality… And so on, and so forth.

"Meant to tell you—Beano has been clean for nearly six months now. How 'bout that?" Judy raised her eyebrows, clearly expecting him to be impressed.

He'd seen too many of her friends go on and off the gear to get too excited about anyone's sobriety.

"Is that a record for him?"

"He stayed straight for a year once." His mother scratched her arms before shooting him a sideways look. "He wanted to know if he could move in here for a while."

Zach gave her his full attention. "Why would he want to live here while you're still using? Wouldn't the temptation be too much for him?"

His mother shrugged, her gaze drifting from his. "Who knows? Seems like a good idea, though. He can help out with the rent."

"Mum." He said the single word heavily. He wasn't in the mood to be bullshitted. There were too many other pressures bearing down on him right now. Despite the way his mother was dressing it up, he knew without a doubt that Beano's moving in was her idea, and any rent money he paid would go straight up her arm, not toward the upkeep of the place.

"What? I'm trying to help a mate out." She hunched her shoulders like a naughty child who'd been accused of a crime she hadn't committed.

"If you need money, maybe you need to think about tapering off."

His mother worked part-time to feed her habit, something that was only possible because Zach covered all her other expenses. If she was scratching around for more money, it meant she was chewing up her wages with drugs, which, in turn, meant her habit was getting out of control.

"I don't need to taper. I'm good."

"Okay. I still don't think Beano moving in would be a great idea."

She considered his response, her head starting to nod again. He made an exasperated noise and stood, taking his half-empty plate and her full one through to the kitchen. He dumped his own food in the bin and covered hers and stowed it in the fridge. When he returned to the living room she'd listed to one side, her eyes closed, her face slack.

The sleeve on her sweater had rucked up and he could see the ugly scar on her forearm, the result of an abscess in an abused vein that had gone bad and had had to be excised, along with a portion of the surrounding tissue. Her body was riddled with scars—track marks, injuries from accidents, wounds inflicted by fellow users or boyfriends.

Which reminded him...

Leaving his mother in the living room, he did a quick tour of the house. The kitchen was clean, the fridge stocked with groceries. A six-pack of beer gave him pause, though. His mother hated beer.

He stopped in the doorway to his mother's room. The

bed was neatly made, a pile of books beside it. To an out-sider, it no doubt looked very ordinary, utterly benign. It hadn't always been like this. When Judy's addiction had deepened when he was in his early teens, they'd slowly lost everything that she'd acquired as a single mother. The TV, the computer, her car, any jewelry she could pawn. At her worst, she'd pawned his Christmas presents from her parents to garner enough money for a hit. They'd been evicted from more apartments than he could remember. The first time had been enough to shock his mother into rehab, but being homeless eventually became something she accepted with equanimity, like so many of the inevitable humiliations that came hand in hand with addiction. After all, the only thing that mattered in her life was heroin. Everything else was white noise.

He turned away, annoyed with himself for checking on her. Nothing he did or said would stop her from making bad decisions. It was futile to waste time and energy worrying that she'd found herself a new boyfriend; far better to prepare himself to pick up the pieces when things went wrong.

As they always did.

She was still out of it when he returned to the living room. He collected the throw from the couch and helped her into a more comfortable position before covering her. Then he obeyed the dictates of his gut and got the hell out of there.

He dove into work when he got home, desperate for the distraction. After an hour he straightened in his chair. His back and neck were stiff. Rolling his shoulders, he went into the kitchen to make coffee and stood at the kitchen counter watching the kettle work itself up to a boil, the growing pressure inside the appliance threatening to push the lid off.

He sympathized. Some months he could walk away from his mother's place feeling nothing, perfectly numb. Other times—tonight—he felt as though there were a scream building inside him and that if he wasn't careful it would find a way out.

Was it any wonder that he'd kissed Audrey? She was one of the few bright, exciting, promising things in his life. The only thing, really, that had nothing to do with either the past or the future. Audrey was about now. About how he felt when he was near her. There was nothing rational or sensible about his attraction to her. If anything, it was the opposite—everything sane in him told him to stay the hell away from her. Yet he felt the way he felt.

He wanted her. Badly.

Only an idiot would go there. Especially at the moment. And you are not an idiot.

He wasn't. He was a ruthless, determined, selfish bastard—because that was what life had taught him he needed to be to survive. He was used to missing out today in order to have what he wanted tomorrow.

He'd add Audrey's name to the list of things he couldn't have and get on with it, like he always did.

Simple.

He switched the kettle off before making himself a strong black coffee. Then he went back to work.

CHAPTER TEN

AUDREY HAD NEVER considered herself a particularly sensual person. She liked sex, but she wasn't mad for it. She'd never stayed awake at night thinking about it, for example. She'd never caught herself daydreaming about it when she was in an important meeting, or during lunch with her best friend, or while she was making toast in the morning.

Until she'd kissed Zach.

In the days following their short but hot encounter against the side of her car, Audrey found herself thinking about him—about them—so many times she began to doubt her own sanity.

The mere sound of his voice was enough to send a tremor through her body. The sight of him sent heat racing into her pelvis as she remembered weight of his body against hers, the taste of his mouth, the scent of his skin. Every time she was forced to look into his eyes and talk to him, she had to concentrate like crazy to stop herself from blushing and giving away the direction of her unruly, steamy, X-rated thoughts.

It was crazy, and disconcerting, and deeply worrying. She didn't want to be so aware of him. She didn't want to sit opposite him in meetings and wonder what his mouth would feel like on her breasts. She didn't want to lie in her bed aching for him. Especially when things were so tense at work.

She'd let the genie out of the bottle when she'd kissed him. She'd destroyed months of determination not to notice the

sexy, cocky man who'd dropped like a bombshell into her
workplace. And now she was a hot mess, pure and simple.

A fact that was confirmed when she looked in the mirror on Saturday morning ten days after The Kiss. Her eyes
were puffy from lack of sleep, her skin sallow. She looked
tired and anemic. As though she were recovering from an
illness—or, perhaps, succumbing to one.

*You need to get on top of this. You need to concentrate on
what's important and get this other stuff out of your head.*

The woman in the mirror didn't look inspired by the pep
talk. She looked a little lost. As though someone had stolen
her internal compass.

She flicked the cold-water tap on and cupped both hands
before sluicing her face with water. The shock of it made her
gasp. She was even paler when she checked her reflection
again, but the slightly dazed look was gone from her eyes.

Good. She needed to stop walking around in a lust-
induced haze and get on with things.

For today, "things" consisted of lunch with her parents
and her sister to celebrate her sister's birthday. Her father had
settled on Vue du Monde as an appropriate venue for such a
special occasion. Audrey hadn't eaten there before, but she
knew from reports from friends that it was the sort of place
that offered a set price degustation menu that went well into
three figures. The wine list, no doubt, climbed into four.

Not her kind of dining, but her parents wanted to mark
the occasion for Leah, and Audrey was hardly going to argue
with that. She thought about Leah's present as she ironed her
dress. She'd wound up settling on another watch, an elegant,
simple piece that she hoped her sister would think was beautiful as well as practical.

It was so hard to know. She and Leah were such different people, in almost every aspect, to the point where
people often looked surprised when they learned they were

related. The only thing they had in common was their brown eyes. Where Audrey was curvy with a medium build, Leah was willowy slender, and instead of being dead straight, her hair had a distinct curl to it. She was also a successful high-achiever, the sort of daughter most parents dreamed of having, whereas Audrey—

Are we really going to do this today? Really?

She yanked the iron cord from the wall so sharply that the plug flew back and smacked her in the shin. Today was not the day to wallow in the past. Today was her sister's day. A happy day.

She tackled her pale complexion with a little more blush than she usually wore and within minutes was zipping up her dress, a black and white and taupe striped tea-dress with a box pleated skirt. It was very Jackie-O demure, with a neat little black fabric belt. She curled her hair under on the ends and toed on her black sling-back wedges and pronounced herself ready.

The restaurant was on the fifty-fifth floor of the Rialto building, and she found a parking garage nearby. She had to blink when she stepped out of the lift and into the dim, modern interior. Dark walls and a dark floor sucked light from the space, allowing the myriad overhead lights to sparkle like stars and throwing the huge floor-to-ceiling windows into stark relief. Her parents and Leah were already seated, and she checked her watch as she was escorted to their table. She was right on time, which meant they were early rather than her being late. Still, she apologized as she arrived at the table and they broke off their conversation to greet her.

"We saved you one of the seats with a view," her father said after they'd exchanged kisses.

It was a spectacular view, too, a sprawling panorama of the city and surrounds.

"This is all pretty amazing," Audrey said as the waiter spread her napkin across her lap.

"We've been wanting to come here for ages but we were saving it up for a special occasion," her mother said, reaching across to squeeze Leah's hand.

"I'm a year older. It's hardly an achievement," Leah said drily.

She was pleased, though, Audrey could see. Which was the way it should be.

"Now, who's having champagne?" her father asked.

They drank a toast to Leah before applying themselves to the menu. Conversation shifted to her parents' work after the waiter had taken their orders. With three doctors at the table, it was natural that medicine was the first port of call when they all got together, and Audrey did her best to keep up. When things became too technical, however, she let her gaze drift to the view.

The city was bathed in sunlight and the buildings sparkled and winked as clouds raced across the sky. It was a truly beautiful day, the kind that lured people out into parks with picnic baskets, or onto hiking trails with water bottles and backpacks.

She found herself wondering what Zach was doing with the perfect weather. Making the most of the glorious day doing something outside? Or perhaps he was tackling one of the many DIY tasks left on the renovation list he'd told her and Megan about that night at the bar.

She tried to picture him with a paintbrush in hand but couldn't quite get there—he seemed far too urbane and stylish to get down and dirty in that way.

"Audrey? Hello?"

Audrey started. "Sorry. I was admiring the view."

Among other things.

Her mother looked exasperated. "You always were a day-dreamer."

"Was I?" It wasn't the way she thought of herself. Not when she was younger and certainly not now. In fact, she'd always characterized herself as an anxious child, always trying to please everyone.

"Oh, yes. You're our butterfly girl," her father said with an indulgent smile.

The waiter came with their meals then and they all fell silent while plates and sides were set out.

"What were we talking about?" Audrey asked once he was gone.

"I was asking about your work. How are things going?" her mother said.

Audrey pulled a face. "It's been a little tense lately. We have a new CEO and he's been restructuring the business. So far we've lost six people from our department. But it turns out we were the lucky ones—he's really cut through the marketing and accounting departments."

"It sounds as though you were lucky to keep your job." Leah was frowning with concern.

"Yeah. It feels that way at the moment, believe me. Morale is at an all-time low. No one feels safe."

Her mother was looking worried. "Do you think they'll be letting more people go?"

"I don't know. I'm keeping my head down and hoping."

And trying not to do anything stupid, like start up an affair with a colleague, even if he was the hottest thing she'd ever seen.

"That sounds scary. I'd be freaking out if I was you," Leah said.

"That won't ever be you, darling. People with your skills don't grow on trees," her father said.

Audrey blinked, caught on the raw by her father's comment. Self-conscious heat rose into her face even as she told herself that he hadn't meant it as a slight to her, more as a compliment to her sister.

Stop being so sensitive.

Conversation shifted to her cousin, Bridget, and it took Audrey a few minutes to clue in that she'd become engaged.

"When did this happen?" she asked.

"A couple of weeks ago. I thought you knew," her mother said.

"No."

"I'm sorry, that's my fault," her father said. "Your aunt asked me to pass the news on but I forgot. The party is next month. I'll email the date to you."

"It's the fifth," Leah chimed in.

"I'll make a note in my diary," Audrey said.

"I meant to tell you, Leah." Her mother's tone was so studiedly casual that Audrey paused in the act of buttering her roll to glance at her. "I ran into Professor Stenlake the other day."

Audrey could feel her sister bristle from across the table. Audrey might not be up to discussing the minutiae of her parents' and sister's day-to-day work, but even she knew that Professor Stenlake was in charge of the cardiothoracic unit at the Alfred Hospital and therefore Leah's boss. She glanced from her sister to her parents, trying to understand what was going on.

"Mum. Can we please not get into this today?" Leah said.

"Get into what? I simply wanted to pass on the fact that he said hello and that you were greatly missed. Which suggests to me that if you asked nicely, he'd be more than happy to take you back into the program before too much damage has been done."

"I've made my decision, Mum. Can we leave it?"

Audrey looked from her mother to her sister to her father. "What's going on?"

"Your sister has dropped out of the surgical program. She's decided she wants to become a clinical immunologist," her father said neutrally.

"Even though she has poured years of her life into a highly prestigious specialty that will ensure she has a brilliant future," her mother added.

Audrey looked to her sister. Leah was blinking rapidly, her face very pale.

"Immunology. That's a bit of a change of pace," Audrey said, feeling her way through the minefield.

"I enjoy it. I have some ideas I want to explore. It's an exciting field with lots of challenges." Leah's chin came up as she spoke and a determined glint came into her eyes.

"Well, good. Congratulations," Audrey said.

"Thank you." There was no missing the pointedness of Leah's response, or the look she threw at their mother.

"I understand that you're infatuated with immunology at the moment. But there is so much more opportunity for you in cardiothoracic surgery, Leah. So many more chances for you to make your mark."

"For the thousandth time, I don't care about making my mark. I want to be a doctor. I want to help people. I don't need my name up in lights. I definitely don't need to stroke around pretending I'm God in a white coat. If you're so keen on cardiology, why don't you look at retraining?"

Their mother sat back in her chair as though she'd been slapped. "We both know I'm too old to go down that path."

Audrey frowned, once again trying to catch up with the conversation. Since when had her mother not wanted to be a GP?

"Mum. Come on." Leah pushed her hair off her forehead, a gesture of frustration since she was a small child. "There's nothing wrong with being a GP. *Nothing.* And you're a great one."

"I don't want you to make the same mistakes I did." Their mother reached for Leah's hand and caught it in her own. Her fingers showed white with tension as she pressed home her point. "Listen to me, Leah—don't settle. Never be less than you can be. Don't let this opportunity slip away."

"It's not what I want, Mum. It's what you want, and I can't live my life for you. Not anymore."

Leah's chair scraped against the floor as she stood. Her eyes were shiny with tears as she spun on her heel and headed for what Audrey assumed was the ladies' room.

She started to push back her chair to go after Leah, but her father beat her to it.

"I'll go," he said, shooting his wife a dark look.

"I told you I couldn't sit by and let her do this to herself," her mother said.

"It's her birthday," he said. "Couldn't we at least have had a cease-fire for a few hours?"

Back stiff, he walked away from the table.

Audrey's mother was very pale as she fussed with the cutlery on either side of her plate.

"Are you okay?" Audrey asked.

"What do you think, Audrey?"

"To be honest, I had no idea this was going on."

"Well, it is. As you can see." Her mother reached for her wineglass.

Audrey stared at the sharp edges of her mother's profile and tried to find the right words to say. "Is immunology really that bad? I'm assuming she'll still get to drive a Mercedes and wear a stethoscope around her neck, right? And that if they ever call for a doctor on a flight she can still put her hand up to be the one to save the day?" She said it lightly, inviting her mother to take a step back from the heat of the situation.

"Your sister is a brilliant woman. She could be a trail-blazer. But she's settling for mediocrity."

"Well, maybe that's what she wants. She seems pretty determined."

And it wasn't as though immunology was a walk in the park or anything to be ashamed of, even if it didn't have the same old-school prestige that cardiac medicine enjoyed.

"Perhaps we should talk about something else," her mother said.

"She's thirty, Mum. And you said it yourself, she's brilliant. You really think she hasn't considered all the angles?"

Her mother set down her wineglass with a thunk. "I can hardly expect you to understand, when you've thrown away every opportunity that's come your way, but your sister is special. I know in my bones that if she passes this opportunity by she'll regret it later. And I don't want that for her. I won't let another of my daughters waste her potential."

Audrey flinched and her mother's expression softened marginally.

"I'm sorry, but it's the truth, Audrey. Even you have to admit that."

It had been a long time since Audrey had dared to defend herself to her parents. Her list of sins was so long, her transgressions so many, she'd always bowed her head and accepted their criticism. It seemed small recompense to pay for all the hurt and fear she'd once caused them. But today she couldn't stop the words that rose up inside her.

"I was sixteen, Mum. It was a long time ago. I'd like to think I've made up a bit of ground since then."

It took her mother a few seconds to respond—apparently she'd become as used to silent compliance as Audrey had.

"When you failed to finish high school, you threw away

any chance of achieving a higher education and ever being anything more than a glorified clerical assistant. Let's not pretend it was any different."

"I have my high school certificate. You know I do. I earned it at night school." It felt like a puny defense against her mother's patent disapproval but Audrey had to say it.

Her mother dismissed two years of hard work with the flick of her fingers. "You could have been so much more. We all have to live with that."

Even though she had always known it was how her mother felt, her words were like a blow to Audrey's solar plexus. For a long moment all she could do was breathe and blink as she concentrated on not shedding any of the tears pressing at the back of her eyes. She was saved from having to say anything further by her father's return.

"Where is she? I'll go talk to her," her mother said, standing.

"Sit down. She'll be with us in a minute." He was uncharacteristically stern, and her mother sat without a word.

Audrey took a swallow from her water glass and tried to regain her composure. The occasion was already a disaster, but she wasn't about to be the one who ruined it beyond all doubt by creating a scene.

"Sorry," Leah said when she slid into her seat a few minutes later, offering everyone a small smile despite the fact that her eyes were red from tears.

"I'm sorry, too. We can talk about this another time," their mother said, patting Leah's hand.

That the discussion was not over as far as she was concerned was more than obvious.

Leah slid her hand from beneath their mother's. "We should probably order another bottle of wine."

Audrey spent the rest of the meal trying not to reveal how much she wanted to be anywhere else. She tried to concentrate on the conversation at the table, but nothing stopped her mother's words from echoing in her head, not even her sister's very genuine pleasure when she opened Audrey's present. One thing that had gone well for the day.

By the time her father signed the credit card slip, Audrey was as taut as a bowstring and desperate to be alone. She managed to say all the right things as she took leave of her family, but it required every ounce of willpower she possessed to not break into a run when she reached the parking garage.

She loved her parents, and she sincerely regretted the fear and sadness she'd caused them in her teens, but sometimes being the black sheep of the family was an impossibly heavy burden to carry. She'd been telling herself for years that one day she would make it up to them, that they'd see her as she was and not as the troubled girl who had scared them and angered them in equal measure, but maybe it was time to face facts. She was thirty-three years old, and she had been a good girl for the past fifteen years. She had worked hard and studied at night school and climbed the ladder at Makers. She'd bought an apartment all on her own, without any financial assistance from her parents, and she had never, ever given them any cause to worry about her again.

Yet her mother still looked at her and saw nothing but disappointment and wasted opportunities.

Audrey slid behind the wheel, started the engine and threw the car into Reverse, accelerating so fast the tires squealed on the concrete. She wanted to be far away from here. She wanted to be gone, gone, gone, away from her mother's disapproval and disappointment and her father's sad eyes.

Your sister is special.... She could be a trailblazer.... You could have been so much more.

"No." Audrey slammed the heel of her hand against the

steering wheel as she zoomed up the exit ramp and out into the busy city street. She *would not* play the comparison game with her sister. It was childish and fruitless and pointless. And it always ended the same way—with Audrey as the loser.

She pointed the car toward St. Kilda and concentrated on driving, doing her best to ignore the thoughts clamoring for attention. She parked in the first spot she found and left her shoes in her car before walking across the sun-heated pavement to the beach wall, down the steps and onto the sand.

It was warm enough that there were a few families camped around umbrellas and sun shelters, and the sand close to the water was dotted with children digging holes and building castles. She walked along the beach until she found a sparsely populated stretch and sat. Looping her arms around her drawn-up knees, she dug her toes into the sand and did her damnedest to concentrate on the world around her and not the turmoil inside her.

The beach had always been her special place, her touchstone when times were tough. There was something about the sound of waves and the smell of seaweed and the freshness of the air that helped her find perspective. Staring at the dark blue sea, she waited for the beach to work its usual magic, but the knot of hard, hot emotion remained tangled tight inside her.

Let it go, she ordered herself. Instead she felt the humiliating push of tears for the second time that day. She let herself fall back against the sand, careless of the fact that she was in a new dress, and flung her forearm across her eyes. She breathed deeply until the threat had passed, once again refusing to give in.

She wasn't a little girl. There was no point crying over things that couldn't be changed. She was who she was, she'd done the things she'd done, and her parents felt the way they felt. It was what it was.

The world was warm and dark behind her eyelids and she lay listening to the sound of her breathing and feeling the wind play against her bare legs and arms and the fabric of her skirt. She was aware of the tension in her body—across her chest and shoulders and through her belly—and she realized that she'd been wound up and tense for a long time.

The pressure at work, the constant need to prove herself to her parents, the push-push-push from within to be good and smart and calm and sensible and always, always, always do the right thing…

She'd been doing the right thing for so long. Working overtime to show the higher-ups she was eager and dedicated and loyal, always wearing just the right clothes, never rocking the boat. She'd dated nice, safe, conservative men; she'd eaten whole-grain bread and broccoli and dragged her backside to the gym three times a week. She'd saved and paid down her mortgage and forgone little pleasures like overseas holidays and the pair of shiny red Jimmy Choo shoes she'd seen in a shop window and the decadent, gooey caramel cream cake they sold at her local bakery.

She'd been good, so good, and the effort of it all, of holding herself to such a high standard, of never losing control, of always doing the sensible thing, the smart thing, was enough to make her want to throw back her head and howl like a banshee.

It was such a visceral need she could actually feel her throat tense, could feel her body bracing itself for the effort of yelling until her lungs ached. She dug her heels into the sand and clenched her free hand around a fistful of the stuff and waited for the feeling to pass, as she'd waited for the need to cry to pass, as she'd waited for so many things to pass.

The feeling didn't go away, though. It sat behind her

breastbone, wanting out. Wanting release. Wanting something that wasn't prescribed and orderly and sensible.

An image swam behind her eyelids—a hard, very male body. Navy eyes, hot with need. A mouth made for secrets and sin.

Her eyes popped open and she stared at the bright blue sky. What she was thinking was insane—or, at best, highly risky. It certainly wasn't smart or safe or advisable.

Exactly.

She pushed into a sitting position, then she was on her feet. Then she was walking to her car. Then she was running. She knew if she stopped to think, she'd stop, period. And she didn't want to stop. She wanted to do something reckless and wild. She wanted to be bad and impulsive. She wanted something that wasn't about duty or ambition or penance.

Something for her.

She grabbed her phone from her handbag as she unlocked her car. Her heart in her mouth, she called up a search engine and tapped in Zach's name. A few seconds later an address filled the small screen.

She flung her phone onto the passenger seat, started the car and steered out into traffic. Instead of thinking or listening to the wet blanket screaming warnings in the back of her head, she punched on the radio and hit buttons until something loud and busy and pumpy blasted through the speakers.

She felt dizzy with both fear and anticipation when she pulled up outside a Victorian workers' cottage in a quiet, leafy street in Surrey Hills. Fear because she was afraid of what she was about to do, of how Zach might react to her arriving on his doorstep, of how she might be about to seriously mess up her life, and anticipation because she had been thinking about him, about this, for too long.

She switched off the engine, grabbed her bag and got out of the car. The road was warm beneath her feet and she realized for the first time that she hadn't put her shoes back on when she'd returned to the car.

Well, she was hardly going to get them now.

The front gate squeaked as she pushed it open. Her heart gave an almighty shimmy in her chest as she climbed the steps, fueled by adrenaline and excitement and trepidation. She could see a fuzzy reflection of herself in the opaque glass of the door, could see herself raise her hand. Her knock echoed in the small porch and sent a tremor up her arm.

What if he doesn't answer? What will you do then?

What if he does?

Footsteps sounded within the house. A shadow moved behind the opaque glass. She heard the snick of the lock. The door opened.

He wore nothing but a sheen of sweat, a confused frown and a pair of low-riding running shorts.

"Audrey."

She'd half expected her courage to dissolve like sugar in water the moment she saw Zach, and maybe it would have had he been fully clothed and perfectly groomed.

But he was about as close to naked as it was possible for a man to get and not be arrested for public indecency, and a wave of pure, blistering lust swept over her. She wanted this. Better yet, she *needed* it.

"Answer me honestly," she said, way past niceties like *hello* and *how are you* and *isn't the weather great today?* "What happened the other night at the bar—has it been on your mind? Have you been wondering what might have happened if we hadn't stopped?"

All confusion left his expression and his gaze was very intent, very focused. "Is that why you're here?"

"Yes," she said. Because the time for playing games had passed.

"Thank God."

He was reaching for her before she could process his words. One second she stood on the doorstep of his house, the next she was inside, her back against the wall, his mouth and body against hers. He tasted of heat, his tongue stroking hers with demanding greed, his body large and powerful as it pressed into hers. Her hands found his bare shoulders, closing over warm, hard muscle, even as his thigh slid between hers, forcing the heart of her into intimate contact with his leg.

It was a pale shadow of what she really wanted, but she pressed herself against him anyway, frantic for satisfaction. For ten days she'd been dreaming about him. She wanted relief. She wanted to know.

As if in answer to her thoughts, Zach's roving hand smoothed down her hip and the side of her leg. She felt the coolness of air as he lifted her skirt, then moaned in encouragement as his palm smoothed its way up her thigh and between her legs. She was wet and hot, so eager for him, and she tilted her hips into his touch. He stroked her once, twice, through the damp silk of her panties before slipping past the fragile barrier. She gasped as he stroked the seam of her sex, and an almost animalistic growl vibrated through his body. Her hands tightened involuntarily on his shoulders as he slid a finger inside her. It was so good, so exactly what she needed that she swore, the single word leaving her on a shocked exhalation.

He surprised her by breaking their kiss and lifting his head. "You know this is a terrible idea, right?"

She blinked, her brain so fogged by lust she could hardly think. "You're seriously asking me that while you have your hand in my underwear?"

"If you want to change your mind, now is the time."

For a moment she was stunned that he could even think of stopping—*she* was so far gone it was a wonder she was still standing. Then she saw the barely leashed desperation

in his beautiful eyes and understood that Zach was trying
to be a good guy, despite the fact that he was hard as a rock
where he was pressed against her hip.

"If you move your hand I will strangle you with those ob-
scenely small running shorts."

There was no mistaking the relief in his eyes.

"You mean, like this?" He stroked her with his finger, his
thumb sliding distractingly over the most sensitive part of
her, his gaze never leaving hers.

By way of answer she slid a hand into his hair and dragged
him down for another kiss. His tongue took her mouth again
as his hand worked magic between her thighs, stroking and
teasing, all thought of stopping and being sensible clearly
forgotten.

Despite the fact that they'd barely started, she could feel
her climax coming, could feel the tension building, and she
wanted him inside her when she finally lost it. Needed it
to be that way, needed to feel invaded and owned and utterly taken. Her hands smoothed down his back and across
his belly. She plunged a hand inside his shorts to grasp his
erection. He was achingly hard, and she slid a hand up and
down his thick shaft, her thumb gliding over the silken head
of his erection.

He shuddered, pushing himself into her hand. She shoved
his shorts down his hips, then reached beneath her skirt to
do the same with her panties. He was quick to help her, then
his hands were on her bare backside, his strong arms bulging as he lifted her. She wrapped a leg around his hips and
guided him to her entrance. The feel of his thick hardness
against her made her sob with anticipation. She tilted her
hips to invite him inside—then froze as cold reality intruded.

She wasn't on the Pill. And he wasn't wearing a condom.

"Wait," she said, wrenching her mouth away from his.
"Condom. We need a condom."

He stilled, his whole body trembling, and she could feel the act of will it took for him to drag himself back from the edge of no return. "In my bedroom."

"How far is that?"

"Down the hall, second door on the right. About a million miles."

She grinned, even though she trembled with unfulfilled desire. At least she wasn't alone in feeling frustrated by necessity.

He eased her down the wall and took a step backward. Her gaze moved down his body to his thighs, to the part of him that had been about to become a part of her. He was beautiful, thick and very hard and just the right length.

She couldn't help herself—she licked her lips.

"Hold that thought," he said. Then he turned on his heel and started up the hall.

For a second she was mesmerized by the flex of his muscular backside as he walked away from her. He had an amazing body. Amazing.

And it was about to be hers.

She followed, hands reaching for the zipper on her dress. She kicked it off as she entered his bedroom, her bra next. He was on the bed, removing a shiny foil square from the bedside drawer. She joined him, crawling up the mattress. She didn't give him a chance to take charge, plucking the condom from his hand before planting a palm in the middle of his chest and pushing him flat onto his back. She straddled him as his hands smoothed up her sides and onto her bare breasts. She watched him watch her as she tore the condom open with her teeth, stroking the thin latex onto his erection, hugely turned on by the dark flush in his cheeks and the knowing glint in his eyes.

She positioned herself over him, ready to take them both to the place they needed to be, but he surprised her by lifting his head and tonguing her nipple. It felt so good, even better when he sucked hard before biting her gently. Her sex throbbed in response, and he took advantage of her momentary distraction to buck beneath her. A second later she was on her back, Zach above her, his arms braced on either side of her body.

"Sneaky," she said.

"You didn't really think I was going to let you be on top the first time, did you?"

She was still trying to come up with a suitable response when he nudged inside her, and then there was nothing but the feel of him, so hard and thick and hot as he stroked into her willing body.

So good. Almost too good.

Wrapping her legs around his hips, she gave herself up to the mindless, perfect pleasure of finally being naked with Zach.

CHAPTER ELEVEN

ARMS BRACED ON EITHER side of Audrey's body, Zach stroked into her again, burying himself deep inside her wet, tight heat. She felt…amazing. Soft and firm at the same time, her skin velvety smooth beneath his hands. And her breasts… God, he loved her breasts.

He lowered his head to draw a pale pink nipple into his mouth, teasing it with his tongue until it was tight and hard. He could smell her perfume and taste clean skin and something that he guessed must be pure Audrey. It was intoxicating, and he couldn't get enough of it.

She made an unintelligible noise, somewhere between a moan and a plea, and he realized she was very close. He didn't think it was possible for him to get any harder but he did, spurred on by her absolute abandonment to pleasure.

Wanting to make her even crazier, he slipped a hand between their bodies. She was already swollen and slick with need when he found her, but he could feel the new tension in her body as he teased her with his thumb. Her fingers dug into his hips as she urged him without words to go harder, faster. He obliged and was rewarded when she arched her back, her head dropping back, her eyes closing. Her breath came out on a shudder, her body tightening around his as she came.

There was something about how lost she appeared, something about the flush across her chest, the small frown between her eyebrows, the way she strained toward him that pushed him over the edge. He'd wanted to last longer, to perhaps help her find pleasure a second time, but she was too hot, and he'd been thinking about her way too long.

Pressing his face into the soft skin of her neck, he breathed in the scent of her as he drove himself home to the hilt. His climax hit him like a fist, squeezing him tight with pleasure so acute it was almost pain. Afterward, he let himself rest on her fully for a few seconds, momentarily spent.

That had been…mind-blowing. Exactly what he'd needed. A million times better than any fantasy he'd ever had. A billion times.

He could feel her heart pounding away, the vibration of it reaching him through their joined bodies. Like him, she was breathing heavily, her chest rising and falling rapidly. Abruptly he realized how heavy he must be. Disengaging, he rolled to the side. He grabbed a tissue from the box beside the bed and took care of the condom and wound up on his back beside her, staring up at the ceiling, his mind a big, echoing void.

No thoughts. No worries. No pressing need to do anything. There was only the pleasant heaviness in his body and the warmth of her arm and leg against his side and the knowledge that he wasn't alone, and that was a good thing. A great thing.

After a minute or two she stirred and he turned his head to look at her. She met his gaze unflinchingly, the way she did everything.

"Well," she said. "I guess that was kind of inevitable."

He couldn't do anything but smile. "Probably."

"Can't shove the genie back in his bottle, after all."

"Nope."

"Good to have it out of our systems, though. Now we can get back to business as usual."

She said it very matter-of-factly, as though they were dealing with a pesky work matter.

He knew better than to think she was feeling matter-of-fact, though, no matter how light her tone was. He'd been inside her. Her fingernails had dug half-moon shapes into his skin. He'd watched her lose herself in spectacular fashion.

He rolled onto his side, propping himself on his elbow so he could survey her at his leisure. He'd dreamed about this body for a long time, after all, and if this was his one shot at living his fantasy, he was going to take it and run with it.

"Sorry to disappoint you, but it's going to take more than what just happened to get you out of my system."

"Yeah?" She didn't look too disappointed by the prospect.

"Definitely. These breasts, for example…" He reached out and cupped one in his hand. Its curve fit his palm perfectly, the weight welcome and warm against his skin. "I'm going to need more time to get over them."

"Is that so?"

He ran a thumb over her nipple and they both watched as it hardened in response, puckering beautifully.

"Absolutely." He smoothed his hand down her breast and onto her belly. Her abdominal muscles jumped as he slid south, past the tiny well of her belly button and into the soft curls at the top of her thighs. "Then there's this. I'm going to need to put some serious man-hours into getting this out of my system."

"Man-hours. Are they different from woman-hours?"

"Hell, yeah," he said, leaning close to press a kiss to her belly. She smelled good there, too. He hadn't shaved this morning and he used the bristle on his chin to gently abrade the soft skin of her stomach.

She shivered, lifting her hips slightly, and he curled his hand over her mons so that his fingers dipped between her thighs.

"You're so soft," he murmured against her skin. "That's going to take some getting over, too."

"Is it?" Her voice was low and husky with need.

He pressed an openmouthed kiss to her stomach, teasing her with his tongue. When he glanced at her again she was flushed, her hands fisted into the sheets beside her body as though she was afraid of what they might do if she let them have their way.

She knew what he was doing, where he was going, and he could see it excited her beyond measure.

Good, because this was one thing he'd always gotten off on, and feasting on Audrey was very high on his fantasy list.

Returning his attention to her belly, he trailed kisses across her abdomen to her hip, licking along the curved ridge before following it into the valley where her belly met her thigh. She smelled deliciously of sex and woman, and he inhaled deeply before kissing her where she needed him the most.

She tensed, a small sound escaping her mouth. He teased her with his tongue before sliding one finger, then two, inside her. She was incredibly wet and tight and he could feel himself growing hard again. Ignoring his own needs for now, he concentrated on giving her pleasure, using his hands and lips and tongue and teeth to drive her wild.

"Zach… Yes…. That feels so good. You feel so good…."

Her breathless words and the small, helpless noises she made almost destroyed his control. He'd never imagined she'd be vocal, but he loved it, especially when she called his name as she came a second time, her body trembling in his grip.

She was still shaking with aftershocks when he slipped another condom on and moved over her, sliding inside her with one powerful thrust. Her hands found his hips, then his ass as he lost himself in her warm, willing heat, reveling in the clench of her body around his.

"Zach… More… Please."

He swore, so turned on he almost came on the spot. Instead, he upped the pace, deepening the angle so that every withdrawal gave her the most stimulation. She tensed beneath him, her breasts thrusting forward as she arched her back. He ducked his head and sucked hard on her nipple and felt her climax roll over her. As it had before, her pleasure fed his and within seconds he was gone, lost on a wave of release.

He was powerless to resist the tiredness that washed over him as he disposed of the second condom. He told himself he would close his eyes for a minute to allow himself some recovery time before he continued to exploit the stunning turn of luck or fate or whatever it was that had brought Audrey to his doorstep. Because no way was two times enough. Not when he had six months worth of half-acknowledged, fevered fantasies to draw upon.

Without saying a word, he pulled the covers over both of them, sparing a moment to press one last kiss to her soft, pretty mouth before succumbing to sleep.

HE WOKE ABRUPTLY to darkness and the dip of the bed as she slipped away.

"Hey." He reached out and caught her wrist as she passed by. "Where are you going?"

He couldn't see her face in the dimly lit room.

"Home."

He didn't want her to go. Not yet. They'd made a tacit agreement that this one time was it, their chance to indulge themselves, but it wasn't only sex he was interested in. He was interested in her, the real her, not the professional her she presented at the office.

"You must be hungry. Let me grab you something to eat before you go."

She didn't respond immediately, and he took advantage of her hesitation to move to the side of the bed.

"I make a pretty mean omelet," he said.

In reality, he wasn't even sure he had eggs, but he was confident he could improvise something.

"Okay. Thanks."

He reached across and flicked the light on, the better to find something to wear. She blinked rapidly in an attempt to adjust to the light. He hadn't had the opportunity to fully appreciate her body earlier—he'd been too busy trying to get close to it—but now his gaze swept over her, pausing appreciatively at her full, rosy-tipped breasts before dropping to her belly and hips and legs. He'd always known she had great calves, but her legs in general were incredibly sexy—toned and athletic, but still womanly. And he'd already worshipped the curve of her hips with his hands and mouth.

Was it any wonder he'd been hot for her since he walked into the Makers building all those months ago? Who wouldn't want this woman?

She was looking around and he guessed she was searching for her dress.

"By the door," he said, and she turned in that direction, offering him a heart-stopping view of her peach-shaped backside, complete with a colorful addition that he'd failed to notice until now: a tattoo, some kind of cartoon animal that occupied the top third of her right butt cheek. The edges were fuzzy, indicating it wasn't a recent addition.

It was the last thing he'd expected to find beneath her crisply tailored clothes. Totally out of keeping with the woman he'd always assumed she was.

He grabbed a pair of cargo shorts from the chest of drawers to his right, tugging them on as she stepped into her dress. He moved forward to zip her up, feeling a definite twinge of regret as the dress closed over the pale, smooth skin of her back.

She was glancing around again, looking for something else. He grinned and stepped out into the hallway. Her panties lay in a small silken pool beside his abandoned running shorts. Had she forgotten the way she'd shoved first his, then her own, underwear down so that they could cut to the chase?

He hadn't. The memory would stay with him for a very long time.

He collected her panties, noting the softness of the ivory silk before returning to the bedroom and handing them over to her. Her cheeks were pink as she bent to pull them on.

"Kitchen's this way," he said, gesturing with a jerk of his head.

He could feel her following him up the hallway, could hear the swish of her full skirt. He flicked on lights as he entered the kitchen, heading straight for the fridge.

"This is nice."

He glanced over his shoulder to find her surveying the white cabinets and dark granite counters.

"It's okay. Needs updating, though."

"You wouldn't say that if you could see the kitchen in my place." She pulled a face. "The seventies are alive and well. I even have burnt-orange countertops."

"Hang on to them long enough, they'll be cool again. Genuine vintage."

"I'm not sure I have the stomach for it."

He opened the fridge and sent a little prayer of thanks out to the universe when he saw he had a carton of eggs. He also had some cherry tomatoes and feta cheese. Dinner was officially sorted.

She slid onto one of the two stools on the other side of the counter as he set out ingredients and reached for the chopping board.

"I didn't realize you cooked," she said.

He shot her a look. "What did you imagine I did, pry cans open with my bare teeth?"

She shrugged. "I don't know. Whatever it is that swinging bachelors do. Eat a lot of takeout, go to a lot of restaurants. Get their women to cook for them."

"I eat my fair share of takeout, I'll own that. But you have an inflated view of my social life."

She combed her fingers through her hair, trying to restore order. A futile task, since she still looked enticingly bed-rumpled.

"I bet it's better than mine." She sounded rueful.

"Not much time left for anything else when you start at seven and finish at eight," he said.

"Exactly."

"Then there's the catch-up work on the weekend."

"And still my in-tray has a hernia."

He smiled as he started cutting the tomatoes into quarters. "You're pretty funny, you know that?"

"Am I?"

He glanced at her. She looked uncomfortable, perched there on the other side of the counter. As though she'd rather be anywhere else.

Maybe it had been a mistake, asking her to stay for dinner. They both knew what this was, after all. Sex. A mutual satisfying of desire and curiosity. So why had he tried to parlay it into a meal and conversation?

"Listen, if you don't want to stay, you don't have to," he said.

She blinked. "Is that you giving me my marching orders or you letting me off the hook?"

"Option B. I didn't want to send you home hungry, but it wasn't meant to be purgatory."

A small smile curved her lips. "It isn't. Not even close. I'm just…out of practice, I guess. And maybe a little worried."

"That I'm going to go to work and let everyone know how I put Audrey Mathews away on the weekend?"

She made a rude noise. "'Put away.' I've always hated that saying. What does it mean, anyway? Put me away where?"

"What would you prefer, then?"

"I don't know. 'Took care of her'? 'Slipped her a bone'?"

He laughed, because he knew she wasn't remotely serious. "Okay. You think I'm going to be bragging all over the office on Monday about how I slipped Audrey Mathews a bone?"

She was struggling not to smile. "No. You don't gossip."

She said it with absolute certainty.

"Neither do you."

Unlike many of their colleagues, Audrey avoided water-cooler speculation.

"Only with Megan, and she doesn't count because she's a vault. What goes in, stays in."

"So if I'm not going to be wearing a T-shirt on Monday letting everyone know I 'took care of you,' what are you worried about?"

The smile faded from her mouth as she considered his question. "I don't know. That I'll act differently around you and people will be able to tell. That Whitman will take one look at us and know. That this was a really bad idea."

"Hey, we both knew that going in."

"I haven't forgotten your timely reminder, don't worry."

"Probably would have been more effective if I'd issued it before I invaded your underwear, huh?"

"You think?"

He moved to the stove and put a frying pan on the burner.

"Don't worry about work. It'll be fine."

"You don't know that."

"Yeah, I do. We both care about our jobs too much for it to be any other way."

"God, I hope you're right."

He whisked the eggs before pouring them into the pan. "Stop worrying. Tell me about something else instead."

"You want me to talk about the weather?"

"Tell me something I don't know about you. Like how you got that tattoo, for example."

She frowned. "I should get it removed, but I figure having to look at it in the mirror for the rest of my life is a fitting punishment for being stupid enough to get it in the first place."

There was a world of self-recrimination in her tone. "You don't like it?"

"A fuzzy, badly inked version of Tweetie Bird? What's not to love about that?"

He couldn't help but smile at her sarcasm.

"How old were you when you got it?"

Her gaze slid away from his. "Sixteen."

It wasn't what he'd expected to hear. "That's pretty young."

"It is."

She didn't say any more, and he decided not to push.

"I was going to get one when I was eighteen, but I know too many junkies with ink to ever trust a tattoo needle."

He said it without thinking, wanting to put her at her ease. Then her eyebrows shot up with surprise and he registered what he'd done.

"That's a nice neighborhood you grew up in," she said after a short pause.

"The mean streets of Footscray. You want some toast with this?"

He could feel heat in his face, hoped that she'd assume it

was because he was standing over the stove and not because he was suddenly feeling burningly self-conscious.

Audrey was the last person he wanted to know about his background. Her parents were doctors. The world he knew, that he'd grown up in, would be as foreign to her as another country. There was no way she could even begin to understand…and he didn't want her to. He wanted her to continue to see him as the guy in the nice suit and the great car who'd done well for himself. That was the important part of who he was. The part that was available for public consumption, anyway. It was why he'd lied to her that night in the bar, telling her both his parents were dead rather than having to shuffle around telling a bunch more lies to cover the truth about his mother.

That part of his life didn't belong in this part. It was separate. A different world.

"Toast sounds good. I can take care of it if you tell me where the bread lives."

She slipped off the stool and looked at him expectantly, and the tension inside him eased. She wasn't going to pursue his slipup.

"In the fridge. Bottom shelf. Toaster is behind that door on the right."

He pulled out two plates while she slotted bread into the toaster and returned to the fridge for butter. Twice they bumped hips as they maneuvered around each other, and both times he had to fight the totally inappropriate urge to grin like an idiot.

Who would have ever thought he'd be jostling for space with Audrey while they rustled up a meal together? Not him, that was for sure.

Five minutes later they sat at the kitchen counter to a meal of buttered toast and omelet. He'd never been particularly fussed about his cooking skills in the past, but he watched warily as she took the first bite.

"Oh, that's good. I never would have thought to put feta in an omelet." She closed her eyes briefly to savor the flavors, and he felt a ridiculous surge of achievement.

It was only a bloody omelet, after all. Glorified scrambled eggs.

"Anything goes when it comes to omelets as far as I'm concerned," he said. "If it's in the fridge and not moving or furry with mold, it's fair game."

"Interesting philosophy."

"I'm all about what works."

"Except for this." She indicated the two of them.

"Except for this," he agreed.

They were silent as they ate. He glanced at her, full of questions now that his brain could move past the stunning fact that she'd arrived on his doorstep with sin on her mind.

Like, what had happened today to bring her here?

Because something had. He had no doubt about that. There had been an almost frantic light in her eyes when he'd opened the door, as though she was running from something. Or, perhaps, seeking something.

Distraction? Release? He had no idea. All he knew was that her arrival had felt like a cosmic gift, especially considering he'd already punished himself with a ten-kilometer run and about a million push-ups in an attempt to get her out of his head. Opening the door to find her standing there, barefoot and gorgeous and wild for it, had almost blown his mind.

He swallowed his questions with his food, aware that his curiosity would not be welcome. Why would it be? She'd offered him her body and her passion for a few short hours, not a free pass into her life. Which was why he hadn't pushed about the tattoo, and why she hadn't pursued his comment about junkies.

They both were well aware that this was a blip. A time-out. And it was about to end, because she'd finished her meal and so had he. He slid off the stool and took both their plates to the sink.

"Something to drink? Coffee? Wine?" he offered.

"Water would be great."

He ran them both a glass from the tap and stood on the other side of the counter as she drank it, studying her, remembering this moment for later.

Her eye makeup was smudged from their nap, her mouth bare of lipstick. Her hair was tousled, far from its usual smoothness. She looked approachable and soft and more vulnerable than he'd ever seen her before. He remembered the way she'd watched him as he'd kissed his way down her belly. The way she'd clenched her hands into the sheets as though she was afraid of reaching out for what she really wanted.

She set down her glass. "What are you thinking about?"

"Guess."

Her gaze dropped to his mouth. "We agreed this was a one-off."

"We did. The moment you walk out the door, that agreement takes effect."

She glanced down, her eyelashes sweeping her cheeks. The corner of her mouth curled up into a small, provocative smile. "In that case…"

She stood, one hand smoothing down her skirt in an age-old feminine gesture. She walked slowly around the counter, stopping only when she was in front of him. Her gaze on his until the last possible moment, she leaned forward and pressed a kiss to his shoulder. He felt her mouth open, felt the wetness of her tongue and the subtle pressure of her teeth. She lifted her head and took a step back. She threw him a challenging look as she braced her hands on the counter and boosted herself up so she was sitting on the edge.

"Come here," she said, her voice rough with desire.

He was already hard, more than ready to accept the invitation, and he stepped into her embrace. They found each other's mouths unerringly, tongues stroking. Her hands gripped his upper arms before sliding onto his chest to find his nipples. She teased him a little before sliding a hand farther south and gripping him through the fabric of his shorts.

She was so hot. He loved the way she'd taken the lead, and he especially loved what she was doing with her hand. He went on his own roaming expedition, shaping her breasts before sliding his hands beneath the fabric of her skirt. Her thighs were already spread wide to accommodate him, and he smoothed his hands all the way to the top of her thighs. He could feel how wet she was through the silk of her underwear and he stroked her with his thumbs, teasing her. She made an approving sound and started fumbling with the stud on his cargo shorts.

Within seconds he was in her hand and she was stroking him confidently. More than anything he wanted to push aside her panties and slide inside her again, but the condoms were back in his bedroom.

"Audrey…"

"Relax."

She lifted a hand to the bodice of her dress and removed a small foil square from inside her bra. It took him a second to understand that she must have grabbed it when they were dressing.

"A little presumptuous, don't you think?" he said as she went to work opening the pack and smoothing the latex onto his erection.

"Are you worried I might think you're easy?" she said, glancing up from her important work.

"I'm worried that if you don't hurry, this is going to be a sad waste of a condom."

She laughed, the sound wicked and saucy and earthy. Then she wriggled closer to the edge of the counter.

"Better do something about these, then," she said, indicating her underwear.

He had them off her in seconds. Seconds after that he was inside her, sheathed in her wet heat. She gusted out her breath and gripped his biceps, her nails digging in.

"Okay?" he asked, worried he'd been too rough, too fast.

"Yes."

She bit her lip and he realized she'd been bracing herself, anticipating what was to come. It was tempting to live up to that, to pound into her and rush them toward completion. But this was the last time he'd have her, and he wanted to savor it. To wring every last second of enjoyment from the encounter.

So instead of driving hard, he withdrew till only the tip of him was inside her, only to nudge forward into her again a few shallow inches. He repeated the action, very deliberate, watching her face, loving the way her breathing hitched and the hectic color that flooded her cheeks.

"Still okay?" he asked.

She gave him a look, her mouth quirking up at the corner. "The worst ever."

"That's what I thought."

His own needs firmly in hand, he set himself to the task of driving Audrey wild.

CHAPTER TWELVE

HE WAS KILLING her. Destroying her inch by inch with his slow, shallow strokes. Audrey could feel the tension coiling inside, could feel her climax building, but it was so slow, each second drawn out until the pleasure was almost pain.

She bit her lip, trying to hold back the plea that was rising in her throat. This was so good, but she needed more. Needed the slap of his body against hers. Needed the urgency of it.

Finally she couldn't hold back a second longer. "Zach…"

"Yes?"

He watched her, was enjoying torturing her.

"Stop messing with me."

"Slow and steady wins the race. Didn't you know that?"

"I want hard and fast," she said.

"I'm not done here yet."

There was something infuriatingly sexy about the way he said it. An absolute acknowledgment that she was at his mercy.

"Zach…"

"Do you have any idea how freaking hot you are?" he said. "How much I love watching you?"

She followed his gaze to where they were joined, watched the slow slide of his body into hers, the equally slow withdrawal. Her inner muscles tightened, her heart rate kicking up another notch as a deeper, dirtier excitement gripped her.

"You feel so good. So tight. So wet."

He slid inside her again, the friction and his voice and

his words and the sight of him inside her all combining to push her closer to the edge. He grinned, and she knew that he knew what he was doing to her.

And still he kept it slow, drawing out her climax so that it built second by second, until she was almost scared of how good it felt.

"Come for me. Do it for me, Audrey," he said, his eyes heavy-lidded and demanding, his dark hair spilling across his brow, his body tense with self control.

It was too much. The final straw. Her climax swept over her, wringing a wordless cry from her throat, making her clench her knees around his hips. It seemed to last forever, tiny, delicious aftershocks rocketing through her as he continued his slow, steady stroking inside her.

Afterward she was limp, utterly spent—and he was still inside her, his grip on her hips possessive. She could see he was close, but she could also see he wasn't ready to let go yet.

Well, two could play at the game.

"You feel so good inside me," she told him, hooking one leg around his hips. "So big and hard."

His mouth hitched at the corner. He knew what she was doing, but she kept it up anyway, telling him how hot he made her, how much she loved his body, loved having him inside her. How she couldn't get enough of him, how beautiful he was.

By the time she was done the veins stood out in his neck, he was keeping such a tight rein on himself.

"What are you waiting for?" she asked.

"This."

He found her with his thumb, then started to pound into her with a primitive, urgent rhythm. She was so sensitized, so aroused she screamed as she came again as Zach rammed himself home one last time, his head dropping back as he called out her name.

If she hadn't already just come spectacularly, the sight of him racked with pleasure, every muscle hard, would have made her lose it on the spot.

Unbelievable.

"Unbelievable," he said, the single word escaping on a breathless pant.

He withdrew almost immediately, turning away to do something with the condom. He dragged his shorts back up his hips before he turned back to face her. They eyed each other across the distance of a few feet, him with his shorts half-zipped, her with her skirt rucked up around her hips, her thighs still spread wide. They were both breathing hard, and she couldn't look away from his steady, knowing gaze.

She'd never had sex this good. She had a horrible feeling that she never would again, either. For some reason, Zach did it for her. Pushed all her buttons in the right order, and then some. His body, the smell of him, the taste of him, the feel of him—it was as though someone had sneaked into her subconscious and pilfered the dirtiest, darkest, deepest corners of her fantasies and designed a man whose sole purpose in life was to get her off.

Yeah. He was that hot.

And she was never going to have him again.

She let the painful reality sit in her gut for a few seconds before she pushed her hair off her forehead. Her brow was damp—no surprises there. She had a rough idea of exactly how abandoned and thoroughly pleasured she must look right about now.

Well, he looked pretty shagged, too. In the best possible way. They'd more than held their own. But it had always been like that between them, hadn't it?

"At the risk of this becoming a habit, do you think you could pass me my panties?" she asked.

Somehow they'd wound up on the opposite counter, sitting next to his egg timer. He passed them over without a word, watching as she slid off the counter. For the second time in an hour she dressed in front of him, smoothing her skirt back down again.

"Thanks for dinner."

"Thanks for dessert," he said.

"I think I should be thanking you for that. That little trick you pulled at the end there… Nice."

"Glad you liked it."

"I did. In case you couldn't tell."

"I had an inkling."

She wanted to stay and banter with him all night, because the moment she was outside on the pavement, this was history. Nothing but a hot, quickly fading memory for her to take out and dust off whenever she wanted to really torture herself.

"Okay. I should go." She said it more for herself, because she needed to hear it, than for him.

"All right."

A little thud of disappointment tightened her belly. Stupidly, there had been a very foolish part of her that had been hoping he might suggest she stay the night.

Not that she would have taken him up on the offer. But it would have been nice for her ego to know that he'd wanted her to.

The guy spent the past three hours making sure you had a very good time. What more do you want from him?

Nothing. She'd come looking for release, for a safe outlet for all the pressure building inside her, and she'd found it. In spades. She'd had her walk on the wild side, she'd transgressed just a little, just enough to make it possible for her to breathe again.

Her work here was done.

"I don't suppose you know where my car keys are?" Like

her underwear, she seemed to have misplaced them in her rush to get him naked.

"No idea." He grinned, and she knew he was remembering the way she'd arrived, barefoot and more than a little edgy.

Together they returned to the front hall, where they found her keys on the runner. Funny, she didn't even remember having them in her hand when he'd opened the door. He stooped and passed them to her.

"Thanks."

She stood back while he opened the door, then moved past him onto the porch. "I had a good time."

"Good. Huh. I clearly need to fine-tune my technique."

She arched a skeptical eyebrow. "Oddly, I find it hard to believe that you're even remotely insecure about your technique."

"Do you now?"

"Yep. But just in case—" she leaned forward and pressed her lips to the angle of his jaw "—I had a great time. A spectacular time."

His hand slipped around her waist, pulling her close as he turned his head to capture her mouth. They kissed deeply, wetly, longingly. She could feel him growing hard again, could feel her own desire starting to reignite.

She forced herself to break the kiss. To take a step backward and slip free of his arm.

"Good night, Zach."

"You can say that again," he said softly.

There was a look in his eyes, a sort of wistfulness mixed with hot lust. As though he was wishing like crazy that this story had a different ending.

"I'll see you on Monday."

His gaze sharpened at the reminder of all they had at stake, his smile fading a notch. He nodded, once, and she knew they were both on the same page. Great sex was one thing, but they both had too much invested in their careers right now to risk blowing it over something so ephemeral and essentially meaningless. Great sex didn't pay the bills, after all. Great sex didn't provide superannuation or sick pay or career advancement.

She turned away and started down the garden path. She beeped her car open and slid behind the wheel. Zach remained silhouetted in his lit doorway, waiting for her to leave. She started her car, then pulled out into the street. Only when she'd turned the corner and was safely on her way home did she let out the breath she'd been holding.

Holy bloody hell.

An incredulous, slightly hysterical laugh bubbled up her throat. She'd had wild, crazy, hot, consuming monkey sex with Zach Black. The Man With the Golden Ass. Three times!

Three times. Who does it three times *in one night?*

Her euphoria lasted all the way home, following her into the shower as she washed the last traces of him from her body. There were a few more lasting reminders that he'd had his wicked way with her, however. A small suck mark on her inner thigh, along with a slight irritation from his beard on her belly. There was also a sort of general tenderness downstairs—more an awareness, really, that her body had been well and truly loved.

Way to break the drought, Mathews.

Afterward, she toweled herself dry and slipped into bed. She pictured Zach doing the same thing across town, lying in his sex-rumpled sheets, and smiled.

It had been stupid to go over there. Crazy, even, given the way Whitman was hacking and burning his way through the head-office staff at present. Now was not the time to slip up, in any way.

But she couldn't regret it. Wouldn't. Refused to, in fact. It had been for her, and she'd needed it, and it had been *good*.

So, no regrets.

Closing her eyes, she rolled onto her side and prepared to dream of Zach.

Definitely no regrets.

ZACH DID ALL the things he'd normally do come Monday morning. Woke, pulled on his running gear, hit the road for a five-kilometer run. Returned home, ate breakfast, showered, dressed, drove into work.

A normal day, like any other working day. Except...

He was aware of a certain urgency within himself to set foot inside the office. His gut was jumpy, and he had to wipe his palms down the side of his pants when he got out of his car.

Stupid, but he was nervous about seeing Audrey. And excited. And, of course, freaking turned on.

Nothing's going to happen, dude. Calm the hell down.

He took a couple of deep breaths as he ascended the stairs to the main level, willing his body to relax. They'd had their time-out, and now it was business as usual. Which meant the dirty little voice in the back of his mind that was urging him to get her alone and naked again was going to be steadfastly ignored, no ifs, buts or maybes.

Zach made his way to the merchandising department, then stopped in his tracks when he saw that Audrey's light was already on.

Immediately all other thought left his mind. Of their own accord, his feet changed direction. Twenty seconds later, he stopped in her office doorway, telling himself that it was far better that they get this first meeting over and done with when no one else was around than do it later when there would be dozens of witnesses.

It was a good excuse to allow himself to do what he wanted—look at her and talk to her and breathe in the subtle vanilla-floral scent of her perfume.

She glanced up immediately. There was a flicker of something in her eyes when she saw him, then her expression became smoothly blank. Her professional mask, the one he'd become so used to over the past six months. He knew what lay behind it now, though. Passion and laughter and sass.

"Hey," he said.

"Hey yourself."

"How was the rest of your weekend?"

Her gaze slid sideways, as though to confirm that no one else was around to hear that they'd spent part of the weekend together.

"There's only us," he reassured her.

Her shoulders relaxed. "I didn't do much. How about you?"

"Just took it easy. I'm not as young as I used to be. I needed to recharge a little."

A smiled tugged at her mouth. "Really? I didn't notice any stamina issues."

"Correct answer, Ms. Mathews. You say all the right things."

She was grinning now, sitting back in her chair, waggling her pen from side to side playfully. She was wearing an oyster-gray silk shirt, the fabric draping her breasts enticingly. "Funny you should say that, since you're the one who has a way with words."

Lured by the mischievous glint in her eyes, he entered her office fully, resting an elbow on the filing cabinet near the door.

"Yeah? What way is that?"

She was a little flushed and he could tell she was enjoying their wordplay as much as he was.

"You know."

He was about to respond when a voice piped up behind him. "Sorry. I got caught in a traffic jam because some idiot ran out of gas and blocked a whole lane. Who does that in this day and age?"

His smile dropped as he glanced over his shoulder to see Lucy standing in the doorway.

"I know you wanted to get a head start on the pricing report." Lucy's gaze was on Audrey. "Hope I haven't kept you waiting."

"Of course not. Zach and I were talking about some stuff that came up at the conference." Audrey shuffled some papers around on her desk. Very busy.

"Oh. Right." Lucy's glance bounced between him and Audrey. "I hope I'm not interrupting?"

"You're good," he said easily. At least, he hoped it sounded easy. Privately, he was kicking his own ass. If Lucy hadn't announced herself immediately, there was no telling what she might have overheard.

Audrey's tense expression said she was thinking the same thing. So much for business as usual.

"I'll leave you to it." He gave Audrey a brief nod.

She returned the acknowledgment grimly.

When he was back at his desk, he tapped out a quick email to her.

Sorry. Won't happen again.

She responded immediately:

No, it won't.

He rested his fingers on the keyboard, driven to write something else. Anything to maintain the connection. Then he dropped his hands into his lap.

He needed to let it go. They were colleagues, and they might be becoming work friends, and for a few short hours they'd been lovers.

God, had they been lovers.

But it had been a one-night-only thing, and it was done, and he should never have let himself stop by her office like that.

Stupid. Really freakin' stupid.

He'd thought it would be easy, slipping back into their old relationship at work, especially given the risks attached to their little fling becoming public.

He'd been wrong. Big-time.

He knew what she looked like naked now. He knew that she made soft, desperate noises when she came, that she arched her back off the bed and dug her nails into his skin. He knew that she liked it when he was a little rough with her, and he knew that he could drive her crazy if he put his mind to it.

He couldn't un-know any of the above. It was burned into his memory, along with the feel of her and the smell of her and the taste of her.

Which meant work was probably going to be a living hell for the next little while.

The thing was, even knowing that, he wouldn't take back Saturday night for anything.

Shaking his head at his own perversity, he dragged the top file from his in-tray. He had an hour to kill before he made his weekly call to Vera, and he planned on using it productively.

LUCY WAS TALKING, but Audrey struggled to take in the words. All she could think about was that moment—that horrible, gut-clenching moment—when Lucy had appeared behind Zach, interrupting the world's most suggestive conversation.

She was almost certain Lucy hadn't heard enough to jump to the right conclusion—her assistant wasn't a good enough actor to cover a realization of that magnitude—but the sheer closeness of the call made Audrey more than a little sweaty.

She'd given herself a little lecture about keeping things on track before she came into work today, too. A little pep talk about how, if she behaved the way she always did, no one would ever clue in that she had spent several hours in Zach's arms on the weekend. Then he'd appeared in her office doorway looking smoking hot in a dark pinstriped suit and deep blue shirt that was almost an exact match for his eyes, and every nerve ending in her body had gone on high alert, like a well-trained dog responding to a high-frequency whistle.

Every good-girl, sensible vow she'd made had gone out the window when he'd smiled and looked at her with that knowing, dirty glint in his eye.

He was irresistible. Utterly charming and sexy and magnetic, and whatever puny power she'd had to ignore him had been well and truly incinerated by their marathon session on Saturday night.

So much for treating him the same as usual—she'd be lucky if her underwear didn't catch fire every time he was in the vicinity.

"…so, if you like, I can double-check that, but I think it should be okay." Lucy waited expectantly, pen hovering above her notepad.

Audrey shook her head, thoroughly ashamed of herself. Lucy had gone to all of the trouble of coming into work early—overtime she would not be paid for—to help her out in a vain attempt to clear some of the backlog they were all struggling to deal with since Whitman had made his cuts. And all Audrey could do was zone out in a sex-induced zombie state.

Pathetic. And more than a little worrying.

"Luce. Sorry. Hold that thought—I'm going to powder my nose." Audrey sprang to her feet before her assistant could respond, circling her desk and heading for the door. Once she was in the privacy of the ladies' room, she locked herself in a cubicle and sat on the closed lid.

You need to get with the program. Now. You cannot afford to drop the ball at the moment.

She took some deep breaths.

She was better than this. Smarter and stronger. Good sex was not going to rob her of her focus and determination. It simply wasn't.

Feeling much calmer, she washed her hands and returned to her office.

"Right. Where were we?"

Resolve got her through the morning and into the afternoon. Then she looked at her calendar and realized she had a department meeting scheduled at three. The first since the layoffs. In other words, mandatory.

Well, damn. The last thing she wanted to do was spend two-plus hours sitting in the meeting room with Zach and a bunch of other people. Not today, of all days. End of the week, sure, she'd be good to go by then. But today she needed some time to get her game face on.

Unfortunately, there was no getting out of the meeting, so at three she buckled on her big-girl panties, grabbed the relevant files and reports, and made her way to the conference room. As luck would have it, Zach was already ensconced at one end, and she chose to sit on the same side of the table at the opposite end so she wouldn't have to look at him for the whole afternoon.

As a strategy it was reasonably effective, except that every time Zach spoke, a little shiver of lust ran down her spine as she remembered him whispering dirty somethings in her ear as he moved inside her.

"You want my cardigan?" Megan asked quietly an hour into the meeting.

"No, thanks, I'm good," Audrey said.

"You're sure? You keep shivering."

"I'm good," Audrey repeated, willing away the heat that was flooding her cheeks.

Clearly, she seriously sucked at flying under the radar. Something it might have been good to know *before* she'd made the decision to turn up on Zach's doorstep for a booty call.

She concentrated fiercely on appearing normal for the rest of the meeting, even if her mind was racing in ten different directions at once.

"Okay, we're done," Gary finally announced. "Don't forget the Makers golf tournament is next Wednesday. We're at Cape Schanck this year, so there will be transport provided if you need it. Jenny's got the list of teams for anyone who is interested."

Audrey barely managed to not roll her eyes as people began to file out of the room. She hated the golf tournament. As far as she was concerned, it was a big old waste of time and money, and it felt like a particularly egregious waste of both when so many of their colleagues had been given their marching orders and they were all still scrambling to pick up the extra load. The powers that be, however, thought that walking around a big swath of grass chasing an itty-bitty white ball was a great way to maintain relationships with their supply base, which meant she had no choice but to put on a pair of stupid shoes and pants and go mix it up on the golf course.

Blurg.

"I hate golf day," Megan said as they left the room.

"Tell me about it. I bet it rains again like last year."

Audrey could still recall the sheer misery of completing eighteen holes in the drizzling rain. Oh, the humanity.

"It's times like these that I remember hardware is a male-dominated industry," she said.

"I know. I would totally make it a spa day if we ruled the roost," Megan said.

"Followed by a shopping spree."

They gave each other a jokey high-five as they parted ways. Audrey diverted by Jenny's desk to find out who she'd be playing with next Wednesday. She was pleasantly surprised to see she'd been teamed with three of her favorite suppliers. At least the day wouldn't be a total bust.

She worked until seven before packing up her desk for the day. As luck would have it, Zach and Gary were about to enter the stairs to the parking garage as she approached. She slowed her pace, hoping they'd get the hint, but Gary stood to one side, gesturing for her to go first.

"After you, madam," he said with his usual friendly smile.

"Thanks."

She carefully didn't look at Zach as she slipped into the stairwell, but she was preternaturally aware of the fact that he followed her down the stairs.

"I was filling Zach in on the golf day," Gary said, his voice echoing in the enclosed space.

"I hope you told him not to try to win."

Gary laughed loudly.

"No, he didn't, as a matter of fact," Zach said.

All the little hairs on the back of her neck stood on end, a physiological response she was powerless to stop. Her body, it seemed, remembered his body all too well.

"The chairman likes to win," she explained as she pushed through the fire door at the base of the stairs. "And he's a sulky loser."

"Just as well that I suck at golf, then," Zach said as he followed her into the garage.

"Looks like you might have some competition for the Lame Duck award this year, Audrey. Better keep an eye out," Gary joked as he moved past them, heading for his car.

"That was two years ago, Gary. Two years," she called after him, shaking her head at his teasing.

"I take it golf is not your sport?" Zach asked.

"My golf skills are marginally better than my ice hockey skills. Which are nonexistent."

He laughed, the sound low and addictive. "I'll be in good company, then."

She gave him a skeptical look. "Right. I bet 'sucking' for you means you have a handicap over ten or something."

"No, I genuinely suck. Small children can drive a ball farther."

"See, you gave yourself away. Only people who play a lot of golf say 'drive.' Rank amateurs like me say 'hit.'"

He laughed again and she found herself racking her brain, trying to come up with something else to say to make him laugh. "I had it drilled into me by a golf pro during the ten most miserable lessons of my life."

"I had twenty and I still hit into the rough every third shot."

"Noted. I'll be sure to hang back when you're teeing off."

"A good idea. Frankly, the way most of us play, this tournament should come with a health and safety warning," she said.

"I bet there's at least one guy who turns up in those knicker golf pants though, right?"

It was her turn to laugh. "Plus fours? Oh yeah. And one of those little hats with a pompom."

He was closer. She wasn't sure who had moved, her or him, but he was definitely closer. His gaze scanned her face before dropping below her chin. She took a shallow breath, painfully aware of her breasts, of how good it had felt when he'd held them and touched them and teased her nipples with his mouth.

She licked her lips. "We could—"

The glare of headlights suddenly swept over them. They both shielded their eyes until the car had straightened up. Gary gave a little toot of his horn and a wave as he drove toward the exit ramp.

It was like a bucket of cold water, straight from Antarctica. Audrey took a step backward, and so did Zach.

"We are really, really bad at business-as-usual," she said, giving him a rueful look.

"I know."

"This has got to stop, Zach. We've got to get it back to normal."

"Okay. It would help if you started wearing a hessian sack to work. And maybe you could shave your head."

She didn't smile. This was serious stuff. They'd been seconds away from doing something stupid before those headlights had swept over them. At work. Everything inside her cringed as she imagined exactly how busted they would have been, framed in bright lights by their boss.

"Maybe we should both do our best to schedule appointments out of the office for the next little while," she said.

"Okay."

"And if situations like this come up, we just walk away."

He frowned. "That's not always possible."

He was right.

"What do you suggest, then?"

"You don't want to know what I'm thinking right now."

Despite everything, a wave of pure lust washed over her at his words.

"That's my cue to leave," she said, taking a step backward.

His mouth tightened for a moment, then he nodded. "Okay."

Without saying another word, they both headed for their respective cars. The nervous-scared-excited feeling didn't fade until he'd driven up the exit ramp, his sleek car disappearing into the night.

Temptation had officially left the building.

Sitting behind the wheel of her car, she let out a long sigh. Despite the slipups they'd had, they'd survived the first day with no out-and-out disasters. That was a good thing. And it had to get easier, right?

Right?

She worried at the problem all the way home but didn't come up with a single viable solution. They were simply going to have to strap themselves to the mast and work through this. They were both mature, rational adults with plenty of incentives to control themselves. Common sense would win out. It had to.

Her phone was ringing as she let herself into her apartment and she rushed to answer it.

"Audrey speaking," she said a little breathlessly.

It was testament to how nuts she was that a little part of her hoped it was Zach calling.

"Audrey. It's me," her sister said.

"Leah." She could hear the surprise in her own voice. She and her sister weren't exactly big on spontaneous phone calls.

"Have you got a minute? Or have I caught you at a bad time?"

"No. I mean, yes. I have a minute. I just got home from work, actually."

"I hear you. My chicken tikka masala is doing laps of the microwave as we speak."

"Frozen meals, Dr. Mathews? I'm surprised," Audrey joked.

"Why? I'm human like everyone else." Leah's tone was defensive. "The last thing I want to do when I get home is slave over a hot stove."

"I was trying to be funny, Leah."

"Oh. Right. Sorry."

"Is everything okay?"

"Yes. I'm tired. Sorry."

"Okay." Audrey sank onto the arm of her couch, trying to think of something else to say. "Um...how's being thirty treating you?"

"Audrey, can we meet?" her sister asked abruptly. "Can we have lunch sometime, or dinner?"

Audrey blinked, blindsided by Leah's request. She couldn't remember the last time they'd caught up, just the two of them. "Sure. We can do that. Lunch or dinner. Whatever suits."

"Good. Great. I can't do anything this weekend, but how about next week sometime? Maybe Friday night?" Leah said.

Audrey could almost see her scrolling through the electronic organizer she always kept with her.

"Sounds good. Where do you want to go?"

"I have no idea. Frozen tikka masala is pretty much my speed these days."

"I prefer the green curry chicken. More rice."

This time her sister laughed. "Noted. I'll try it."

"I'll ask around for recommendations and get back to you."

"Look at us, two sad workaholics with no idea where to get a good meal. Mum and Dad trained us well, huh?" There was a dark note to Leah's tone, something Audrey had never heard before.

"Still getting heat over the immunology decision, are you?"

"Probably until the day I die. Listen, my other phone is ringing so I need to go."

"No worries. I'll see you next Friday, okay?"

Audrey was thoughtful as she went into the bedroom and started undressing. Something was clearly up with her sister. She wondered what it was. Something to do with the disagreement with their mother? It seemed highly probable, given the vibe at Leah's birthday lunch.

She made a face as she walked into the bathroom for a quick shower. If Leah was expecting her big sister to have some pearls of wisdom for dealing with their mother, she was so out of luck it wasn't funny. If anything, it should be the other way around. Leah had always been able to bring a smile to their mother's face; Audrey, on the other hand, had a knack for stimulating her critical gland.

She felt a distinct flutter in her chest when she thought about having dinner with her sister, about what they might talk about and where they might go. It took her a second to understand it was nervousness.

The truth was, she and Megan saw each other more often, talked more intimately and shared more than she and her sister did. There was a very real chance their dinner could be a stilted, awkward nightmare.

You'll find out soon enough.

Indeed. In the meantime, there was dinner to nuke, and some reports to read before she went to bed. Which meant it was time to leave the warm shower.

It wasn't until she dried off that she noticed that the small red mark on her inner thigh had all but faded away. Only two days, and it was almost gone.

Yet if she closed her eyes, she could still feel the weight of Zach pressing her into the bed. She could still feel the delicious tug of his mouth at her breasts, the firm pressure of his hand between her legs.

She sighed and opened her eyes.

If they didn't work together, if they'd met at a different time and place and under completely different circumstances...

But they did, and they hadn't, and sighing and wafting about the house feeling horny and wistful wasn't going to change any of that.

Big-girl panties, Mathews. Remember?

Feeling distinctly flat, she went to make dinner.

CHAPTER THIRTEEN

ZACH WASN'T THE type to indulge in false modesty where his sporting prowess was concerned. He was a good runner, a pretty great basketball player, and he'd competed in the Portsea Pier to Pub open-sea swimming competition four times, each time achieving a spot in the top ten.

Not too shabby, if he did say so himself.

But when it came to golf, any athletic ability he possessed evaporated into thin air. He simply didn't get the appeal or point of the sport, and consequently his technique sucked the big one.

No amount of practice at the local driving range or lessons with pros was going to change that—and yet here he was, less than twenty-four hours before tee-off at the Makers annual golf tournament, whacking away at a bucket full of small white balls, until his shoulders ached and his palms burned against the grip of the club. What he should really be doing was trying to get on top of his ever-increasing workload, but his ego had demanded he at least make an attempt to lift his golf game out of the toilet.

Intellectually, he understood that it wasn't the end of the world that golf was not his thing, but there was no getting away from the fact that if he had a choice, he'd really prefer not to look like a complete dick in front of Audrey tomorrow.

She may have reassured him that she was an average player, but he knew her too well to accept her at her word.

Average for Audrey probably meant that she didn't get a hole-in-one every time.

He swung the club back and addressed the ball, watching as it soared in a long, swinging arc to the left. Why did he keep hooking it? It was beyond him. And, frankly, he was a little over it.

Which probably meant it was time to head home and re-sign himself to a humbling day tomorrow. No doubt his ego would survive, even if Audrey trounced him thoroughly.

It occurred to him that an outside observer might find it telling that even though there were over a hundred and fifty men and women competing tomorrow, Audrey was the one he was fixated on.

In his defense, she was pretty damned hot, and it had been a tough few days. As per their agreement, he and Audrey had done their best to not be in each other's faces at work. He'd scheduled appointments off-site and kept to his side of the department, and she'd done the same. He'd even canceled out of a meeting they were both scheduled to attend, only to find out later that she had, too.

He'd hoped that time and distance and lack of proximity would dull the thud of desire he felt whenever he was near her, but only this morning she'd walked into the kitchen as he was making himself a coffee and he'd taken one look at her and gotten hard. The urge to grab her and push her against the counter had been so strong he'd abandoned his cup and left the space, unable to guarantee his self-control.

It has to get better sometime.

He tossed his keys on his bedside table when he got home, only too aware that the "it'll get better" line was one he'd fed himself after their kiss, too. And look how that had turned out.

Still, it wasn't as though there was an option B. Not one that he was prepared to allow himself to fantasize about, anyway. A long run took some of the edge off, and a twenty-page marketing proposal from one of his suppliers did the rest. By eleven he was tired enough to sleep and he turned off the light.

He started awake hours later, dragged to reality by the phone ringing. He was instantly alert, adrenaline coursing through him as he reached for the handset.

"Black speaking." The glowing numerals on his clock told him it was two in the morning.

"It's me, love," Vera said apologetically. "Sorry to wake you, but I wanted to let you know your mum's in a bit of a bad way. She called me an hour or so ago, and I've done my best, but she's burning up, can hardly walk. Can't keep anything down, either. I'm pretty sure it's not just withdrawal."

He swung his legs over the edge of the bed. "It sounds like she's got an infection. Maybe cotton fever. Or an abscess."

"How would I check for that?"

"You don't. I'll be there in twenty."

"All right. I'll be here." Her creaky voice sounded immeasurably relieved.

He ended the call and reached for the nearest piece of clothing, which happened to be his work pants. Shoving his feet into sneakers, he grabbed the hoodie from the chair beside his bed, scooped up his wallet, phone and keys, and left the house.

His mother's place was lit up like the Fourth of July. He bounded up the front steps and rapped once to announce his arrival, then let himself in.

"It's me," he called.

"In the bedroom, love."

Vera was hovering by the bed when he entered the room, her broad face creased with concern. His mother lay with her eyes closed, a frown furrowing the skin between her brows, an indicator that she was both conscious and in pain.

"Thanks for coming over so fast," Vera said.

He shook his head. She shouldn't be thanking him. She had no obligation to be mixed up in any of this, and he would be grateful until his dying day for her simple generosity and decency.

"It's the other way around and you know it," he said as he knelt beside the bed and pressed his palm to his mother's forehead.

Her eyes opened slowly and she focused on him briefly before closing them again.

"Not feeling so good," she said. Her cheeks were sunken, her face flushed.

"Don't look so good, either," he said lightly.

She was burning up, as Vera had said. He lifted the sheet and did a quick check of her arms and legs. He found the culprit on her inner thigh, near her groin.

"Jesus, Mum," he said, sitting back on his heels, appalled by the ugly red mess she'd made of her femoral vein.

Only truly desperate junkies shot up into their neck or groins. Usually it meant all other means of getting the drug into their bodies had collapsed. That his mother had been playing this particular game of Russian roulette shouldn't have had the power to surprise him, but it did. Judy had seen more than one of her friends lose limbs to infections like this over the years. She knew better.

"Was only for a little while," his mother said without opening her eyes. "Until my arm recovered...."

He was already pulling his phone from his pocket. "You need to be in the hospital."

She didn't say a word and he assumed she was resigned to her fate. She was no stranger to the emergency room.

He gave the details to the dispatcher and then did a quick round of the house to ensure his mother didn't have a stash anywhere. While it was unlikely that the police would turn up with the ambulance, it wasn't unheard of, and the last thing he needed was his mother being arrested for possession again.

He checked all her usual spots—in the freezer, inside the cushions on the couch, taped beneath the basin in the bathroom.

Nothing. Good. Returning to the bedroom, he put together an overnight bag for his mother. He was folding her dressing gown when a knock sounded.

"That'll be them," he said.

"I'll get it," Vera said.

"Thanks, Vera." He made a mental note to do something spectacular for her. Maybe treat her to a holiday in Queensland or something.

When he turned his mother was watching him, tears pooling in her eyes.

"I've messed up again, haven't I?"

He moved to the bed and took her hand. The tendons and bones were visible beneath the skin, and he wondered when she'd last had any fluids.

"They'll look after you at the hospital."

She closed her eyes, sending a single, fat tear rolling down her cheek.

"It's okay, Mum," he said.

What else was there to say?

The paramedics bustled through the door then, stretcher banging against the wall. Zach stepped out of the way as they did an assessment of his mother before plugging her into a saline drip and loading her onto the stretcher for transport to the hospital.

He followed them out into the street, stopping only to lock the house and thank Vera for her endless patience before trailing them to the hospital.

There he watched as his mother was greeted by name by

long-serving doctors and nurses who'd seen her far too many times over the years. He did his best to answer questions and resigned himself to a long wait while they rounded up a vascular specialist. It was five in the morning by the time his mother had been seen and a course of heavy-duty IV antibiotics prescribed by a grim-faced woman in her late forties.

Afterward, Dr. Fawkner called him out of the cubicle to talk.

"You understand that if this infection had gone another day or two, there's a real risk your mother could have lost her leg, possibly her life?"

"She's going to be okay, then?" Strange that he had enough hope left in him to be relieved.

"It's going to be a close run thing, and one of our surgeons is going to have to excise the necrotizing skin around the abscess, but my best bet is that she's out of the woods. This time."

Meaning his mother would have yet another scar to add to her collection.

He asked some more questions and listened carefully to her answers. Afterward, he returned to his mother's bedside. She was dozing, her face slack. Even though he needed to get home and get some sleep, he resumed his seat beside the bed. He didn't have it in him to abandon her while she was sleeping, even though he knew she was in good hands now.

So he sat, and he waited.

EVEN THOUGH THE company had hired a bus to transport everyone to the golf course en masse, Audrey chose to drive there the next morning. That way she could make her escape as soon as possible.

Seated in her car in the dusty gravel parking lot, she tucked her hair behind her ears and slipped on her Makers cap, inspecting the result in the rearview mirror. She'd already smoothed SPF 30 sunscreen onto her face and arms, all the better to withstand a day beneath the warm spring sun.

"Okay. Let's do this," she told herself before getting out of the car and hefting her clubs out of the trunk. She'd bought them secondhand after she'd been promoted to buyer, back when she'd kidded herself that she might actually develop an affection for the game. She'd given up that particular delusion after her first tournament, but held on to the clubs anyway. It didn't hurt to look the part, after all, even if her heart was decidedly not in it.

The buggy wheels bounced over the gravel as she approached the clubhouse, shaking her head a little when she saw the crowd of loudly dressed men milling beneath the broad veranda. Bright pink and yellow and lime-green polo shirts were the order of the day, sartorial statements that had been matched in some instances with equally bright plaid trousers.

She wondered what it was about golf that encouraged middle-aged straight men to dress like children's entertainers. Truly bizarre.

She spotted a couple of suppliers she knew and headed over to say hello. That was what the day was all about, after all—making them feel special, so that next time she asked them to bend over on pricing and cooperative advertising dollars, they'd touch their toes with a smile instead of a frown.

She chatted with suppliers for nearly forty minutes, all the while a part of her was keeping an eye out for Zach. She didn't even try to quell the urge these days. What was the point? Despite the time that had passed since they'd been naked in his bed, her awareness of him hadn't simmered down one iota. Telling herself to get over him was clearly a futile gesture.

She wasn't sure where that left her, but at least she wasn't wasting a whole lot of energy pretending she wasn't feeling the way she was feeling.

One of the organizers began calling for groups to tee off around about the same time that Audrey started to worry about Zach's failure to appear.

He was never late. Like her, he was a stickler for punctuality. Which meant one of two things: he'd either gotten lost, or something had happened.

A dart of fear tightened her chest and she rolled her eyes. She was being a drama queen. Zach was not lying in a ditch, bleeding to death after a car accident. The odds of that were so high as to be absurd. He was simply held up. Or something.

Chewing on her lower lip, she abandoned her buggy and went to find Gary's assistant, Jenny. Armed with a clipboard, the other woman was looking frazzled as she tried to organize groups and send them off onto the course.

"Jen, have you seen Zach at all? I need to check if he heard back from Black & Decker about the new rechargeable range," Audrey said.

She felt stupid the moment she added the explanation to her request. Jen wouldn't care why she wanted to talk to Zach; the woman was clearly more than a little overwhelmed. Paranoia was turning Audrey into an idiot.

"Haven't seen him. But if you find him, tell him to come see me. There's been a change to his team."

"Sure. Will do."

Frowning, Audrey moved off to one side of the crowd and pulled her phone from her back pocket. She dialed Zach's number and swore in annoyance when it immediately went to voice mail. He was on another call or his phone was dead. Either way, he was not contactable.

She glanced over her shoulder. Jenny was talking to Gary, pointing to her clipboard, her face a picture of frustration.

Any minute now she was going to run out of teams to send out onto the course and everyone was going to notice that Zach wasn't here. If it was last year's tournament, Audrey was almost certain she wouldn't have broken a sweat over it. But this year... Things were so tense at work. Everyone was doing their damnedest not to put a foot wrong. If Zach didn't turn up for some reason, it wasn't going to look good.

She tried his number again, and again got his voice mail. She walked to the head of the driveway and squinted up the highway. Was that a black car she could see on the horizon? She waited until it drew closer, revealing itself to be a mini-bus full of tourists.

She tried his phone again and swore softly when she got his voice mail for the third time.

"Call me when you get this, Zach. You're about to miss your tee-off time. If you need directions or...anything, just call, okay?"

She made her way back to the clubhouse. The crowd had thinned considerably and Jenny waved her over when she spotted her.

"There you are! I was beginning to think you'd disappeared. You and your guys are up next, okay?"

"Okay, thanks."

Jenny started to turn away, but Audrey caught her arm.

"Also, I just spoke to Zach. He had a flat tire, but he said he'd be here as soon as he could."

"Oh, thanks. I might send his team out without him, then, and he can catch up with them."

"Sounds like a plan." Audrey smiled brightly before moving away.

Good one, idiot girl. What happens when Zach turns up and doesn't know he's had a flat tire? Or what if he doesn't turn up at all?

She would look like a big fat liar. Or something.

Well. So be it.

She cast another look toward the freeway.

Come on, Zach. Move your ass.

Unsurprisingly, his car didn't miraculously appear. She pulled her phone out and left one last message on his voice mail, telling him the excuse she'd concocted on his behalf. By then Jenny was hollering for her to go tee off with her team and she grabbed her buggy and headed for the first hole.

Zach was on his own. Wherever that may be.

More than anything, she really hoped he was okay.

ZACH EASED OFF on the accelerator as he rounded the final bend and saw the turnoff for the golf course. The car bucked as he hit the gravel driveway, and he throttled back some more to turn into the crowded parking lot. He swore when he saw there was only a handful of staff hanging around the clubhouse.

He'd missed tee-off. Awesome.

He'd been pretty certain he would, given how late it had been by the time he dropped by his place to change and grab his clubs after leaving the hospital, but there'd still been a seed of hope in his heart.

He found a spot and grabbed his clubs and buggy, trying to decide what was best to do. Strike out on his own in an attempt to find his group? Chase after the closest team and latch onto them?

He was still tossing up options when someone called out to him and he realized that one of the women he'd mistaken for clubhouse staff was actually Jenny, Gary's assistant.

"You got here!" she said as she strode toward him, a relieved smile on her face.

"Yeah. Sorry I didn't call, my phone was dead and the charger chose this morning to die." He shrugged ruefully, not even attempting to hide how frustrated he was. "Sorry if I put a spanner in the works."

"No worries. Audrey told us about your flat tire, you poor thing. At least you know how to fix it on your own—I'm so hopeless I'd have to wait hours for the car club to come find me," Jenny said, laughing self-deprecatingly.

He narrowed his eyes. Flat tire? What flat tire? Then he understood what Audrey had done for him and gratitude warmed his chest.

"Yeah. I managed to get a message through to her before my phone died completely."

Jenny was busy consulting her clipboard. "Your team left about half an hour ago. The pros tell me we should allow about twenty minutes per hole, so if you cut across there—" she pointed across the fairway "—and head through that stand of trees you should be able to catch them at the second green. And if you want to leave your phone with me, I can stick it on my charger, since I brought it with me."

"Great. Thanks, Jen. And sorry again for the hassle," he said as he handed over his phone.

"All good, don't worry."

Zach tugged his cap lower on his brow as he set off across the grass. Even though he was so tired he could barely see straight thanks to his all-night vigil by his mother's bedside, he couldn't keep the grin from his face as he made his way to the second green.

Audrey had covered for him. She'd been worried, and she'd made up an excuse for him and put her own credibility at risk by offering it up to Jenny, even though she'd had no guarantee that he wouldn't land her in it by inadvertently blowing her story or even by not turning up full stop.

She'd put herself on the line for him.

It was a little ridiculous how happy the realization made him. She liked him, so much so that she'd tried to prevent him from getting into trouble. The thought made him grin like an idiot.

He hit the second fairway and glanced around to get his bearings. Tee off to his right, green to his left.

As Jenny had predicted, the suppliers he'd been assigned to host for the day were taking their turns to putt. One of them spotted him, alerting the others, and they gave him a round of applause as he climbed the slope to the tightly clipped green.

"Nice of you to join us, Mr. Black," one of them called.

"Thought I'd better give you guys a head start. Don't want to make you feel too bad when I wipe the floor with you," he said.

Pure bravado, given his golfing skills, but a bit of macho bull was the order of the day at these kinds of events. He figured he could be forgiven for stretching the truth a little.

The rest of the day went smoothly enough. He managed to avoid complete humiliation by finishing in the middle of the field for his team of five players, not too bad a showing, and the sunshine and fresh air went a long way toward blowing away the smell of the hospital and keeping him awake and alert.

It helped that every now and then he caught sight of a trim, neatly dressed figure playing farther along the course. Even from a distance, he knew it was Audrey. There was something about the way she walked, the way she held herself, that he would have recognized in a crowd of millions.

He watched her from afar and wondered what had been going through her mind when she'd lied for him, and found himself grinning like a fool all over again.

He shouldn't be. He knew he should be worried that after nearly two weeks, he wasn't even close to moving on from their one night together. He should be busy writing off her act of charity as a gesture of comradeship from one colleague to another, instead of reading all sorts of things into it.

He didn't care. Maybe that was because he was so tired, or maybe it was because he'd spent the night beside his sick mother, and turning his back on something—on someone— who felt as good and life-affirming and *right* as Audrey did seemed nuts.

He didn't want to stop at one night. He didn't want to stop, period. He wanted to see her again. Screw the consequences. He'd dotted his *I*'s and crossed his *T*'s and paid his dues. He figured he deserved something that was just for him. Something good. Something that made him happy.

They could sort out the work stuff later. Somehow. They were both intelligent, articulate adults. There had to be some way that they could negotiate a relationship without it impacting on their careers.

Relationship. Getting a little ahead of yourself, aren't you?

He was. Big time. He knew there was no guarantee that Audrey would be prepared to risk the inevitable flak that might come their way if they embarked on something longterm. God knows, it wasn't as though the situation at work had gotten any less tense or fraught. There was no guarantee she wanted anything more from him at all, apart from one night of scorchin', smokin' sex.

So be it, but he had to try. He'd regret it for the rest of his life if he let her slip through his fingers without a fight. He knew it in his bones.

As for the myriad complications that would arise the moment they decided their one night was the beginning of something more…well, they could cross those bridges when they came to them.

CHAPTER FOURTEEN

AUDREY WAS HOT and tired by the time her team trudged the final few meters to the clubhouse. The men separated to find the bar and make phone calls, and she found a bench beneath a shade tree and drank a whole bottle of cold, cold water in one fell swoop.

Better. Much better.

Resting her elbows on the backrest of the bench, she watched the other teams straggle in. There was lots of ragging and catcalling as people compared scores, and she found herself smiling more than once at some of the slurs and jokes.

It hadn't been too awful a day. She'd surprised herself by finishing first in her team, a minor miracle that said more about how bad her teammates were than her own skill. Still, not too shabby. And best of all, the ordeal was almost over for another year.

Her gaze caught on a tall, broad-shouldered figure among a group of men returning to the clubhouse.

Zach.

Her stomach did the familiar nervous-excited dance that it always did when he was around.

She'd spotted him from a distance midmorning and been relieved—he'd arrived in one piece, so she could put the worst-case scenarios chattering away in the back of her head to rest once and for all.

Whether he'd maintained her impulsively offered cover story was something she was yet to discover. Jenny hadn't rushed over with a "please explain" yet so that was a good sign. She hoped.

Glad of the privacy offered by her sunglasses and the bill of her cap, she watched Zach as he approached the clubhouse.

He was dressed in slim-cut chinos and a navy polo shirt, a navy Makers baseball cap casting a shadow over his sunglasses, and he looked far hotter than any man had a right to in any of the above. But he always looked hot, no matter what he was wearing. Especially when he was wearing nothing.

We've had the "not helpful" chat before, right?

She batted away her inner nag. There was no harm in enjoying one of nature's simple pleasures. Just because she was looking didn't necessarily mean that she would be touching. She understood that Zach was out of bounds.

She knew the exact moment he spotted her—his head came up, and she felt his gaze on her, as warm and real as a caress. Any ease she'd felt fled for the hills as he abandoned his buggy and made a beeline for her. She glanced around, hoping no one else had noticed the very intent way he was homing in on her, all the while trying to quell the excited rush of awareness rocketing through her.

He was coming over to talk to her. Nothing more. She needed to calm the hell down.

"Hey," she said when he stopped in front of her.

His shadow fell across her as he looked at her. "I owe you," he said bluntly.

She shook her head. "No, you don't. You'd do the same for me."

He sat beside her on the bench. It wasn't the longest bench in the world, and the two of them were a cozy fit. She didn't move, though. This was the closest she'd been to him in days, and, God help her, she wanted the contact.

There would be plenty of time for her to flagellate herself for her weakness later.

He copied her posture, propping his elbows on the backrest, his gaze focused on the course, not on her. For a moment they were both silent as they pretended to be people-watching.

"I *would* do the same for you. In a pinch." His voice was gravelly and very low.

"I know."

"What do you think that means?"

"All this self-sacrificing behavior, you mean?"

"Yeah, that."

"That we're friends?"

He was silent for a long beat. "I don't feel very friendly toward you."

She turned her head to look at him. "Don't you?"

"Not at all. I've been thinking about it, and I realized that if you and I didn't work together, there's no way I would have let you go the other night."

It was such a frank, raw admission, for a moment she couldn't think, let alone speak.

"I believe they've opened the bar in the clubhouse if you're feeling a powerful urge for an out right about now," Zach said.

She didn't move.

She cleared her throat. "If you want another night—"

"I want more than a night. I want to take you somewhere nice for dinner. I want to go to the movies with you and get it on in the back row. I want to do the Saturday morning crossword puzzle with you in bed."

Her heart was pounding. She was so excited and uncertain about what she was hearing, she felt a little sick.

Zach wanted to see her. To date her. To have a *relationship* with her. Or to try to have one, anyway.

He stood. She opened her mouth to protest, but he shook his head.

"I'm not going to push you. Think about it. I know it's not exactly an easy option. Take as long as you like. You know where to find me."

Before she could speak he was gone, striding toward the nearest group of men.

She felt shell-shocked. As though someone had stolen her center of gravity. Deep inside, she'd hoped that Zach would suggest they spend the night together again. She hadn't for a moment considered that he might want more. It certainly hadn't occurred to *her* to want more.

She wasn't sure why that was. Perhaps because it had been a while since she'd had a man in her life, and it simply wasn't the first place her mind went to.

Or maybe it was because she was a little afraid of wanting too much where Zach was concerned. It would be so easy— too easy—to fall in love with him. He was amazing in bed, he stimulated her, he challenged her, he made her laugh. When she was with him she felt more alive, as though she was her best self. Sharper. Smarter. More attractive. Sexier.

Okay. So what? So what if you start really seeing Zach and you fall in love with him? Would that be the end of the world?

It might be. If he didn't fall in love with her in return, it would be damned awkward. And sad and hurtful and all the other things that came with a broken heart.

But that was the same risk everyone took when they started seeing someone, wasn't it? The only difference in their case was that a love affair gone wrong had the potential to make work hell on earth in addition to casting a blight over their private lives.

And that was without considering how their burgeoning relationship might be viewed by the powers that be. While there was no official nonfraternization rule within the company, Makers was a conservative organization. She knew eyebrows would be raised, questions asked. After all, how could they possibly have fallen for each other when they were supposed to spend every living, breathing moment working for the company's good? Especially now, when it was supposed to be all hands on deck to lift the load created by Whitman's *rationalizing*.

Granted, embarking on a proper relationship with someone was a different proposition from a one-night hookup, but she wasn't going to kid herself—she and Zach going out together would not be viewed favorably. It simply wouldn't.

She twisted the cap on her water bottle back and forth, torn and tempted in equal measures.

If they didn't work together, she wouldn't hesitate. She liked Zach more than she could remember liking a man for a long time. They were supremely sexually compatible. It was a no-brainer that she'd want to see where it might go.

But she'd worked so damned hard to get where she was. She'd started in the warehouse at Makers when she was nineteen years old. She'd studied at night to finish high school, and she'd put her hand up for every training program the company offered. By slow, painful degrees, she'd edged her way from the warehouse and into the main building, starting out in clerical support roles and ending up where she was now. Fourteen years of perseverance, sucking it up, unpaid overtime, working while she was sick...

Not for a second did she doubt that she'd earned her current role, but there was a tiny part of her that would always feel insecure about her humble beginnings. Unlike Zach, she didn't have qualifications up the you-who to help her score another job if things went south with Makers. She had experience, and her reputation within the business—neither of which was particularly portable, she suspected. Certainly she wouldn't want to pit it against someone like Zach in the job marketplace.

Her gaze followed Zach as he moved from one group of golfers to another. There were taller men, men with broader shoulders, men who earned more, men who had more status—but he was the man who drew her eye. He was the man who had always drawn something in her, hence her months-long battle to pretend otherwise.

Was she really prepared to turn her back on what had happened between them the other night for the sake of her career?

Her own words came to her then, like the ghost of Christmas past: *I'm the only person in the world I can rely on, and if I don't make things happen, they don't happen. I'm not ashamed of being ambitious.*

She wasn't. But ambition didn't make her laugh. Ambition didn't warm her bed or her heart. Ambition didn't infuriate her and challenge her and make her toss and turn at night.

Work-life balance wasn't a philosophy she'd ever aspired to—she'd been too busy proving to herself and her parents and the world that she wasn't a screwup, that she was worth something. But maybe it was time to reassess her priorities. Maybe it was time to allow herself some comfort.

Maybe it was time to allow herself some happiness.

"Audrey. You gotta come help me out here. These guys don't believe I got a birdie on the fourth."

It was Terry, one of her team members. She pasted on a smile and pushed herself to her feet and pushed her thoughts into the background. This was a workday. Never let that be forgotten.

"How many witnesses do you want? I'll swear on a stack of Bibles," she said as she joined the men.

Over the next few hours she smiled and talked and laughed as dinner was served and joke awards presented, but she never stopped thinking about Zach's question. How could she, when he'd offered her something she secretly wanted very badly?

The evening wound down after dessert. She said her good-byes and good-naturedly accepted some final ribbing about the shot she'd hooked into the rough on the ninth and gathered up her jacket and keys. The lot was half-empty when she walked to her car. The dark was punctuated by the occasional laugh and the sound of engines starting. She got into her hatchback and checked her phone for messages, aware that she was stalling and not really sure why. Then she saw Zach heading toward his car and understood that she'd been waiting for him.

She watched him, as she had all night, savoring the length of his stride, the cowboy certainty of his gait. He walked like a man who knew where he was going and what he wanted when he got there.

He slipped his cap off, running his hand roughly through his hair. His profile was illuminated as he opened the driver's door and tossed his cap inside.

He didn't get in immediately, instead rubbing a hand up the back of his neck as though it was stiff. Then he bowed his head, his whole body very still for a handful of heartbeats.

Something sharp pierced her chest as she watched him. He looked…lonely. Isolated. And infinitely weary and worn.

She pressed her fingertips to her chest, trying to ease the sudden pain there.

After a second he seemed to shake himself, climbing into his car. The engine fired to life, the brake lights flashing red.

She reached for her phone, punching in a text message before she could check herself. After all her agonizing and weighing and considering, it came down to this: she cared about his happiness. A small but profound revelation, and it had taken witnessing that small, private moment for her to get it.

She didn't want him to be lonely. She knew only too well what that felt like.

She hit Send. His reverse lights were on. He was about to leave. Then his brake lights came on. The driver's door opened and Zach exited the car. He scanned the parking lot until he found her hatchback. She could feel the heat of his gaze across the feet that separated them. Smiling, feeling sexy and dizzy and more than a little scared, she sent him a second text.

This time it was her address.

She didn't wait to see if he followed her onto the freeway. She knew he would.

ZACH WATCHED AS Audrey's car disappeared around the corner of the parking lot. He glanced down at the two messages still displayed on his phone screen.

Yes.

Unit 6, 17 White Crescent, Ringwood.

If he was a fist-pump kind of guy, now would be the time for one, but he wasn't so he settled for grinning like a madman as he got back into his car. He entered Audrey's address into his GPS and made his way out onto the country-dark streets of Cape Schanck. It took him an hour and a half to drive to Ringwood, and he used some of the time to call the hospital and check on his mother.

He spoke to the nurses first, learning she was scheduled for surgery first thing tomorrow to remove the dead tissue around the site of the abscess. His mother was disoriented and defensive when he was put through to her, a sure sign she was experiencing the hell of withdrawal. No doubt the hospital would do what it could to alleviate her symptoms, but they weren't in the business of keeping junkies happy.

He offered what comfort he could, given her state, then spent the drive focusing on Audrey, on what he would do with and to her when he reached her place.

He deserved some happiness. And even if he didn't, he was going to make a grab for it, anyway.

Her apartment was in a small block of six on a leafy, well-kept street. He parked out front and made his way to the security entrance. She answered the moment he hit the buzzer.

"It's on the second floor," she said, her voice sounding slightly breathless through the speaker.

She had the door open when he arrived, light spilling into the corridor. She smiled almost shyly. "It's small but perfectly formed," she said, leading him into an airy living room.

If he had to guess, he'd say the complex had been built in the fifties. The ceilings were high and unembellished, the windows large. He could see a small kitchen through a doorway to his left. Another doorway led off to the right toward her bedroom, he guessed. Both her couch and armchair were midcentury spare, and a couple of vintage travel posters in bright colors graced the walls.

"Do you want something to drink?" she asked.

He didn't say a word. She gave a nervous laugh.

"Okay, stupid question. Would you like a shower, then? I know I've been dreaming of one since the eleventh hole."

He reached out and hooked a hand behind her neck, drawing her close. He kissed the nervous smile off her lips, inhaling the scent of her skin.

"That sounds good," he said when he broke the kiss. He didn't want to let her go, but a shower was a necessity. Plus it meant they'd both be naked in a small space, which could only be a good thing.

"It's through here…"

He followed her into her bedroom, glancing at the queen-size bed with its fluffy white duvet. The bathroom had been renovated in the past ten years, all clean, modern lines, and he watched as Audrey collected two towels from a storage tower to the left of the vanity.

"Here," she said, passing him one.

He set it on the vanity and pulled her close, letting his hands slide down her back as he reacquainted himself with her mouth. He shaped her hips with his hands, then cupped her backside and pressed her against him so she could feel what she did to him.

She made an approving sound, and the next thing he knew she was palming him through the cotton of his chinos, stroking along the length of him. They tortured each other for a few more minutes, pushing polo shirts out of the way and tasting each other's salty skin before finally stripping each other naked.

He pushed her hair out of the way as she leaned in to turn on the shower, tonguing the nape of her neck and smiling as she shivered in response. Any minute now, he was going to be inside her again and she was going to be making those soft, desperate noises that had been haunting his dreams.

She drew him into the shower and they kissed beneath the streaming water, slicking their hands with soap and dividing their time between washing each other down and revisiting their favorite body parts. When he was so hard it hurt and she was breathless with need, he leaned out of the shower to collect a condom from his pants pocket and sheathed himself.

She closed her eyes as he lifted her, pressing her against the tiled wall as he pushed inside her.

"That feels so good," she breathed, her hands gripping his shoulders tightly.

"No kidding."

She laughed and he kissed her, swallowing her happiness

as he started stroking inside her. The water and the tight heat of her body and the feel of her breasts flattened against his chest pushed him hard, but he held off until she gave a small, strangled cry and he felt her pulse around him. Only then did he allow himself to come, his face pressed into the sweet, soft skin of her neck.

She stumbled against him as he released her and he caught her arm. "Sorry." She blinked dazedly.

He loved that he could make her look that way. Loved how swollen her mouth was, how pink her nipples.

He turned off the shower, then dried her with slow, leisurely passes of the towel. She smiled as he bent to attend to the soft skin behind her knees, one hand resting on his shoulder as he lifted her foot.

"You're establishing a dangerous precedent here," she said, her voice low and lazy and tired.

"Am I?"

He had others he wanted to establish, too, and once he'd dried her feet he pressed a kiss to her belly and dipped his tongue into her navel.

"Zach," she moaned as he urged her to widen her stance and started kissing her inner thighs.

He teased her with his mouth and tongue until her legs were trembling with the effort of remaining upright, then he carried her into the bedroom and laid her on the bed and really drove her crazy.

He licked and teased and tasted until she trembled, her hips lifting involuntarily. Then he slid a finger inside her and searched for that one elusive spot....

She gasped when he found it, her back arching, her hands clutching at his head as she came and came and came. He rode out her pleasure, then soothed her down to earth with gentle kisses and caresses.

"If you get sick of the corporate world, that's a career for you," she said when he lifted his head.

He grinned. He loved how bold she was sometimes. How shameless.

"I'd hate to ruin the purity of my art by putting a dollar value on it." He kissed his way up her body.

"How very noble of you."

She collected a condom from the bedside table, then pushed him until he straddled her hips. Her gaze avid, she took him in her hands, stroking him firmly, knowingly. He watched through half-slitted eyes as she tore open the condom and eased it onto him, inch by inch.

He was harder than titanium by the time she'd finished, pushed to the limits of his control. Pulling her hands away, he lowered his head and drew one of her already-hard nipples into his mouth. He bit her gently but firmly, just enough to let her know he knew she'd been torturing him on purpose. She responded by lifting her hips and widening her legs as she guided him to her entrance.

One flex of his hips and he was inside her, part of her, sheathed in slick heat. She started to move at the same time he did, their bodies working as one.

"I love how wet you are. How good you feel," he whispered in her ear, because he knew she liked it.

She made a sound in the back of her throat, her fingers clenching as she gripped his ass.

"I love how tight you are, how it feels to be inside you," he told her, upping the tempo.

She started to pant, her breath warm against his neck. He slid a hand between their bodies to where she was wet and swollen.

"Is that what you want?" he asked, sliding his thumb over her.

She gasped, losing her rhythm as she lifted her hips, silently begging for more.

"Is that what you need?" he asked, pushing himself deep inside as he stroked her.

"Yes. Please. Please, Zach…"

She came then, pulsing around him, her body as taut as a bowstring as pleasure took her. The sight of her tightly shut eyes and bared teeth pushed him into his own climax and he held her close as he nudged even deeper inside her.

They were both limp, their breathing heavy as they lay side by side on the bed. After a while, he felt her hand on his forearm. She slid her hand down until it found his, her fingers weaving with his.

"Let's not wait two weeks again, huh?" she said.

He laughed quietly, feeling tired and empty and utterly at peace. "Deal."

He had enough sense to take care of the condom before he drifted into sleep. The last conscious thought he had was both simple and profound: *she said yes.*

CHAPTER FIFTEEN

SHE WOKE TO the unfamiliar sensation of another person in her bed. Her eyes popped open, then she smiled as she remembered.

Zach.

The shower.

After the shower.

After, after the shower.

She stretched out a hand and laid it on his warm, hard body and simply lay there for a moment, listening to his breathing and feeling his chest rise and fall beneath her hand.

He was in her bed, in her apartment. This was real. They'd decided to do this. To try to build on sexual chemistry and lots in common and see where they might end up.

She gazed at the dimly lit ceiling, doing a quick internal audit, and decided giving him her address, saying yes to him, to this, was one of her better decisions.

She rolled closer to him, pressing her lips against his shoulder, inhaling the scent of him—the lingering remains of yesterday's aftershave, warm skin and the faintest tang of clean sweat. It was so delicious she wanted to lick him, to somehow absorb the essence of him into her own body. She settled for pressing a row of kisses along his shoulder until she came to his collarbone.

She lifted her head to consider his profile, only to be drawn to the glowing neon numerals on her clock.

Three in the morning. They both had work tomorrow—today. She needed to send him home.

"Zach," she said softly, not wanting to startle him. "It's three o'clock."

He didn't stir, and she kissed his shoulder and tried again. "Zach."

When he still didn't respond, she turned on the bedside light. He didn't so much as flinch.

She frowned, noting for the first time the weary lines around his mouth and eyes. He hadn't offered an explanation for his lateness this morning, but he'd clearly had a rough night last night.

She turned the light off. She didn't have the heart to force him awake and out into the cold morning when he clearly needed to sleep. She pulled the covers high up over his shoulders and closed her eyes.

The room was lighter the next time she woke, but since her alarm hadn't yet sounded she figured it must be before six. She checked and saw that it was five.

Zach was still out of it, his breathing slow and regular. She hated to wake him, but he really did need to go now or he'd be late for work.

Still, there was waking someone, then there was *waking someone*.

Feeling more than a little saucy, she slipped beneath the covers. Zach's body was warm and firm, and she ran her hands over his belly and thighs before homing in on her true goal. He was already semihard—morning glory was a wonderful thing—and she settled herself comfortably before stroking him once, twice with her hand, then taking him into her mouth.

She felt the surge of blood as his body responded to her ministrations, and she allowed herself a small, private, wicked smile before she applied herself to her self-appointed task.

Last night he'd made her climb the walls, and it seemed only fair to return the favor.

It didn't take long before he stirred to life, his legs moving restlessly against the sheets. A warm hand landed on her shoulder. She pictured him blinking to wakefulness, pulled out of sleep by pleasure.

"Audrey," he murmured, the hand on her shoulder trying to pull her back up the bed.

She took him deeper into her mouth and teased him with her tongue until his grip relaxed and he gave himself up to her.

She stroked him with her hand and used her lips and tongue. His body grew tense beneath her, his hips jerking as he neared his peak. The hand on her shoulder tightened… and then released as he let himself go.

She waited until he finished before pushing back the covers and sitting up with a Cheshire cat smile.

"Good morning."

"Now who's setting a dangerous precedent?" His face was flushed, his eyes heavy-lidded with sated desire.

"You're not objecting, are you?" Because she knew it would drive him wild, she licked her lips.

"Last thing on my mind."

He pulled her up the bed again and this time she went, laying her body over his, pressing a kiss to his bristly jaw.

"I didn't want to wake you, but it's five and you'll need to go home to grab some clothes."

"I will."

He didn't seem in any hurry, though, smoothing his hands over her back and pressing kisses to her cheekbone, the bridge of her nose, her jaw.

It was seductive and sexy, and she was warm and alive to

the possibilities inherent in having a hot man beneath her—but she was also aware of the time, ticking inexorably on.

She was about to draw his attention to that fact when he broke their kiss and sighed. "Okay. I should start moving."

He suited words to actions, rolling to the edge of the bed and pushing himself to his feet. She leaned across to get the light and watched as he gathered his clothes together.

It was like watching Michelangelo's *David* come to life, his body lean and powerful in equal measure. She admired the play of light over the long muscles of his thighs, the mysterious shadowy indentations on the sides of his glutes.

"What's your day looking like?" he asked as he pulled his polo shirt over his head.

"I've got a meeting in the afternoon, but otherwise I'll be in the office."

Thinking about Makers, about the day ahead, burst the bubble of contentment rising inside her. She sat and tugged the duvet up to cover her breasts.

"We should probably talk about work," she said. "Don't you think?"

He glanced at her, then sat on the bed to pull on his socks. "You think we need ground rules?"

"No. But maybe we should make sure we're on the same page."

He twisted to face her. "Okay. You show me your page and I'll show you mine."

"All right. I think we should keep work work and this private."

"Okay."

"You don't agree?"

"I think it's the smart thing to do. Especially with things the way they are at the moment."

"That's what I thought." She felt uncomfortable, though.

As though they'd both agreed to something neither of them really wanted.

It wasn't exactly an auspicious way to start a relationship—covertly, carefully, warily. But there was no getting around the fact that people would talk if they were open about what was going on between them. Makers was a hotbed of gossip and rumor at the best of times. Aside from the added pressure created by Whitman's staff cuts, there were unofficial factions—warehouse versus admin, marketing versus finance—and plenty of political game-playing. So far in her career, she had made a point of never drawing attention to the fact that she was a woman in a male-dominated industry—not by being one of the boys, but by doing her job very, very well. The moment it became known she was seeing Zach, people would look at her differently. It was a given.

And if things didn't work out between her and Zach... Well, a whole new can of worms would be breached. And she would have compromised her professional life at what could only be described as a precarious time for nothing.

"If we didn't work together..." she said, because she didn't want him to think that her preference for privacy was a vote of no confidence in them. In the potential them, anyway. She was simply being practical. Conservative.

"It's okay." He stood and rounded the bed, leaning down to kiss her. "There's a reason we didn't jump each other's bones six months ago. Apart from the fact that you thought I was a trust-funded asshat. We both know work's not exactly a barrel of giggles at the moment."

She brushed the hair away from his eyes, something she'd been dying to do since the day she met him.

"You didn't want to jump my bones when you first met me. You were too busy deciding if I was a threat or not."

"Want to bet?" He cocked an eyebrow, then kissed her

one last time before straightening. "I'd better get going. Can we do dinner tonight?"

Probably she should pretend to have a very busy schedule, but who was she kidding?

"Yes, please."

"I need to take care of something after work, so it might not be till eight, if that's okay?"

"Eight is great. Where do you want to go?"

"Where is your favorite place?"

She laughed. "The frozen food section of the supermarket?"

He smiled. "Leave it to me. I'll come up with something."

She sank back onto the pillow once he'd left the room, holding her breath until she heard the front door click shut behind him. Then she grabbed his pillow and pressed it over her face and indulged herself with a jubilant teenage squeal into its muffling feathers, complete with horizontal dancing in the bed.

She had a boyfriend. Not just any boyfriend, either. She had Zach Black in her bed, and he wanted to take her out for dinner tonight, and afterward they would no doubt come back here or go to his place and he would do insanely good, needful, delicious things to her body....

It might be complicated. It might even be genuinely risky, career-wise. But she was still glad it was happening. Then and there she made a promise to herself: no matter what happened, she wouldn't forget this moment. She would hang on to the happiness and pleasure he'd brought her, and she would enjoy the ride for as long as she could. For both their sakes.

ZACH SPENT A good half hour of his lunch break trying to decide where to take Audrey for dinner. He finally settled on a modern Chinese place in Camberwell he'd always loved and made a booking for eight-thirty.

He liked thinking about what might please her. He liked thinking about her, full stop. Her soft, pale skin. Her luscious mouth. The golden warmth of her eyes. The sound of her laughter.

She'd been troubled this morning when they talked about work. He understood her concerns and shared them to a degree, but for the first time in his life he found himself wanting to argue against work being the number one priority. He'd put his career first for so many years, he didn't want to do that with Audrey. And not only because he knew it would be a sure way to kill what was happening between them before it was even off the ground. He wanted things to work between them for him, too. Because when he was with her, the world felt right.

Normally, his head was full of a million things at once. Projections for various product lines, proposals he needed to assess, displays he needed to finesse with suppliers. His mother, what needed to happen with the house next, what was happening in the broader economy.

But when he was with Audrey, the world stopped. He breathed. He listened. He watched. He enjoyed. He laughed. He savored. She made him want to relish each moment, not rush on to the next thing, and the next. She made him want to live his life, rather than view each day as a challenge to be overcome or endured.

It was a foreign concept to him, but one he was surprised he was only too ready to embrace. He'd been driving himself hard, driving himself ragged, for so many years. Surely he deserved to stop and smell the roses? Surely he could allow himself a few moments of respite?

Once he'd settled the matter of the restaurant, he rang the hospital. He'd already called that morning to see how his mother had coped overnight, and now he was told that she was still in recovery after her surgery but would be more than likely up to a quick visit that evening. Accordingly, he left work at six and went straight to the hospital, only stopping to buy some craft magazines from the gift shop.

Once, a long time ago, his mother had enjoyed making things with her hands. He had no idea if that remained true today, but he couldn't think of anything else to take her.

She was drowsy but pleased to see him and he tried not to show how worried he was by her pallid complexion. Maybe it was the brutal lighting in the hospital, or perhaps he was seeing her clearly for the first time in a long time, but she looked old and sick and incredibly frail. He was overcome by a painful rush of emotion as he tried to make conversation with her. He'd spent years shepherding her away from danger, had wearied of his guardianship long ago, but the realization that perhaps they were nearing the end of the road made it hard for him to breathe.

As messed up and damaged and damaging as she was, he wasn't ready to let her go. Which probably meant he was messed up, too, but she was his mum. He could still remember enough good times to hang on to some remnant of his childish affection for her.

"Do you remember the time we went berry-picking down near the beach?" he asked suddenly. "I think I was eight or nine. We spent the day down there, came back with buckets of fruit?"

His mother turned her head toward him, her eyes blinking owlishly. He thought she was going to blank him, deny the memory, but suddenly she smiled, the movement carving deep lines in her face.

"You were covered in juice. Kept pretending you'd cut off a body part and it was blood."

He grinned. "Yeah. And you made jam, but didn't put enough pectin in so we called it sauce."

"Never could cook worth a damn. It's a wonder you didn't die of malnutrition." She closed her eyes, clearly exhausted.

"I'll go. Let you get some rest," he said.

He started to rise, but her hand slid across the sheet and caught his. Her grip was surprisingly strong as she tightened her hand around his. She didn't say a word, and neither did he, but he settled into his seat.

After a few minutes, her grip grew slack as she slipped into true sleep. He untangled their hands and tidied the sheets and left the room. A nurse was at the ward desk and he stopped to talk to her.

"I'm Judy Black's son, Zach."

"Hi, Zach. What can I do for you?" The nurse's gaze was bright, assessing him in one quick glance.

"She seems really fragile. When was the last time the doctors came by?"

"As you know, Zach, your mother is very underweight. Pretty typical for someone with her problems, but it means she doesn't have a lot of resources to deal with something like this. We'll do our best to get calories into her, keep her hydrated, but she's going to be slow to heal. We're talking about a pretty compromised immune system here."

He nodded. "Okay."

"She's tough, though. And we're keeping a close eye on her. I'll make sure to let you know if anything changes."

"Thanks. I appreciate it."

He handed over one of his business cards so she would know how to contact him and headed for the car. He made a deliberate attempt to slough off the experience as he drove to Audrey's place. He didn't want the bad part of his life infecting the good.

She was ready to go when he arrived, dressed in slim black pants and a soft-looking black velvet top that made him want to run his hands all over her.

"You smell good," he murmured as he kissed her hello.

She took his hand and placed it on her breast and held it there. "I've been thinking about you all day."

"Me, too."

"About this." She squeezed his hand so that he, in turn, squeezed her breast. "And this." She slid her hand onto his hard-on, stroking him through the wool of his pants.

"This is the part where I ask how hungry you are," he said, hands already delving beneath her top.

"Starving. But I can wait."

It was tempting, but he really wanted her to experience the mushroom-stuffed gar fish and basil-leaf chicken at Choi's. Every cell protesting, he pulled back.

"Come on. Torture me some more over dinner," he said, taking her hand and tugging her toward the door.

She pouted. "Really? You really want to go?"

"No. I really want to show you a good time."

"Well…"

He grinned at the sly look on her face. "Come on."

She allowed him to lead her to the car, and they talked about the day's battles on the way to the restaurant. Audrey announced herself at his mercy in terms of menu selection and he ordered all his favorites and enjoyed watching her ooh and ah over them.

It was good being out in public with her, good watching her enjoy something he'd made happen. If he could, he'd take her out and spoil her every night. And then he'd take her home and spoil her some more.

"That was so good," she said in the car.

"Worth the sacrifice?"

"I was under the impression it was more a case of delayed gratification than actual self-denial."

"That's a good point."

"I thought so. By the way, if you take the freeway from here we can save ten minutes' travel time."

He did, and they did, and the moment they arrived at her place he pushed her onto the couch and followed her down onto the cushions.

They kissed slowly, lazily, enjoying the fact that they had all the time in the world. He undressed her by slow degrees, unwrapping her like a present.

"I haven't made out on the couch since I was sixteen," he said as they maneuvered into position so he could tug her pants down her legs. "I'm remembering why now."

"Lucky you, I never got to make out on the couch."

He pulled back so he could see her face and check if she was serious. "Really?"

Her cheeks were flushed, her hair mussed. She shrugged, the movement making her bra strap slip down her shoulder. "My parents were pretty vigilant. They didn't approve of boyfriends. I didn't have my first kiss till I was sixteen, and he was *not* allowed in the house."

"Those are some strict parents you had there."

"They wanted the best." She shrugged again, but there was sadness behind her eyes.

He brushed a thumb along her flushed cheekbone. "What did you want?"

"Too many things," she said, pulling him down for another kiss.

It was a make-do answer, a side step, but he didn't push. He was hard, and she was wet and willing, and now was not the time for a heart-to-heart. Instead, he filed the moment away and continued the important work of getting her naked.

He entered her as slowly as he'd undressed her, easing in, biting her plump lower lip as he slid all the way home.

"Zach," she said, already breathless. "I need…"

"I know."

He gave her what she needed, but he did it his way, slowly, savoring each stroke. She was silky and tight, her nipples firmly puckered as they brushed his chest with every pump of his hips. He watched her face and read the tension in her body and knew when to reach between her legs and give her the final push she needed.

She came with her knees clenched around his hips, her body trembling beneath his, and somehow he managed to hold on to his self-control long enough to bring her to the same place again a few minutes later before finally letting himself go.

When he tried to take his weight off her afterward, she wrapped her arms and legs around him and held him close.

"Not yet."

He let himself relax into her warmth, resting his head on her shoulder and closing his eyes. It was the first time he'd truly let his guard down all day, and he was aware of a tightness in his chest and throat as the rest of him relaxed. An image of his mother's pale, worn face flickered across his mind's eye, and he remembered the feel of her cool fingers gripping tightly to his own.

He took a breath, opened his mouth… And caught himself in the split second before he let his past bleed irrevocably into his present.

Audrey did not need to know about his mother. She didn't need to be a party to the ugliness of his childhood or the reality of his mother's addiction. There was nothing she could do or say that would undo what had happened or what would inevitably happen in the future. Which meant there was no reason to burden her with it.

No reason at all.

It was enough that he was here, with her, that this was the memory he would take to bed with him, not the one where his mother was in a hospital bed, her body reduced to a sinewy husk by her disease.

"Do you want to come to bed?" Audrey asked after a while.

"I should probably go," he said reluctantly.

"You're welcome to stay."

He pressed a kiss against the place where her shoulder joined her neck. "Thanks, but I didn't bring any stuff with me."

"Oh. Okay."

He liked that she sounded a little disappointed. The truth was, he'd debated dropping past his place en route from the hospital but he hadn't wanted to assume anything.

They levered themselves up off the couch and spent the next few minutes collecting their scattered clothes. He threw her an assessing look as he pulled on his trousers. He wanted to see her again, soon, and he wanted to nail down when that might be, even though he was aware he risked looking more than a little desperate.

"Are you busy on the weekend?" he asked.

"I have dinner with my sister tomorrow night. Other than that, I don't have any plans."

"Can I pencil in Saturday?"

"You can. Can I pencil in Sunday?"

He grinned. "Deal."

She saw him to the door wearing nothing but her bra and panties. He raked her with a look, shaking his head in disbelief at himself.

"I can't believe I'm actually walking out the door right now," he said.

"You must be insane."

"I think you're right. Deranged in the extreme."

Because he couldn't resist, he lowered his head and tongued her nipple through the silk of her bra. She made a small sound, her hand slipping around to grip the nape of his neck.

After a moment he lifted his head. "Sweet dreams."

"As if I'm going to slip peacefully into sleep after *that*."

He was still smiling when he exited the building and unlocked his car. One day, he needed to thank Gary for pairing him with Audrey for the report.

Luckiest day of his life.

CHAPTER SIXTEEN

"I'VE BEEN THINKING," Megan said.

Audrey glanced up from the catalog page she'd been proofing—even though what she'd really been doing was thinking about Zach—to find her friend propped in her office doorway.

"Yes?"

"Yes. And the conclusion I've come to is that you should ask Zach out."

Audrey stared at Megan. Was she messing with her head? Had she guessed that she and Zach were conducting an under-the-radar relationship? Had they been *that* obvious already?

"I'm not sure I agree with you," she said, because that was what she normally said in these sorts of conversations.

She'd done her damnedest to keep her face poker-straight whenever she was around Zach. This morning, she'd had the most inane conversation with him in the staff room while Megan hovered in front of the fridge. Sure, she'd been remembering what his clever hands had done to her last night the whole time, but she was almost certain she hadn't given anything away.

She hoped.

"I really think you should give him a chance. I know you were pissed about the whole giving-the-report-to-Whitman thing, but I think he's a good guy. I like him," Megan said.

Audrey opened her mouth to say something, then shut it

again. What could she say that wouldn't be an out-and-out lie? She didn't want to deceive her friend. But she also wasn't even close to being ready to go public with what was happening between her and Zach. It had been *three days,* after all.

"He is a good guy," she finally settled for saying.

Megan clapped her hands together and made a "gotcha" noise.

"You *do* like him. I *knew* it. I knew you wouldn't be able to hold out forever."

Audrey fought the need to squirm in her chair. She felt like such a liar, liar pants on fire.

"How did it go with that missing order?" she asked, desperate to change the subject. "Did it turn up?"

Megan's smile faded as she shook her head. "No. Sometimes, I want to go out to that warehouse and crack their heads together like coconuts. How hard is it to lose ten pallets of grass seed? Pretty hard, from where I'm sitting. But not for them."

Lucy appeared at Megan's side "Hey. Want some apple cinnamon tea cake? Jen made it."

She offered the plate to Megan, along with a napkin. Audrey was about to pass with a thank-you when she saw her friend's face.

"Are you all right?"

Megan was white, with a definite hint of green. "I think I'm going to throw up."

Pushing her way past Lucy, she broke into a jog as she headed for the ladies' room. Audrey was frozen in shock for a full second before she got herself together and went after her.

The first thing she heard when she entered the washroom was the sound of her friend retching in one of the cubicles.

"You okay?" she called.

"What do you think?" Megan's tone was anguished.

"Okay, that was a dumb question. Is there anything I can do?"

"A glass of water would be good."

"Water. Right."

Audrey exited the restroom and grabbed a plastic cup from the dispenser next to the nearby water cooler, filling the cup to the brim.

All was quiet when she returned to the bathroom.

"I have water."

"Thanks."

The cubicle door opened and Megan looked at her, her expression miserable. "I really hate throwing up."

"I don't think there are many actual, card-carrying, die-hard fans of regurgitation," Audrey said as she handed over the water.

She waited until Megan had rinsed her mouth a few times before voicing the thought at top of her mind.

"So. When was the last time you did a pregnancy test?"

"I had my period a couple of weeks ago. I'm not pregnant."

"Except you've been eating enough for a small island state and now you've tossed your cookies."

Megan frowned.

"I'm going up the road to the pharmacy," Audrey said, very firm.

"It's a waste of time," Megan said, but there was a lack of conviction in her tone.

Since it was nearly lunchtime, Audrey didn't feel even remotely guilty as she ducked up the road to grab a pregnancy test. She chose one with two tests in one box. If what she suspected was right, Megan might need some convincing.

Audrey understood her friend's refusal to allow herself to get her hopes up, but there was cautious, then there was crazy.

Megan was in her office when she returned and Audrey tossed the bag across the desk to her.

"Go do your thing, puke girl."

"Puke girl. That's lovely." But Megan was smiling faintly as they walked together to the restroom.

Five minutes later they were both staring at the twin blue lines on the test strip.

"But I just had my period. There's no way these things are sensitive enough to pick up a two-week-old pregnancy."

"What if that last period wasn't really a period? That happens. I've read about it in a magazine or something."

"You mean it was a bleed?" Megan's voice trembled with worry. Megan had lost one pregnancy, so Audrey knew that it was going to be hard for her friend to wholeheartedly embrace the news she'd received.

"I'm not a doctor. Let's make you an appointment. And maybe you should call Tim. Tell him there's a good chance he's going to be a daddy."

Megan stared at her. Then a slow smile curved her mouth. She pressed her fingers against her lips. Audrey wrapped her in a hug.

"Told you you'd get there, puke girl."

Megan thumped a fist on her back. "Stop calling me that or I'll come up with a worse nickname for you."

"I dare you."

Megan took the rest of the day as a sick day and raced off to the doctor, calling at three to confirm the diagnosis. She was so happy, Audrey felt a twinge of guilt that she was holding back her own good news from her best friend. She and Megan had shared their hopes and dreams and fears for a long time now. It felt sneaky not to let her in on what was going on.

But if things didn't work out with Zach, she would feel like such an idiot. And she didn't want Megan feeling obliged to keep a secret on their behalf, even though the odds were good she'd revel in the subterfuge.

She made a deal with herself as she ended the call—the moment she was confident things with Zach were solid, she'd come clean to Megan.

As for telling the rest of the office…she wasn't sure. But she knew it was unrealistic and unhealthy to try to keep their thing under wraps for too long.

Just until I'm sure. Or as sure as I can be, she promised herself. *Until things settle down at work.*

Even though her desk was heaving with work, she left earlier than usual to go home and change before driving into the city for dinner with her sister. One of Leah's colleagues had recommended Chin Chin as a great place to eat and they'd agreed to meet there at seven.

Audrey showered and dressed in jeans and a cowl-necked sweater, then changed her mind and pulled a black wrap dress out of her closet. She was staring unhappily at her reflection in the mirror on the back of her bedroom door when she caught sight of her bedside clock in the mirror.

She was going to be late if she didn't hustle.

Shaking her head at her own stupidity, she pulled on black knee-high boots and dropped a string of colorful beads over her head for a little brightness. Then she forced herself to leave, before her nerves could inspire another wardrobe change.

It was crazy to be nervous about having dinner with her own sister. This was Leah, after all. Conservative, top-of-the-class Leah who always said and did the right thing. She probably wanted to talk about what to buy their parents for Christmas. Or maybe she was feeling nostalgic or something.

Not that there was much to be nostalgic about in their shared childhood. Not from Audrey's point of view, anyway.

But maybe Leah saw things differently. Maybe she had much fonder memories of it all than Audrey did.

She tried to shake off her trepidation as she walked the block from the parking garage to the restaurant, but her breath got caught somewhere between her lungs and mouth when she spotted her sister waiting for her out in front of the restaurant. Dressed in creased linen pants with an equally creased linen shirt, Leah looked pale and uneasy.

"Hey. I forgot to mention to you that this place doesn't take bookings. I've put our name down for a table and they'll text me when it's ready. We can have a few drinks in the bar while we wait," Leah said, her delivery rapid-fire, her movements jerky.

"Okay. Sure." Audrey studied her sister out of the corner of her eye as they made their way downstairs to the dim bar. She couldn't decide if her sister was as nervous as she was or wired on caffeine and stress.

They were shown to an alcove with upholstered banquette seating and handed a fan of menus. Wine, bar food, cocktails.

"You want a drink? My friend at work said the cocktails here are really good. I'm going to have one. You should, too. I know you're driving, but you can have a couple without it being a problem. Trust me, I'm a doctor." Leah laughed a little too loudly.

"I'm up for a drink." Audrey breathed in through her nose, trying to calm her suddenly racing heart. Why did she feel as though something bad was about to happen?

They were both silent for a moment as they scanned the cocktail menu, the groovy vibes emanating from the speakers doing nothing to relieve the tension. When the waitress came, they both ordered a lemon fizz.

They made small talk until their drinks came. And all the while Audrey wondered why they were there.

Leah swallowed nervously once the waitress had delivered

their drinks, the sound audible in the pause between tracks. "You're probably wondering why I asked you here tonight," she said. Then she laughed awkwardly. "I sound like I'm in an Agatha Christie movie, don't I? *And the murderer is...*"

The table was trembling and it took Audrey a moment to work out it that was because her sister's leg was jiggling nonstop underneath.

"Leah. Whatever you've got to say, spit it out. The waiting is killing me," Audrey said.

Leah stilled. Then she nodded. "Okay. How about this? I'm really sorry for being such a shitty sister."

Audrey stared at her. Not what she'd expected. By a long shot.

"I have no idea what to say to that, Leah. Except you haven't been a crappy sister, obviously. I know we're not the closest, but it takes two to tango, right? And you have every right to be a little wary of me given some of the things I did when we were younger."

Like breaking into her parents' house when she was seventeen and living on the streets, raiding every possible source of ready cash that she could get her hands on—including her sister's piggy bank and portable CD player, which she'd promptly sold at the nearest secondhand shop.

She'd apologized to Leah when she'd finally given up her wild bid for freedom and come home a year later, but her sister hadn't looked her in the eye for months afterward.

"Don't let me off the hook, Audrey. I need to say this. I've been wanting to say this for years, but I always felt as though it would be a betrayal of Mum and Dad and they've always been so good to me... Which is the point, actually." Leah took a big swallow from her drink. "I'm just going to say it, put it right out there—I was the favorite. Hell, I still am. And I would be lying if I said I didn't enjoy being the golden child, able to do no wrong. Who doesn't want to be the best, the favored one, right?"

Leah's eyes had filled with tears and Audrey reached across to grab her sister's hand. "You don't need to do this. We don't have to have this conversation. It's all water under the bridge."

And it wasn't going to change anything. Audrey had long since resigned herself to the fact that she would never meet with her parents' wholehearted approval. Leah flagellating herself wasn't going to change anything.

"We do. God, we so do, Audrey. Because we both know that in order for me to be right and good and perfect, you had to be wrong and bad and damaged, don't we? That's what it comes down to, in a nutshell. I sat back and let that happen for thirty years. I accepted that, because it made me feel good, and I want you to know how...*ashamed* I am of that. And of Mum and Dad and what they did to you. What they still do to you...."

Leah's face was streaming with tears now and she shook her head impatiently, using one of the cocktail napkins to mop up.

Audrey lay her hands palm-down on the table. "Listen to me. This is not your fault. You have nothing to be ashamed of. Nothing, okay?" There was a tremble in her voice. The only clue to how profoundly her sister's words had affected her. "Let's have a nice dinner and you can tell me about your new speciality and I can tell you about my scary, seagull-eyed CEO."

But instead of taking the out she was offering, Leah tilted her head, her eyes narrowing as she studied Audrey.

"You don't want to talk about this." It wasn't a question.

"No."

"Why not?"

"Because it won't change anything." And because it had

taken her years to get to a place where she could protect herself and still be a part of the family.

"It might," Leah said.

"No, it won't. It's been like this since before you were born, Leah. For whatever reason, I don't measure up. So be it."

"God, it kills me to hear you say that. I can't stand it, Audrey."

To her everlasting surprise, her sister scooted along the curved bench and flung her arms around Audrey.

"You are amazing. You are gorgeous and stylish and so smart. And strong. You are *so* strong, Aud. Even when I was a spoiled little princess I used to admire the way you endured everything they threw at you. And then you made a break for it when you were sixteen, and I didn't know whether to cheer you on or be terrified of what might happen to you...."

Audrey sat stiffly in her sister's embrace, stunned all over again by her sister's words, her sister's perspective.

Leah released her, but didn't return to the other side of the banquette. "Do you know, I have never said no to them? Not about anything important. I have always been their good little girl, playing my part. And then I dropped out of the surgical program and got a small taste of what you've had to put up with for years." Leah huffed out an incredulous gust of laughter. "Phone calls. Dire predictions. Guilt trips. Hand-wringing. Recriminations. You'd think I was going to throw medicine in and run off to join the circus the way Mum carries on. I can't tell you how many times I've come close to caving purely to get her to let it go."

"Mum sees herself in you. If you achieve, she achieves." It had always seemed obvious to Audrey.

Leah shook her head slowly. "No, I don't think so, Aud. I think she sees herself in you. Did you know she always wanted to be a surgeon instead of a GP?"

"No." A memory tickled at the back of Audrey's mind the moment the words were out of her mouth. She frowned. That day at Leah's birthday lunch, her mother had said that she didn't want Leah to make the same mistakes she had.

Audrey closed her eyes for a brief moment as she understood something she probably should have worked out years ago.

"Mum fell pregnant with me, didn't she? And had to settle for being a GP."

Leah nodded. "She had all these plans. Wanted to make her presence felt in the boys' club."

"And instead she had me."

"Yes."

Such a small, insignificant piece of the puzzle, yet now that Audrey had it, so many other things made sense. The pressure she'd felt from the very youngest age to be the smartest, the best, the most advanced. The disappointment her mother hadn't even tried to hide when she'd failed at all of the above. Oh, she'd been smart enough, but not the smartest. She'd had a speech impediment early on that required therapy to correct, and she'd always struggled with math.

Then Leah had been born and started showing signs of being a gifted child from an early age. All of a sudden Leah became the focus, and the pressure was off for Audrey.

She'd been relieved at first. Then, in the way of children, she'd done her best to earn back some of the attention and focus she'd once enjoyed. She'd never been as smart or as good as Leah, though. For a brief period she'd acted out, but that got her little joy. By the time she was sixteen, she'd resigned herself to being the also-ran daughter.

And then she'd met Johnny and he had looked at her with desire and hung on her every word and worshipped her. And she'd been so hungry for all of the above that she'd given him whatever he asked for and followed wherever he led her—to parties, to clubs, to squats he and his friends were illegally occupying. And, finally, out her bedroom window so they could start their life together—a bold experiment that had encompassed sleeping rough on the streets when they couldn't find a suitably vacant house or building, and stealing and begging to buy food and drink and drugs. She'd survived a torrid, scary, blurry eighteen months before being admitted to the hospital with life-threatening pneumonia after collapsing at a train station in the city.

Audrey could still remember how scared and hopeful and desperate she'd been when she'd finally allowed the hospital to contact her parents. She'd wanted them to love her so badly. For her absence to have somehow elevated her in their eyes to someone worthy of their affection and attention. They'd come running, gratifyingly tearful and grateful she was still alive. And angry, so very angry, that she'd put them through eighteen months of hell.

"You want another round?"

Audrey blinked, dragging her thoughts from the past and focusing on the tattoo-covered waitress hovering at the head of their booth.

"Um, sure. Yes, thanks," she said.

"Me, too."

Leah waited till the waitress was gone before speaking again. "I had a feeling you didn't know about the surgery thing. She only told me recently. A cautionary tale in case I was planning on getting close enough to another human being to have sex. I saw your face when we were talking about it at my birthday lunch and it hit me that you didn't know. I haven't been able to stop thinking about it since."

"No. I didn't know. I always thought I was a disappointment. And sometimes I thought I was imagining all of it, that there was something needy and small in me that reacted against you being praised. That I was simply jealous. Envious."

It was hard to articulate the things she'd always kept a lid on. The ugliest parts of herself. Because, of course, she *had* envied Leah at times. She'd coveted the smiles and approval her sister seemed to receive so effortlessly, simultaneously hating herself for being petty and jealous and needy.

Such a vicious cycle, all of it. The only way she'd even come close to stopping it was to build her own life, a world that existed independently of her parents and her sister. The moment she'd earned enough from her warehouse job at Makers to make it financially viable for her to leave home, she had, and she hadn't looked back.

Hadn't wanted to. Hadn't needed to, because she'd been too busy building herself an unassailable fortress. A career she could be proud of. Financial security. Achievements she could hang her hat on. A sense of self-worth that came from within, not from anything her parents might bestow on her.

And mostly it worked. Mostly it protected her.

And now her sister was asking Audrey to lower the drawbridge and let her in. Telling her she'd been right to build her walls, that she admired her for it. That she was ashamed of the part she'd played in the sad family drama that had led them here.

"You wouldn't be human if you hadn't been jealous. As for what happened with Johnny… It's hardly a miracle, is it, that you took off when there was so little for you at home."

"No."

Audrey reached for her drink, only to realize it had been taken away and the new one hadn't arrived yet. Her hand was shaking, and she dropped it into her lap and clasped it with her other one. Holding it steady, even though the last thing she felt was steady.

"Are you okay?" Leah asked, frowning.

"Yes. I might…" Audrey stood and gestured toward the bathrooms. She didn't wait for her sister to respond, making her way there. She wasn't sure what would happen once she arrived, her insides were in such turmoil. The answer burned its way up her throat as she entered the cubicle and shut the door. She didn't throw up, even though she really felt as though she needed to.

Shaky and on the verge of tears, she rinsed her mouth and washed her face. Megan was right—nausea was horrible. Definitely one of her least favorite things in the world, right up there with the anxiety that was jangling its way through her body. Drying her face, she tried to find some calm.

It was beyond her. Her sister had torn the scab off old wounds, and feelings and thoughts Audrey had buried years ago were rising up to assail her. No matter how many deep breaths she took she couldn't seem to get enough air, and the walls still felt as though they were closing in.

I need to get out of here. I can't do this.

She didn't question the impulse. She left the bathroom and returned to her sister.

"I'm really sorry, Leah, but I need to go. I need to…process some of this, I guess. I feel a bit like I've been kicked in the head."

Leah's face was creased with concern. "Because I dumped all this on you like an idiot. I'm so sorry, Audrey. I was so caught up in wanting to get this all of my chest, wanting to clear my plate, but I've dumped it all on you instead, haven't I?"

"It's fine. It's good. And I'll be okay. It's just… I try not to think about this stuff too much, you know?"

"I know."

"But maybe we could do this again some time soon? Dinner, I mean."

"I would really, really like that." Leah stood and embraced her, pressing her cheek against Audrey's.

It took her a moment to return the embrace, and when she did she did so fiercely.

"I do appreciate you being brave enough to bring this stuff up," Audrey said.

Because how many families sailed along and ignored all the hurts they inflicted on each other?

"I love you. I haven't said that to you nearly enough, but I do. I love you, Aud."

"I love you, too, Leah."

They broke their embrace and Audrey took a step backward. Needing to be outside now. Alone. That was the way she was used to dealing with the tough stuff—on her own.

She made her way upstairs and outside and sucking in big lungfuls of cool night air. It didn't stop the tears from flowing as she strode toward the parking garage, but that was okay. There were only strangers to witness them and she could live with that.

Somehow she managed to slot enough money into the machine to get out of the lot, then she was driving home, the need to be in her place, with her things around her, to be safe, almost overpowering.

She was nearly home when her phone rang. She wasn't going to answer it, then she thought it might be Leah, checking on her, and she didn't want her sister to think she'd driven into a tree or something.

"Hello?"

"Audrey. Hey. I figured you'd still be out for dinner with your sister. I was going to leave a dirty, desperate message on your voice mail." Zach's voice filled her car, deep and resonant and familiar.

Suddenly the tears that had been tapering off started again, filling her throat, stealing her breath.

"Audrey? Are you still there?"

She sucked in a breath, using her forearm to wipe her face. "I'm here. Sorry. Now isn't a great time to talk. Can I call you later?"

"Are you okay? You sound upset."

"I'm fine." She injected a note of brightness into her voice. "Just a little tired."

He was silent for a moment. "Okay. Call me if you need anything, okay?"

"Thanks. I will." She managed to hold it together until he hung up, then she pulled over and rested her arms on her steering wheel and howled her eyes out.

She felt so hollow, so sad, so alone. Feelings she'd been fighting all her life. Dumb to let them swamp her now at this age. She had a great life. Sure, her family was a little messed up, but whose wasn't? There was no reason for her to be distraught because Leah had shone a light on the monsters under the bed.

Audrey started her car, glancing around to get her bearings. Suddenly the thought of spending the evening alone seemed unbearable. She didn't want to be alone with her thoughts and memories.

Call me if you need anything.

Zach's words echoed in her head. She couldn't show up all tear-soaked and pathetic and launch herself at him. They'd been seeing each other less than a week. No way was she subjecting him to that.

It would be pathetic. And needy. He'd probably run a mile. He'd probably wonder what he'd gotten himself mixed up with.

Megan. She could go to Megan's place. Megan would listen and offer tissues and get angry on her behalf and hold her while she cried.

But she didn't want Megan.

She wanted Zach. She wanted to put her head on his shoulder. She wanted the already-familiar weight of his body pressing hers into the bed. They didn't need to talk. They could have sex and then she could fall asleep in his arms and simply being surrounded by his solid warmth and confidence and sureness would make things recede to their proper perspective.

She tightened her grip on the steering wheel, undecided. Then she signaled and made a U-turn, driving toward the city.

The light was on in the front room at Zach's place so she figured he was still awake, a not unreasonable assumption given it was relatively early. She grabbed her handbag and walked up the path and knocked, both hands fisted around the leather of the strap.

He looked surprised when he answered. "Audrey."

"You said if I needed anything, I should call you."

"I did."

"Okay. I need you to take me to bed and not ask any questions. Can you do that?"

He was silent as his gaze scanned her face. "Yes. Of course."

She felt the press of tears again and she blinked rapidly to dispel them. "Thank you."

"Come here."

He held his arms open and she walked into them. He kissed her temple, then her forehead, and she lifted her head so he could access her mouth.

It didn't take long for desire, sweet and sharp and demanding, to replace the shaky feeling inside her. She pushed Zach inside his house and shut the door before tugging at the tie on her dress.

He frowned slightly, and she could feel his concern, but

she pressed kisses to his neck and slid her hand into the waistband of his jeans.

"Take me to bed," she whispered against his skin. "Make me forget my name for a little while."

CHAPTER SEVENTEEN

EVEN THOUGH EVERYTHING in him wanted to ensure that Audrey was okay, that there wasn't some guy he needed to pound into hamburger or some other act of vengeance he needed to wreak on her behalf, Zach honored his promise and led her into his bedroom.

He didn't turn on the light, instinctively knowing that the dark was more comforting. He helped her slip her dress off and unzip her boots, then he shed his own clothes and joined her on the bed.

His mind might be preoccupied, but his body knew what it was doing, and soon there was only the silk of her skin beneath his hands as he made love to her. She was silent and intense, her body quivering with need, and he wrapped his arms around her as he slid inside her. She clung to him, the two of them rocking in a shared rhythm. He knew when she was close and he stroked her to climax, quickly following her. When he kissed her temple afterward he tasted the salt of tears and never wanted to let her go.

She fell asleep almost immediately, curled against his body, and he ached for her, wanted to right the wrong that had caused her so much pain. Whatever it was. Whoever it was.

That she had come to him, that she'd chosen him to trust with her hurt, filled him with a fierce sense of gratitude. He wanted to make this woman happy. He wanted to protect her from the world's harshest blows. He wanted to cherish her.

So much so that it was a little scary. He refused to be

scared, though. Audrey was the woman he'd been waiting his whole life to meet. Strong and vulnerable, courageous, clever, kind, generous... He could go on.

And she'd come to him in her hour of need.

She stirred after half an hour, pushing away from him. He let her go, then rolled out of bed and went into the kitchen. He poured a glass of water and headed to the bedroom. At the last minute he detoured to the bathroom and grabbed a box of tissues, too.

He didn't turn on the light, setting both items on the bedside table before climbing into bed.

"Water," he said, passing the glass to her.

"Thank you."

She drank, then set down the glass. He lifted his arm, silently inviting her closer, and she rested her head on his chest and fitted her body along his.

"Sorry," she said after a moment.

"For?"

"Using you as a sex aid."

He laughed. "Was that what that was?"

"Not really. I didn't want to be alone tonight."

He knew that feeling only too well. "Want to talk about it?"

She shifted her head slightly, as though the question made her uneasy. Just when he thought she wasn't going to answer, she spoke.

"My sister apologized to me tonight."

He listened in silence as she poured it out—her sister's confession, her mother's unfulfilled ambitions, the endless pressure and lonely negligence of her childhood. He dropped a kiss onto her head when she told him about running away with her boyfriend, Johnny, at sixteen, and the scraping-by existence they'd lived together on the streets.

It was a life he was only too familiar with, for other reasons. He'd spent more than his fair share of nights in shelters with his mother when he was a teen, and he'd known dozens of desperate junkies over the years. He had a fair idea the things she'd faced, the dangers she'd survived.

He felt himself getting angry when she described her disgraced return to the fold, her parents' relief and then angry laying of blame and guilt.

"I decided a long time ago that they simply didn't understand me and I didn't understand them. When I was a kid, my favorite fantasy was to pretend that I was adopted, because it explained so well why I didn't fit with their idea of who I should be, and why they didn't fit with my idea of who they should be," she said. "Hearing my sister say out loud that she is the favorite, something that I've always tried to convince myself wasn't true, and, when I failed, chastised myself for being a whiny-little-bitch, poor-me loser...I can't explain how it made me feel. *Validated* is the best word I can come up with. As though all the feelings and moments and memories of not quite measuring up weren't figments of my imagination. That it wasn't about me having a jaundiced view or being jealous of perfect Leah or sulky because I was the eldest and she was the baby. It really happened. It was real.

"Now I feel kind of liberated, but I also have this spot in my chest—" she tapped it with her fingers "—that aches for that sad, messed-up little kid who could never do anything right."

He ached, too. And he didn't know what to say to her to take away her pain. That he'd like to burn her parents to the ground was a given, but it wouldn't solve anything. It wouldn't change the past, and it wouldn't heal her. It seemed to him that she'd done a pretty amazing job of doing that for herself.

"I don't want to blow smoke up the skirt you're not wearing," he said when she'd fallen silent, "but I hope it's occurred to you that it takes a will of iron to rise above the kind of shit you're talking about. To get to where you are, all on your own. Not because of your parents, but despite them. Do you have any idea how exceptional that makes you, Audrey Mathews? How gutsy and brave and determined?"

"Don't. You'll make me cry again."

"Then cry. I've got you."

She did then, a little, and he rubbed circles on her back and passed her tissues and listened some more as she tried to make sense of the thoughts and feelings churning around inside her.

She fell silent after a while, and they sat with their own thoughts.

"You're a really good listener," she said.

"It's an art form."

She propped herself up on her elbow so she could see his face. "You're joking, but it is. You didn't try to fix anything, you simply let me bleat to my heart's content."

"Can't fix a lot of what makes the world suck." He shrugged. "Being able to have a good bleat about it seems like the bare minimum in my book."

"I like your book, Zachary Black."

"Excellent. I have another chapter for you to get familiar with. Roll onto your stomach."

"Is this about to get perverse?"

"Only if you want it to."

He started rubbing her shoulders and neck and she gave a low groan.

"Sweet Lord, you have good hands."

He set himself to massaging the tension out of her body, working his way down her back to her sacrum and glutes before finally arriving at her feet. He'd forgotten about their conversation at Al's regarding her foot fetish, but she almost levitated when he started digging his thumbs into the ball of her foot.

"Oh, God. Don't ever stop doing that," she groaned into the pillow.

Eventually she fell silent, and he knew she was drifting toward sleep. He pulled the covers up to her shoulders and stretched out alongside her.

Never would he have imagined that he'd be grateful a woman had chosen him as her first port of call in an emotional crisis. Yet he was, profoundly so.

She trusted him. Lying in the dark, she'd spilled her secrets and trusted him not to judge her. He hoped he'd risen to the occasion. He hoped she'd come to him again if she was hurting. He hoped she'd turn to him for everything, because he was wild about her.

Crazy, wild, devoted. Maybe even a little sexually obsessed.

Rolling onto his side, he rested his lips and nose against the nape of her neck and inhaled the soft scent of her skin. Being careful not to wake her, he slid his arm around her body.

Then and only then did he let himself fall asleep. Holding the woman that he was crazy, head-over-heels in love with.

THE BED WAS empty when Audrey woke. She sent out a searching hand for Zach's warm chest or back and met with cool sheets. Sitting up, she pushed hair out of eyes that felt sore and gritty from too much crying.

Last night had been…messy. Not her finest hour. She was still a little astonished that she'd not only allowed herself to take solace from Zach on a physical level, but that she'd spilled all her inner turmoil out for him to see, too.

Not her usual deal with men. With anyone, really. But Zach was not the usual kind of man. She already knew that, of course, but he continued to reveal new aspects of himself that hammered home that notion.

He was special. Very special.

He was also an excellent masseur.

She flexed her feet, remembering the firm pressure of his thumbs in her instep last night. Heaven.

"You're awake. Great."

Zach entered holding a glass of orange juice and a plate heaped with toast. "No bacon or eggs, sorry, but I thought Vegemite toast might get us through." He was wearing only a pair of navy boxer briefs, and she noticed he had the newspaper tucked under his arm.

"I love Vegemite toast."

"I sensed as much. I have an instinct for these things. Plus there was nothing else to offer you."

"Always helps narrow down the options."

He passed her the juice and set the plate on the sheets beside her before plumping his pillow and settling onto the bed.

"Would I be wildly wrong if I guessed that's the crossword?" she asked.

"It is. Do you want to be in charge of the pen or will I do it?"

He offered her the pen. She didn't take it.

"I have a confession to make. That night when you talked about doing the crossword puzzle with me...I don't want you to feel as though you've embarked on this thing under false pretenses, but I probably should have told you that I'm really bad at them. I'd almost go so far as to say I am crossword-impaired."

He smiled. "I'll be in charge of the pen, then."

"I'm serious. I totally suck."

"I believe you, don't worry. I, on the other hand, am pretty freakin' awesome. If I do say so myself. So I think this'll even out okay."

He reached for a piece of toast, and after a moment's hesitation she did the same. He read out the first question, and she surprised herself by guessing the answer. Half an hour later, the bed was full of crumbs and the crossword puzzle was finished.

"That was fun," she said, surprised.

"Guess what else is fun?" He rolled toward her.

They made love, then showered and dressed and went to collect fresh clothes for her before Zach took her to Maling Road in Canterbury for lunch. Afterward, they inspected the antiques and other specialty shops along the quaint Victorian shopping strip. Zach bought her a pretty notepad with her name on it and she reciprocated by getting him an antique letter opener with an embossed leather handle.

"I should go shopping with you more often," he said as they made their way back to the car.

That night, they went to the movies before going to her apartment.

Sunday was equally relaxed and fun. More than once Audrey had to pinch herself at how easily she and Zach fitted into one another's grooves. But they'd established many times how much they had in common, so maybe it wasn't too surprising.

That first weekend set the pattern for the next month. They worked late, scrupulously sticking to their work-is-work rule even when they were the only people left in the building apart from the cleaners. Then they went to her place or his, only occasionally missing an evening when one of them had an interstate trip or an early meeting. Once, they both flew into Sydney for a store visitation and bent their rules enough to make good use of the spa bath in Audrey's hotel room that night.

They ate out some nights, got takeaway others, and every

now and then cooked a meal together, just to prove to each other that they could.

Life was good. And not only because of Zach, although he constituted the majority of the goodness. Audrey had dinner with her sister a week or so after their first attempt, and this time they talked of things other than family, including touching on her sister's love life, with her sister revealing that there was a special guy she'd like Audrey to meet one day. Audrey discovered that her sister had a sly sense of humor while being surprisingly naive about some things, which made her very easy to tease.

It seemed to Audrey that there was a chance for them to become friends if they wanted to take it, and all signs pointed in that direction.

The only black spot on the horizon was the increasing guilt she felt about keeping her relationship with Zach on the down-low with Megan. It was impossible to keep the happiness she felt from flowing over into her work life, and even though Megan was brimming with her own happiness and preoccupied with baby plans, she had noticed. Who wouldn't, when there was precious little to be thrilled about given their workloads and the flatlining morale among many of the staff? Megan kept joking that she wanted to know what vitamins Audrey was taking, and every time she brought it up, Audrey had to stop herself from blurting out the truth.

Nearly four weeks to the day after her tearful gut-spill on Zach's shoulder, Audrey waited until they'd finished the Saturday morning crossword—now one of her favorite pastimes simply because Zach enjoyed it so much—to raise the subject.

"So. About work," she said.

"What about work?" He folded the paper and set it on the bedside table.

"I was thinking that if it's okay with you, I'd like to tell

Megan what's going on." She watched his face, trying to gauge his reaction.

"Okay." He appeared to be unruffled about the prospect of going public with their relationship.

"She won't talk. But I don't want her to feel as though it's a big secret she needs to protect with her life or anything, either. That's not fair," she elaborated.

"I agree."

She studied him. "You're really not fussed about this? Even though things haven't settled down yet?"

"Why would I be? People will find out eventually." He said it so matter-of-factly.

"That doesn't bother you at all? Especially after hearing about Dean?"

Dean was another of their fellow buyers. He'd been called into Gary's office yesterday and given his marching orders. "Budget constraints" had been the official line. Whitman wanted them to do more with less, the modern corporate mantra.

"I'm not going anywhere, Audrey. How about you?" His expression was very serious.

"No. I'm right where I want to be," she said quietly. It was a little scary saying it out loud. Neither of them had made any declarations yet. But it was getting harder and harder to bite her tongue when her feelings grew stronger every day.

He smiled, a slow, sweet smile that made her chest get tight in the best possible way. "Good."

He leaned across to kiss her.

"So I should go ahead and tell her?"

"Yep. Tell whoever you like. I can hire a sky writer, if you like."

She couldn't help laughing, even though the thought of going public made her feel distinctly jittery. Zach's expres-

sion grew more serious and he reached across to tuck a strand
of hair behind her ear.

"We work like dogs, do overtime every day. I know you're
worried about being judged or censured, but they can suck
it up. We're allowed to have lives."

She let her breath out in a rush. He knew her so well. He
knew all her secrets, and he understood she had an almost
pathological need to get things right in her professional life.
It was something she knew she should work on, but it was
hard to separate herself from any criticism she might receive
for her work. She didn't have to go far to understand why.

She knew he was right. The company might command
their attention and focus for the bulk of their waking hours,
but it didn't own this time, right now. This was for them, and
she was not going to pretend that Zach wasn't one of the most
important—if not *the* most important—things in her life.

"Right. Now that we've solved the world's problems, I'm
going to squeeze in five kilometers. You coming?" he asked.

They'd been through the same routine for the past three
weeks and she settled against her pillows with a big smile
on her face. She kind of liked the idea that they were developing their own shtick.

"I don't run unless there's a flesh-eating zombie with a
chainsaw chasing me."

Last week it had been an ax-wielding psychopath. She
knew from his smile that he appreciated her changing things
up.

"I'll get you out there one day, you know."

"You can keep trying if you like. But this body was not
made for speed."

"We'll see."

He tossed off the covers and stood, stretching his back.
She ogled him unashamedly as he pulled on running shorts,
socks and sneakers before shrugging into a T-shirt.

"Won't be long, okay?"

"Make sure you're all sweaty when you get back, okay?"

He gave her an amused look. "Are we developing another fetish?"

"The foot thing is not a fetish. It's completely asexual. The sweaty-man thing I'm not so sure about."

"I'll keep that in mind."

He dropped a kiss onto her lips before leaving. A few seconds later she heard the heavy thud of the front door.

Probably she should get out of bed. There were dishes to clean, the remnants of last night's takeout, and Zach would surely appreciate it if she put on a load of washing. They'd been spending so much time together they'd both let household chores pile up.

"Okay, Mathews, ass in gear."

She threw back the covers and was about to roll out of bed when her phone rang on the bedside table. She leaned across to grab it. The caller ID said it was Judy, but it wasn't until she'd hit the button to accept the call that it occurred to her that she didn't have anyone named Judy in her contacts list.

"Hey, baby. I just wanted to hear your voice and let you know that I'm doing really well. They're really pleased with me. I feel good about it this time, Zachy. I feel really good."

Audrey cleared her throat, deeply uncomfortable. Clearly, she'd picked up Zach's phone instead of her own, an occupational hazard when they had the same model. She really needed to get around to fancying up her cover or something to distinguish hers.

"I'm really sorry, um, Judy, but Zach's not here right now. I can give a message to him, if you like." She knew she sounded stiff, but it wasn't as though she had a lot of practice taking phone calls from women who called her boyfriend *baby*.

"Oh. Okay." There was a long pause and Audrey frowned.

There was a slowness to the other woman's speech, an uncertain quality that made Audrey wonder if she was drunk. Maybe this was one of Zach's exes, making a not-quite-sober booty call. "Who are you, anyway?" The question was abrupt and to the point. "Not to be rude or anything."

"My name is Audrey. I'm Zach's girlfriend."

It was a little freaky how easily the words fell off her tongue. As though a part of her had been wanting to say them for a while now.

To her surprise, a crack of laughter sounded. "Well. How about that? Good for him. About time he did something about his tragic love life. Listen, Audrey, you tell him his mum called. He knows where to find me. And maybe we'll talk again sometime. Or maybe not." She laughed again. "He's a hard man to pin down, that boy of mine."

She disconnected but Audrey was frozen in place, the phone pressed to her ear. Slowly she lowered it.

Zach's *mum?* How was that possible when Zach had told her both his parents were dead?

Maybe she's a stepmum. Or a foster mum.

That could be it. That must be it. Because the alternative was that Zach had lied to her about something pretty damned basic and fundamental.

"He wouldn't do that." Audrey's words echoed.

Mind whirring, she set down his phone, only then registering that she'd had to reach to grab it—of course it had been his phone. If she'd been thinking with even half her brain, she would have realized that before she answered. And then she would never have spoken to Judy, Zach's "mum," and learned that Zach had potentially been lying to her.

It was a little scary how ambivalent she felt about that fact. Things had been going so well. She'd been so happy. Zach had been happy, too. She was sure of it. She had the awful feeling that that phone call would throw an almighty spanner into the works. It would have been nice if they'd been able to enjoy a little more time in the sun before things blew up.

She closed her eyes and pressed the pads of her fingers against her closed lids. Why on earth would Zach lie to her about his parents being dead? And what else had he been lying about?

A memory came flying at her as though her subconscious had been waiting for this moment—the golf day, Zach running so late she'd covered for him. She'd been too busy grappling with his dinner invitation to register it at the time, but he'd never told her why he'd almost missed the tournament. Granted, she hadn't asked, but he hadn't offered, either.

He was never late. Ever. And that night, he'd been so bone-weary she'd been unable to wake him up. Her intuition told her the two things were linked.

She wasn't sure what to do with herself. Zach would be back in thirty minutes or so. She needed to hang on to that and stop speculating, because the scenarios her brain was creating were not helpful.

Because she needed to be busy, she made the bed, then tidied last night's mess in the kitchen. She'd showered and dressed by the time Zach returned, bright-eyed and sweaty, clearly energized by his run.

"Man. That was hard work today. Not sure why it's easier some days than others, but today was a tough one. Maybe you wore me out last night."

He kissed her before heading to the kitchen. She followed and watched as he poured a glass of water and drank it.

"I accidentally answered your phone while you were out. Sorry, I thought it was mine."

He gave her an amused look, as though he thought she was getting anxious over nothing. "No biggie."

"The woman I spoke to said she was your mum."

He didn't say anything, but there was the smallest of hesitations before he filled his glass a second time. She knew, absolutely, that he was using the action to buy himself some thinking time. Her stomach sank.

"I thought your parents were dead, Zach."

He set down the glass and turned to face her. His expression carefully composed.

"My father is."

"But your mother is alive?"

"Yes."

"Okay." She crossed her arms over her chest, trying not to show how shaken she was. "Why would you lie about something like that?"

"It's complicated, Audrey. It's also got nothing to do with us, so it's really not that big a deal."

"You lying about your *complicated* mother has nothing to do with us?"

"Look, I didn't do it to be sneaky or malicious or anything like that. There's simply no good reason to get into any of this, and so I didn't. My mum is not a part of my life. Ergo, she's not a part of your life."

"But she called you. You have her as a contact."

He sighed and ran a hand through his hair. He looked cornered and wary, his body tense. "This isn't a big deal, Audrey. Honestly. My mum isn't someone you need to worry about. Can we let it go, please?"

"I don't understand why you won't talk about this." He'd been so fantastic when she lost it over Leah's apology, but suddenly he was closing the shutters because his mother had called.

"Because it's not fun. And I don't want to inflict it on you if I don't have to."

"Fun. Okay. You think I'm only in this for fun? That's what we're about?"

"I didn't mean it like that. You know I'm serious about

you, about us. I wouldn't have even laid a finger on you in the first place if I wasn't."

"Then tell me what's going on, Zach."

"There's no point. It won't ever affect you, because I'll make sure it doesn't. What we have is separate from that, so why should you have to wade through tons of shit for no reason?" His expression was tight now, his delivery clipped.

She stared, more than a little overwhelmed by what this conversation was revealing. Zach had something going on, something difficult, yet he didn't want to share it. He wanted to compartmentalize it, keep their relationship on one side, while whatever else was happening remained on the other. Because she shouldn't have to "wade through" his shit.

"Don't you trust me?" She couldn't think of any other reason for him to quarantine her from his real life. "Don't you think I'm up for complicated?"

"This is not about you, Audrey."

"Then what is it about?"

"It's about me being able to have my own life."

"What life is that? The one I'm allowed to be a part of, or the other one, the one where you have a mother and God knows what else?"

"This is my real life. This is who I am," he said.

"No, Zach. This is one part of you. The part you trust me to share."

She was afraid of what else she might say, so she turned and left the room. In the bedroom she straightened the bed again, fussing with the pillows, smoothing the duvet cover.

She felt as though someone had given her a vicious shove in the middle of the back. She felt blindsided. She'd thought she and Zach were on the same page. She'd thought they were building the foundations for a lifetime commitment. She'd fallen in love with him: besottedly, wholly, completely in love. And all the while he'd been sharing only part of who he was.

She felt rather than saw him enter the room.

"Audrey. This is nothing. Trust me."

"I do trust you, Zach. But you clearly do not trust me. Here I've been, thinking about the kind of renovations we could afford on this place when we sell my apartment—getting a little ahead of myself, I know, but I'm like that when I want something. When something's important to me. And you've got this whole other thing that you won't share with me."

"That's because it's not worth sharing."

She stared at him across the expanse of the bed, hollow with fear, because this was a deal-breaker conversation they were having. She was terrified of how it might end.

She loved him so much, had invested so much in him. If he wasn't prepared to let her in…they had nowhere to go. Surely he must be able to see that?

"Zach, don't you get it? I don't care if it's good or bad or awful or farcical or tragic. If it's a part of your life, if it's a part of you, I want to share it with you. I want to understand. I want to help you."

He stared at her, his jaw tense. She could practically hear him grinding his teeth together.

She had a sudden flash of intuitive insight. "Have you ever told one of your other girlfriends about your mother? About this other part of your life you're so determined to keep to yourself?"

He didn't answer, but he didn't need to. She knew the answer: he hadn't. Of course he hadn't. He could barely bring himself to address the topic obliquely, let alone directly.

It was the final blow. She felt sick as it hit her that he didn't consider her any different from his past girlfriends. He stood head and shoulders above any man in her world. She'd shared things with him, revealed more of herself than she ever had with another man. He was a treasure she'd stumbled upon, the soul mate she'd been searching for all her life.

And she was just another woman he didn't want to become truly intimate with. Another woman he was prepared to share only so much with.

It physically hurt to realize how stupid she'd been. How misguided and blind. She'd offered herself to Zach on a platter—and he'd rejected her with his lack of trust. The enormity of her folly, of her foolishness yawned before her. Her throat closed.

She'd believed in him. In them. And it had all been a mirage. A lovely fantasy that existed only in her mind.

She teetered on the brink of control. Then her pride kicked in. She'd bared her soul to this man once. She wouldn't—*couldn't*—do it again.

"I guess we both know where we stand, then. And I guess it's better that we had this conversation sooner rather than later." She searched for her overnight bag.

"Audrey. Come on."

He moved into the room as she started stuffing her things into her bag—her purse, yesterday's shoes, the earrings and necklace she'd left on the bedside table. She was about to stuff her skirt inside when he tugged both it and the bag from her hands.

"You can't go. I don't want you to go home."

She fought desperately to stop herself from breaking down. She was absolutely determined to preserve that last, small shred of her dignity.

"I don't think there's much point in me staying."

"None of this changes how I feel about you. Audrey, I love you."

How she would have loved to hear those words from him a couple of hours ago. Now they made her feel incredibly sad and empty. What sort of relationship did he imagine they had when he only allowed her to know the parts of himself he considered acceptable for public consumption?

"Zach—" She pressed her fingers to her lips to stop them from trembling. "Zach, I think you're a wonderful man, I really do. But what sort of future can we have together when you cut me out of part of your life? How could that possibly work?"

They were standing so close she could feel the turmoil inside him, the battle that was taking place behind his stormy blue eyes.

Hope flared. Maybe she was wrong. Maybe he wanted to trust her. He'd obviously been holding on for a long time. No wonder it was hard to let go.

But she couldn't pry the truth from him. He had to want to share it with her. He had to trust her. Otherwise, they were doomed.

I don't want to lose this man.

But it was possible she'd never had him, not in the sense that she'd once believed she had.

"Whatever it is, Zach, it's not going to change the way I feel about you. It's not going to change us."

She willed him to say the words she needed to hear. Willed him to put his faith in her the way she had in him.

"Then why make a big deal out of it?" There was no heat behind his words, no conviction. He'd already made his decision. He would let her go rather than invite her into his life. She could see it in his face.

"Because I want all of you, Zach. Not just the great lover and the smart business guy and the goofy crossword addict. I want the sad and the mad, too. I want the hard stuff, because I trust you with my hard stuff. I trust you to want to be there in the morning, to hang in there even when I'm maybe not making sense or being fair. I need you to trust me in the same way. I need you to let me love all of you, Zach."

His chin jerked as though she'd landed a punch. He looked so bewildered, so blindsided, as though he couldn't quite grasp how quickly things had shifted.

He wasn't alone.

Her chest aching, she flung her arms around him. She squeezed him tight, resting her cheek alongside his. Because this was a tragedy. This was the greatest, most painful could-have-been of her life.

Then she stepped away and grabbed her bag and strode for the door.

CHAPTER EIGHTEEN

AUDREY MADE IT to her car before she started to sob, the sadness welling up from deep inside her. Not only for herself, but also for Zach. She'd always sensed a loneliness inside him. An apartness. It made sense now—how could he ever truly connect with people if he was always holding a part of himself back?

It made her feel so heartbroken that he felt it had to be that way. She didn't even want to think about what might motivate a man like him to partition his life so meticulously, so thoroughly.

What happened to you, Zach?

It was possible she would never know.

Her car didn't unlock the first time and she hit the remote button several times before she heard the click. She gave the door pillar a frustrated thump before sliding in and slamming the door behind her.

She started driving, but she was barely five minutes up the road before dizzying anxiety gripped her, so powerful she had to pull over to the curb.

This felt wrong. Driving away from Zach wrenched at something inside her. She kept picturing his face, the turmoil behind his eyes. He had been utterly torn. She'd *felt* it, felt the battle he was waging with himself.

He can't help being the way he is. Something happened to make him this way, and he's done what he had to do to cope. Who are you to judge what that is? Who are you to try to take away the walls he's built to protect himself without knowing all the facts?

After all, no one knew more than her how important walls could be. Sometimes they were absolutely essential to surviving and functioning and staying sane. She took a deep breath, hiccupped, then used her sleeve to wipe her face.

Before you do this, make sure you know exactly what you're opening yourself up to. He may never be the man you want him to be. He may never be able to share himself with you fully. Are you that desperate for some love in your life that you're prepared to accept half a loaf?

There was only one answer: she loved him. If she could make him happy, give him some comfort… That would be enough. She would make it enough.

Another swipe with her sleeve, then she performed a highly illegal U-turn across oncoming traffic.

Zach's front door was unlocked and she let herself in without knocking, too impatient to wait. She heard the shower running. She didn't hesitate, walking down the hall and into the bathroom. Zach raised his head as she entered, but she didn't stop, pulling the door open and walking straight into the enclosure with him, clothes, shoes and all.

She wrapped her arms around him and pressed her head to his chest, holding him as tightly as her puny girl muscles would allow. "I'm sorry. I'm sorry for pushing. If it's that hard for you, that painful, it's okay. We'll work around it. And if you ever decide you want to invite me in, that's okay, too. Whatever you need, okay? Whatever you need."

"Jesus."

His arms came around her like steel bands, his grip so strong and tight she couldn't breathe. It didn't matter. She could feel how much this meant to him, how much he loved her—that was all that mattered.

He kissed her forehead, the bridge of her nose, her cheekbone, and finally her mouth, each contact fervent and almost violent, as though he couldn't quite contain his feelings.

"How did I get by without you?" he said against her skin. "How did I even wake up in the morning?"

She kissed him with everything in her. "I love you, Zach. I love you so much."

"Audrey. I don't want to lose you. I don't want to stuff this up."

"I know. It's okay. I know."

They held each other close until the water started to cool, needing the contact, the reassurance.

"I think we've sucked the water tank dry," he said.

They spent a couple of minutes wrangling her out of the soaked, clinging clothes and shoes, leaving them in the shower, before toweling each other dry.

"Let's go back to bed," she said.

They lay skin to skin, kissing occasionally, looking into each other's eyes, letting all the adrenaline and emotion drain away.

Audrey very deliberately didn't think about the future, about how this issue might manifest itself next. She loved Zach, and she knew he loved her. As she had said, they would work around it.

He was worth it. They were worth it.

She was starting to doze off, lulled by the warmth of the bed and his breath on her cheek and the calm after the storm, when he stirred beside her.

"Is your bag in the car?" he asked.

She opened her eyes. "Yes. Why?"

"You're going to need dry clothes."

He didn't say anything more, slipping from the bed and pulling on jeans before leaving the room. She heard him in the bathroom—taking her car keys from her wet jeans, no doubt—then she heard his tread in the hall and the sound of the front door closing. He was back in minutes, her bag in hand.

She didn't ask where they were going. There was a grim set to his face that told her all she needed to know. She wasn't going to make this any harder for him than it already appeared to be.

He went into the kitchen to make a quick phone call, then they managed to cobble together an outfit out of yesterday's work clothes and a few loaner items from his wardrobe—a dress shirt and one of his jackets with the sleeves rolled up. It didn't quite go with her skirt and high heels, but that was probably something she should have thought about before she'd stepped fully clothed into his shower.

"Ready?" he asked when she'd finished tying her hair into a ponytail.

"Yes. But we don't have to do this now if you don't want to." She meant it. Whatever he was about to show or tell her, she could wait until he was ready.

"It's not going to get any better. Let's go."

They took his car, driving into the city and then out again until they were entering the inner west. Greenery became more sparse; the parked cars were older. A sign above a store announced they were in Footscray, where Zach had grown up. He kept his gaze on the road, but she could feel his tension.

"Whatever I'm about to see, Zach, it won't change how I feel about you."

He glanced at her, then refocused on the road. She had no idea what was going through his mind.

He turned off the main road, wending his way through quiet residential streets until he stopped in front of a neat weatherboard house with a cracked concrete driveway and trim lawn. Zach glanced at the house, then fixed his gaze on the street. His chest rose and fell with a breath.

"My mum is a heroin addict. Has been since I was about eight or nine. Mostly she's functional, meaning she's got a part-time job and manages to work it around her habit. I found this place for her about six years ago. I pay the rent, make sure she gets food once a week, and she shoots her income up her arm."

He said it as though he was reciting his grocery list, his tone flat and dead.

She wasn't sure what she'd been expecting, but it wasn't this. She looked from him to the house and then back again as his words sunk in.

She'd hung out with junkies when she'd run away from home. She'd even been offered heroin on more than one occasion. But she'd seen what it did to people, how desperate it made them. It hadn't appealed to her one iota.

Zach had grown up with that kind of single-minded desperation, though.

"When did your father die?" she asked.

"About the same time Mum started using heavily. They were both casual users. They loved to party together. Then he came off his motorbike one night and that was it. I guess him dying tipped her over the edge. There's a saying junkies have—heroin abhors a vacuum. She went from using socially to having a habit in the space of a few weeks. Then it was pretty much all over."

He looked at her for the first time, and she saw a sort of watchful wariness in his eyes, as though he was waiting for her to do or say something.

Recoil in horror?

Judge him and his mother?

Then it hit her like a blow that he was ashamed, that the reason he'd been so damned reluctant to share his story was because he'd been worried what she would think of him, that she'd pity him or paint him as a victim or think less of him because of who his mother was and where he'd come from.

Zach was a strong guy, a determined guy. He wasn't a victim. He was a fighter. A survivor. He would hate being pitied. He would *despise* it, but she bet Zach had been exposed to hundreds of card-carrying professional pitiers over the years. Social workers and police and teachers and medical staff and the kindly, good-intentioned parents of school friends. She bet Zach had had it up to his back teeth with people who wanted to bleed for him.

So even though she wanted to throw her arms around him and say she could not imagine what his childhood had looked like and the sorts of nightmares he must have had to stare down, she didn't.

He didn't need her pity or sympathy. He needed her understanding and support. He needed her to help him shoulder this burden, because that's what it was. A son looking after his mother. Doing the right thing, because that's who he was, down to his bones.

So instead of cradling his head in her hands and saying she wanted to weep for him, she studied the house, the neighborhood. "Is she expecting us?"

"I told her we might drop by."

"Okay, then." She climbed out and waited until he'd followed suit before slipping her hand into his. She could feel him watching her but she kept her expression impassive as they crossed the road and walked up the path to the front door.

Zach knocked, and she could feel his unease as he waited for his mother to answer. She turned her head to look at him and waited until he met her eyes.

"It's okay, Zach."

He nodded, and his hand relaxed around hers a notch. The lock rattled and then a split second later the door swung open.

"Zach. You came. So good to see you, sweetheart."

The woman in the doorway had gray-streaked dark hair pulled back into a loose bun on the back of her head. Her eyes were the same navy-gray as Zach's, but any other resemblance there might have been was muddied by the fact that she was clearly underweight, her cheekbones and collarbones pushing at her skin.

She wore jeans and a fluffy blue sweater, and she smiled slowly as she looked at Audrey.

"Let me guess—you're Audrey. Great to meet you." She held out her hand and Audrey shook it.

"Nice to meet you, too, Mrs. Black."

"Get out of here—I'm Judy. Come in. I'll make you some coffee. Or tea, if you prefer."

She reached out to touch Zach's arm. "Good to see you, kiddo."

"You, too, Mum."

"Liar." She laughed faintly, the sound more sad than amused. "Coffee's this way."

Gesturing for them to follow her, she started up the hallway. Audrey started after her, then realized Zach wasn't beside her. She turned and found him frozen on the doorstep.

The look on his face...

It took everything she had not to cry for him then.

She held out her hand silently, and after a beat he took it. Together they went into the house.

ZACH LEANED AGAINST the sink and listened to his mother make conversation. Apart from the slowness of her speech and her general scrawniness, he doubted an observer would guess that a month ago she'd been slavishly addicted to illegal opiates.

Is *addicted, idiot. Don't fall for the spin. You're smarter than that.*

His mother had been clean since being discharged from the hospital. They'd set her up on a methadone program, and she'd assured Zach that this time she would stay clean.

He'd heard it before. Too often.

"I've got some biscuits here somewhere… You always buy biscuits for me, don't you?" his mum said, glancing over her shoulder at him.

"I thought you liked them," he said.

"I do—when I remember them. Ah, here we go."

His mother pulled a packet of assorted cookies from the cupboard and slit the plastic, arranging them on the plate. She'd already fixed them both up with coffee, and he watched as Audrey accepted a cookie and then casually dunked it in her drink.

As though this was a normal, run-of-the-mill meet-the-parents visit. Nothing to see here, please move on. Not by word or deed did she give the impression that she was freaked out or appalled or overwhelmed by what he'd revealed.

It was too good to be true. Or maybe she was buying his mother's I'm-just-your-typical-suburban-mum routine. Maybe she thought his mother was always like this and was wondering why he'd made such a federal case out of the whole deal.

"Why don't you sit down, Zachy? Or maybe we should go into the living room? Yeah, why don't we do that?" his mother said.

"That sounds great." Audrey stood and collecting both her coffee and the plate.

They trooped into the next room, he and Audrey gravitating to the sofa, his mother to the armchair. The ashtray on the coffee table was empty, but the smell of cigarettes lingered. His mother's smoking always took off when she was clean. No doubt she was spending a fortune on cigarettes.

"I suppose Zachy's told you about my situation." His

mother perched on the end of her seat. Her legs were crossed, one foot swinging rapidly the only sign that she wasn't completely at ease.

He'd never brought a woman to meet her before. She was doing her very best to make a good impression, he knew.

"A little," Audrey said cautiously, glancing at him.

"Four weeks and three days I've been clean now. Feeling pretty good about it, too. So much of it's a head game. If you can get that right, you're on the home stretch, and I think I'm there."

Zach reached for a cookie, even though he wasn't hungry. He chewed mechanically, listening to his mother talking up her recovery, the counselor she'd been assigned at the clinic, the new "headspace" she was trying to cultivate.

He kept glancing at Audrey, wondering if she was buying any of this. Then he reminded himself that she had no reason to doubt his mother. She didn't know how many times he'd heard Judy say almost exactly the same things.

And she had always relapsed. Always.

"Is that Zach?" Audrey indicated the framed photo on the mantel.

"It is. That's his first day of high school. He was so pleased with his new uniform he wanted to wear it during the summer holidays." His mum crossed to the mantel and handed the frame to Audrey.

"Look at you. Ready to break some thirteen-year-old hearts." Audrey smiled at him, totally at ease.

His mother started talking about the girl he'd asked to the seventh-grade school dance, but he was too busy watching Audrey to really pay attention.

Slowly, as the minutes ticked by, it sunk in that she didn't care. She really didn't care.

This wasn't a deal-breaker for her. This was simply one

of life's curveballs. A thing to be dealt with or endured as painlessly as possible.

She wasn't overwhelmed with pity for him. She wasn't terrified or fascinated or repulsed. She was simply letting it roll over her, absorbing, observing. Taking it as it came.

She'd meant it when she said she wanted the good as well as the bad of his life.

He let the realization sink into his bones. The next time his mother had an emergency—and there would be a next time—Audrey would be there with him, if he let her, waiting in the hospital or the police station or wherever he needed to be. If he wanted her to, if he asked, she would accompany him on his monthly dinner dates with his mother, too. He knew without raising it with her. If he asked, she'd come.

She loved him. She wanted to share his life, truly share it. Messed-up, addicted mother and all.

He was dragged out of his thoughts by Audrey's hand coming to rest on his forearm.

"Your mother was wondering if we were going to stay for lunch," she said.

"I'll have to pop up to the shops for some ham for sandwiches, but it's no bother," his mother said.

He glanced at Audrey. She smiled, telling with her eyes that the decision was his. She was fine. She would do whatever he wanted or needed to do.

"We might go, Mum. I've got a few things I need to take care of this afternoon," he said.

"Oh. All right, then."

They talked for a few more minutes, then said their goodbyes. Zach led the way to the street, stopping to glance at Vera's house as it occurred to him that he'd really like for Audrey to meet her.

"What?" Audrey asked.

"The woman next door, Vera. She keeps an eye on Mum. I call her once a week for an update."

"We should go say hello, then. I'd like to meet her," Audrey said.

He held her gaze. She didn't look away.

"You don't have to. You don't have to do any of this, ever again."

He'd handled it for years. It would be enough that he could talk to her about it. More than enough.

"Zach. It's not optional. Love doesn't work that way. At least, my love doesn't. I'm an all-or-nothing girl, in case you hadn't noticed."

So they went next door and had another cup of coffee with Vera and he tried to ignore Vera kicking him under the table and giving him not-so-subtle thumbs-ups to indicate Audrey had her approval. They left an hour later.

Audrey was silent as they drove, her head turned away as she gazed at the passing streetscape. Then she turned to him and put her hand on his knee.

"Do you think you could pull over for a second?"

He shot her a startled look. "Are you okay?"

"Yes. There's something I need to do."

He pulled over, and she immediately unbuckled her seat belt and climbed over the central console, clambering into his lap.

"What—"

She silenced him with a kiss, wrapping her arms around him. She held him for long minutes, her body trembling with the urgency of her feelings.

Finally she pulled back enough to see his face.

"Sorry, but I needed to do that. Not because I feel sorry for you, Zach, but because I'm so bloody glad that you survived all of that. You are a miracle. An amazing, gorgeous miracle, and I cannot believe that I have the right to sit in your lap and kiss you and call you mine. Because you are mine, okay? Now that I've found you, I'm not letting you go."

Something slipped its leash inside him then, the iron-hard control he'd always kept on his emotions falling away. He turned his head, blinking rapidly, trying to hide the tears pushing at the back of his eyes. Audrey cupped his face in her hands and gently drew his head around to face her.

"I love you, Zach Black. You don't need to hide your tears from me."

He stared into her golden-brown eyes and saw her love, her sadness for him, her pride in him, and understood that sharing his shame hadn't diminished him.

"You need me, and I need you," she said. "It's that simple. We were made to fit."

"You always say the right thing," he said, his voice husky with emotion, his chest expanding with it.

"No, I don't." She laughed. "Remember the clitoris incident? And the time I gave you a hard time about your polo pony?"

"That's right. I forgot about that." He slid his hand up to capture the nape of her neck. Her hair was warm from being against her skin, sliding over his fingers like heated silk. "You never did tell me what you and Megan were talking about that day."

"What a shocking oversight." She smiled, and he knew she was going to make him work for it.

"It's going to be like that, is it?"

"You couldn't have it any other way. Admit it."

He wouldn't. He wouldn't trade this woman, this perfect moment in time for anything. And the best thing was, it was but the first of many.

"I guess I'll have to persuade you, then."

And he did, despite the fact that they were on a very busy, very public road in the middle of the city.

Some things just couldn't wait.

EPILOGUE

Six months later...

A<small>UDREY</small> <small>PUSHED</small> <small>HER</small> chair back from her desk when she read the email, the words *new category manager's role* and *we'd like to encourage you to apply* emblazoned on her brain.

Oh, boy.

She shot to her feet, keen to go talk to Zach and share the news. There had been rumors lately that after cutting them to the bone, Whitman was looking at rebuilding things his way. But she hadn't expected this.

Then it hit her that her news might not be so welcome for Zach, and she sat down with a thump.

Once upon a time she would have crowed about being in this position, but not anymore. Now, his happiness meant the world to her. She wanted him to succeed, was his biggest cheerleader.

Her nervous excitement soured. It wasn't as though there were many ways to handle this situation. She could either politely decline the offer, and hope that Zach would never know she'd been offered a chance at the job. Or she could be honest with him and trust that he could deal with it, as he'd dealt with everything else life had thrown at him.

She stood. There was only one choice. The cornerstone of their relationship was honesty. She wasn't about to change that now, even if it was potentially for a good cause.

He was sitting behind his desk when she entered his office and she took one look at his face and knew.

"Gary asked you to apply, too, didn't he?"

Zach gusted out a breath. "I've been sitting here trying to work out how to tell him I'm not interested."

"You're not doing that, Zach. You idiot," she said fondly, even though she'd been contemplating the same radical solution. "You have to apply."

"What, and you step back?" His expression let her know what he thought of that solution.

"There will be other promotions." She shrugged.

"Fine. Then I'll step back, and you can apply. Problem solved."

"I can't let you do that."

"And I can't let you do that, either."

She stared at him. She knew the stubborn look on his face all too well. He wasn't going to back down.

"Then, what, we both walk away?" she said.

"Or we both apply."

She sank into his guest chair as she digested what he'd suggested. "Zach... That's a recipe for disaster, pure and simple. One of us is going to miss out. And that's the best-case scenario."

"The other way we both miss out. What's wrong, Mathews? Not up to the challenge?"

Despite the gravity of the situation, she fought a smile. Zach could always make her smile, and he used his secret weapon mercilessly, in the same way that he'd used foot rubs to lure her into Saturday morning runs and his best bedroom moves to convince her to live with him sooner rather than later.

"Don't try to turn this into a competition. You know it'll get ugly," she said.

"Because you're so competitive."

"Right. That's *my* problem." She rolled her eyes to let him know the shoe was on the other foot.

He rounded his desk, parking his butt on the edge. "We can do this, Audrey. We can handle it. If you get it, I'll be happy for you. If I get it, you'll be happy for me. It's a win-win."

"Since when did you become an incurable optimist?"

He glanced over her shoulder and she knew he was checking to see if anyone was watching. Their relationship was well and truly public these days—although she had made sure that Megan enjoyed a good few weeks of feeling smugly in the know before she and Zach had agreed to start commuting together. It had only taken a few days of them coming and going in the same car for the word to get around.

At the time, Lucy had sent her an animated email of a cartoon cat dancing Gangnam Style, the young generation's equivalent of a high five, Audrey figured. Gary had had a quiet word with her in his office, the gist of the conversation being that he didn't want any personal shenanigans affecting work matters. She had assured him they wouldn't, then wondered—perhaps unwisely—if he would be having the same conversation with Zach. Something Zach had thanked her for later, naturally.

Twice she and Zach had arrived at the same time as Whitman, the CEO noting their exit from the single car with his usual cool, assessing demeanor. If he had an opinion about their relationship, he hadn't let on, not by the flicker of an eyelid. But Audrey figured it was more his style to sack the people he didn't approve of. So much cleaner and easier.

Neither of them had been sacked to date. And now they were both being asked to apply for a promotion.

The coast must have been clear over her shoulder because

Zach moved his knee forward, nudging it ever-so-slightly between hers. She pressed her knees together, trapping his, reassured as always by having his skin next to hers. Even if her stockings and his wool pants were technically in the way.

"This was always going to happen," Zach said. "It was only a matter of time."

She agreed, but she hadn't envisaged it happening quite like this, with both of them being encouraged to go for the one job.

"Maybe this is Whitman's cunning way of making one of us resign."

"Well, he can be cunning all he likes, but we're both great at what we do and we both deserve a shot at that job."

She stared at him. He'd had a haircut over the weekend and he looked even more handsome than usual, his unruly fringe for once behaving itself.

She loved him so much, in so many ways, for so many reasons.

She really didn't want work to come between them. But he clearly wouldn't tolerate her bowing out of the competition. And—honestly—she would probably lose a big chunk of respect for herself if she did that. Just as she would hate it if he bowed out because of her.

"All right. It'll probably end in tears, but if you think we can handle this, I guess we've got to do it."

"We can handle it."

His knee rubbed against hers, a subtle reassurance. As always, it only took the barest touch and the right kind of smile and her body started to burn for his.

She pushed back her chair, breaking the contact. "Stop using your powers for evil."

"I can't help it. I can see down your top from here."

She snorted out a laugh and stood. "Later."

"Count on it."

He meant it, too, which was good, because she did, too. The day she didn't, she wouldn't have a pulse.

They talked about the job some more that night, then helped each other finesse their résumés. Audrey felt a lot calmer by the time they'd gone through the process. Zach's academic credentials far outweighed the piecemeal, part-time education she'd patched together for herself over the years. He was a shoo-in for the job. A cinch.

She would do her interview, but she had already resigned herself to the fact that the job was his. Something she could more than live with.

It was no surprise that they were both invited to interviews, Zach's in the morning, hers in the afternoon of the following week. Zach tried to fill her in on the questions he was asked in the interim but she stuck her fingers in her ears and refused to listen.

"That's an unfair advantage, and I always fight fair," she told him.

Zach had laughed at her, and there was a part of her that regretted her stance as she was being grilled by Whitman and Gary later that day. But it was the right thing to do. And the job was Zach's, anyway.

Whitman surprised her as she dragged her limp and sweaty body out of the hot seat at the end.

"I've been meaning to say to you, Audrey—that report you and Zach coauthored has been instrumental in a lot of the new strategies you'll be hearing about in the next month or so. I've been meaning to thank you for your good work on it for some time."

She was so stunned she gaped at him stupidly, like an overgrown baby pelican waiting to be fed. "Um. Thank you. That's good to hear."

Gary gave her a wink as he followed Whitman out.

Zach and Megan were waiting in her office.

"Well?" Megan asked.

"I have no idea. They asked tough questions. Gary was a bit of an asshole, actually." Audrey thought of one question where Gary had really hammered her.

"Yeah, he went in hard on me, too. We can egg his car after work." Zach's eyes were worried, though, and she gave him a small smile to indicate that she was fine.

He pushed away from her filing cabinet. "Better get back to it."

Megan made a rude noise once he was gone. She rubbed a hand over her very round belly, a habit she'd developed early in her pregnancy. She was under two months away from delivering now, a thought that made Audrey both sad and glad, since she'd be losing her awesome work buddy to maternity leave but gaining a baby to coo over.

"You guys. I hate it when you do the telepathy thing. It makes me feel like I'm looking through your bedroom window."

"What on earth are you talking about?"

"You and Zach have this little Morse code thing you do with your eyes. It's creepy."

Audrey laughed. "Okay. If you say so."

"I know you have probably thought about this, but how will Zach handle you getting the job? In case you hadn't noticed, the care and feeding of the male ego can be a precarious thing."

"Megsy, you are so good for *my* ego, but there is no way they are going to pick me over Zach. He has degrees coming out his ears, his department is one of the top five performers this quarter… It's his."

"You landed an exclusive on that new European lighting range. You headed the development committee for in-store tutorials and staff training. And your department is the third-highest performer this quarter. Zach's is fourth." Megan ticked her points off on her fingers.

"That's only because he had some sales data that tipped into the next quarter thanks to a reporting snafu." Audrey dismissed those arguments with the wave of her hand.

Megan leaned across the desk and grabbed her hand. "Don't be an idiot. You could get this. You need to think about how Zach might feel when he learns you're going to be earning more than him."

"If that happens, he won't care," she said instantly.

"You sound very sure. Tim would have to go chop wood for a few years to reclaim his macho if that happened to us."

Audrey doubted that, since Megan's husband was a sweetheart, but perhaps she didn't know him the way his wife did.

"I'm sure," she said.

She and Zach had always admired and applauded each other's drive and ambition. She had to believe that one of them earning this promotion over the other wouldn't change that. Even if that person was her.

Gary had indicated they would have an answer tomorrow, and she and Zach went home to pizza and spreadsheets, followed by a cool shower and hot sex.

Lying in the tangled sheets afterward, she rested her chin on his chest and looked at him.

"No matter what happens tomorrow, I love you."

He smiled. "I love you more than a job, sweetheart. Don't worry, okay?"

"Ditto. A million times ditto."

She had a crappy night's sleep, and had to force herself to eat breakfast. They drove to work together and broke convention by kissing each other long and lingeringly in the car before heading inside.

"Go get 'em, champ," Zach said as they parted.

She was edgy all morning, jumping every time the phone rang. Lucy kept checking in with her, along with Megan, and after a while she promised that they would be right at the top of the list of people to know when she heard. At midday her sister called, and for a second Audrey wished she hadn't told anyone what was happening. But only for a second. Getting to know Leah—and her man, Will—had filled holes in her life she hadn't even known existed. She would never regret their new closeness.

It was nearly three before Gary called and asked her to come to his office.

Whatever you do, don't look disappointed. Even if you feel it.

Honestly, it was hard to know how to feel, because she wanted Zach to have this opportunity, too.

"Grab a seat," Gary said when she entered.

She did, gratefully, since her knees were feeling distinctly rubbery.

"As you know, it was a tough choice. Both you and Zach are outstanding candidates. At the end of the day, experience tipped things in your favor, though. That, and your nose for innovation. Everyone's been very impressed with your tutorial initiative."

Audrey sat and blinked, not quite sure if her ears were working properly. Did Gary just say "in her favor"? Had she heard that correctly?

"Sorry. This is going to sound dense—but are you offering the job *to me?*"

She was aware she sounded like Oliver Twist, putting her

bowl out for more, but she was genuinely dumbstruck. They had picked *her* over *Zach?*

"We picked the best man—person—for the job." He shook his head at his own political incorrectness. "And that person is you. Congratulations, Audrey."

"Wow. I'm not—I didn't—I thought Zach would—"

"So I gather. But he didn't." Gary smiled indulgently.

"Okay. Thanks. This is amazing. Really, really cool," she said dazedly. She realized she was rambling and she stood, smiling apologetically.

"You have stuff to do. So I'll go. But…thank you. Thank you."

She left Gary's office, waiting until she was around the corner before she leaned against the wall and closed her eyes, one hand pressed to her crazily beating heart.

Bloody freaking hell, she'd gotten it!

Hard on the heels of jubilation came trepidation.

Because her getting it meant Zach missed out. That was always going to be the outcome for one of them, but the reality of it hit her in the solar plexus.

She needed to go talk to him. She needed to tell him her news and look into his eyes and see for herself what this meant to him, if this was going to be a problem for them or not. And if it was… She had no idea what she was going to do, because now that Gary had dangled the carrot, she wanted it, so badly.

She walked to Zach's office on wooden legs, stopping in the doorway and swearing under her breath when she found it empty. She swiveled on her heel and scanned the open-plan area, but she couldn't see him anywhere. It occurred to her that maybe he was waiting in her office, maybe he'd gotten wind that something was up. She raced across the department, but he wasn't there, either.

Maybe he does know, and he's gone somewhere quiet and dark to punch a hole in the wall so I don't see how disappointed he is.

The thought filled her with dread. She had a vision of them over dinner tonight, both of them choking down obligatory champagne, pretending it was just dandy that she'd come out on top.

Desperate for someone to download to, she went to Megan's office, but her friend wasn't there, either.

"Has someone sounded the evacuation alarm or something?" she muttered to herself.

Disgruntled and worried, she drifted toward the staff room. Maybe she'd find one of them in there.

She saw the banner the moment she turned the corner—a run of printer pages strung together to spell out the word *Congratulations*. Then she registered the crowd—all her colleagues crammed into the one small space, grinning madly as they tooted on noisy horns and popped party favors and yelled out "Congratulations, Audrey!"

And in the middle of them all was Zach, grinning like the lunatic he was, looking so proud and happy for her that she knew instantly, with one hundred percent certainty, that this was okay with him. That this was more than okay, that he celebrated for and with her, that her happiness meant everything to him, more even than his own.

But Zach had always been a giver, right from those early, dark years when he'd had to shoulder the burden of looking after his lost, broken mother. How could she have expected anything less from him?

"Sweetheart, don't cry," Zach said, his face creased with concern as he moved to comfort her.

"Zach." She looked into his eyes, wanting to tell him all

the things in her heart right now, but very aware of all the people watching them.

She wanted to tell him she loved him, beyond measure. That she couldn't and didn't want to imagine her life without him. Most of all, she wanted to tell him how lucky she was. So damned lucky.

"I know," he said, taking her into his arms. "I know, sweetheart."

Then he kissed her, right in front of everyone.

Screw being professional.

* * * * *